'TILL *Death* DO US

L . C .   S O N

www.LCSonBooks.com

Ebook Cover Design by PoppyPremades
Paperback Cover Design by L.C. Son
Formatting by EmCat Designs
Editing by Alexa at The Fiction Fix

ISBN 979-8-9862237-8-0

For my brother.

Contents

Content Advisory

The contents of this book are suitable for mature adults aged 18 and up. For a full content advisory, including triggers, tropes, and more, please visit my website or refer to the full product description available online.

https://www.lcsonbooks.com/content-notices--spice-index.html

Something Special Just For You

Interested in reading a prequel bonus chapter? Sign up for my newsletter now and grab this short and sweet prequel, 'Till We Meet.

CHAPTER 1
Desephone

"Pour me another," I groan, sliding my short stout glass across the bar.

Arius grins his normal charming, crooked smile. "That would be your fourth whiskey smash, Des. Are you sure you don't want to call it a night?"

I let out the most unladylike snort ever. Covering my mouth, I shake my head, waving my hand around. "Pretty sure I can manage, Ari. I live across the street." I jump up from my barstool, just barely clinging to the side of the bar. "I can just bunny hop to my brownstone," I laugh, curling my hands into a would-be rabbit pose.

Scrunching his face and narrowing his dark gaze at me, Arius tosses his towel from his shoulder onto the holster near the sink behind him. I'm almost impressed at how he does so without even turning around, but my heel sticks to something sticky on the floor, and I lose my footing.

"I got you, gorgeous," a husky voice, reeking of a foul mix of garlic and bourbon, whispers behind me as two bulking arms wrap around my waist.

Looking up, I'm pleasantly surprised to find a hulk of a man, with steely gray eyes and dirty blond hair pulled back into a ponytail, smiling down at me.

"Oh, thank you," I grin, allowing my fingers to smooth over his large, warm hands as I steady my footing.

"Pleasure's all mine," he adds with a small peck against my wrist, offering a most gentlemanly bow. "The name's Derek," he continues, brandishing a polished white smile with just the faint point of his fangs showing.

Ooh... a wolf, I think to myself. I haven't had one of those in a long time.

Twirling my long, thick black tendrils around my finger, I bat my eyes just enough to show interest. "Hi," I begin, now shaking our hands together. "I'm—"

"Leaving!" Arius growls, taking my wrist in his palm and pulling me back from Derek.

"Damn it, Arius! What the–"

Arius doesn't look at me. Instead, after a heavy sigh, he steps in front of me, blocking my view of Derek while keeping a tight squeeze on my wrist. "You should keep moving, pal. She's in no condition to consent to whatever your intentions are."

Yanking myself free, I shove Arius away from me. "You've got some nerve," I snap as I make my way to Derek's side.

An arrogant smirk crowds the side of Derek's mouth as his once-gray eyes flash to gold. He throws his arm around me and pulls me close.

"Well, I think the lady knows what she wants. Now, why don't you be a good–" Derek pauses, taking a sniff at Arius to discern his scent. His nose crinkles some, unable to make out Arius' origin, so he waves a dismissive hand. "Whatever the hell you are, just go mind your libations and keep them coming!"

Arius doesn't respond. He just stands there, arms folded, dark eyes narrowed, staring at me with that cute, singular, dark curl of hair that hangs against his forehead like Superman.. Yet, despite looking at his face every day for the past fifty years since I moved here, I've never seen Arius look at me like this.

From the sheen of sweat resting over his well-manicured mustache to the tint of red rising beneath his tawny brown skin, it doesn't take a genius to see that my favorite bartender and friend is angry...*with me*.

It's not like it's the first time he has seen me with a guy—or guys, for that matter. I haven't the faintest idea what could make this night any different. But from the way he's looking at me, you'd think I broke his heart.

And that is a ridiculous thought.

Arius Knight can have any woman he wants.

In fact, he has had plenty.

We've even gone on doubles and partied until the next day with pairs of siblings—more than once. Most folks around here even think we're cousins or related in some way. We're not; he's half-Bulwark, half-human, nothing remotely close to who and what I am. Still, people take one look at how we carry on and assume we must be related.

Maybe that's it.

Perhaps he has taken his big brotherly affections for me too seriously. I don't answer to him, and it's about time he knows that.

Arius digs his gaze deep into mine. His jaw slacks some, as though he wants to say something, but I won't deal with any more of his posturing tonight.

"Want to take this party back to my place?" I breathe, tiptoeing my fingers up Derek's broad chest, only to rest my palm against his well-sculpted pectorals as I stare over my shoulder at Arius.

"You read my mind," Derek answers, using his large palm to turn my head back to him. "Shall we?" he says with a sly smile and a quirked brow.

Shooting a wink to Arius, I glide my hand up to Derek's collar, pulling just enough to lower his head to mine. "I thought you'd never ask," I playfully coo, adding a tap to the bridge of his nose.

With a frown, Arius' dark brows cave together as he watches us, balling a fist against his hip, but he doesn't say anything. He stands in the center of the bar, brooding with something that so strangely resembles jealousy. I'm intrigued.

Arius is hardly bothered by the swarms of folk mingling around us. No, he has his sights fixed on me and Derek. He's not even phased by the flirty ladies strolling along, who add an extra sway of their hips and flip of their hair, hopeful to get his attention, as they walk by. Nor is he concerned by the looks of some of the brawlier vampires, lurking with crimson eyes in the corner, watching our every move.

His stance right now says it all.

He doesn't give a fuck.

While a part of me admires this brash new side of my normally cavalier and relaxed friend, I refuse to blur the lines any more than whatever damage has been done tonight.

I need to leave.

Likely sensing my trepidation, Derek threads his fingers together with mine as he leads us away from my friend's scornful glare. Adding a light peck to my hair, he leans into my ear. "Let's get out of here."

Offering a small nod, I curl into his hulking embrace as we make our way toward the exit. Everything in me wants to turn and make sure Arius is okay, but I can't.

I have to stay my course.

Tonight might be the night.

CHAPTER 2
Arius

*F*uck.

Why do I let Des get under my skin?

I've got enough on my plate trying to maintain the peace and keep this place afloat. The last thing I need is to worry about a hell-bound primordial princess who can obviously take care of herself.

But *I do* worry about her.

In fact, all I do is worry about her.

Perhaps it's that tight, red pencil skirt that she was wearing, hugging her curves in all the right places, setting off my alarm. The way it accentuates her round, plump ass, and the sweet sway of her hips is enough to drive any man insane. Even with her sporty denim jacket and white tee, there's no playing down just how alluring she is.

So hell yeah, I'm worried about her alone with that damned wolf. How can I not?

Since she walked into my bar fifty years ago, I've done nothing but think of her. Worry about her. Care for her.

I'm a Bulwark– or at least, half one. My only job as a gatekeeper is to ensure the peace between the earthbound supernaturals, nothing more. Sure, I hear more than my fair share of their gripes as I pour copious amounts of blood or alcohol for them night after night, but still, she's the only one I care to listen to for hours on end.

Desephone clouds my judgment and invades my every thought. That's why I've worked hard at playing the dutiful best friend. Hellish expats like the daughter of Hades often seek the company of Bulwarks like me, since we are considered the most neutral of supernaturals. We don't ruffle feathers, nor do we seek out trouble.

My bar, *Dram Deaux*, has remained a quaint refuge for vampires, wolves, and others to numb their cares or corral for mates on neutral ground.

Des has spent night after night charming any man she fancies, looking for her soulmate.

Thankfully for me, she hasn't found him.

And for the past few years, I've watched her parade around my bar, offering sweet smiles to whosoever will. Before, it was a mere frustration. Now, however, it's a viable threat.

The Queen of the Underworld has given her daughter nearly three millennia in the earthbound realm to find a suitor. Des, however, has spent most of her days, and a great deal of her nights, doing anything but finding a husband. Playing the field is more than a hobby for the princess—it's a full-time occupation.

While a part of me wonders whether Des even wants a mate at all, a greater part of me wishes what she wanted was me.

But here I am, stuck in neutral.

Not only am I her friend, but as a Bulwark, I am forbidden from marriage or taking a life partner. I know better. I understand the risks. Then again, I suppose I'm just like my father in that regard.

"Hey, puppy-eyes!" I feel Cade give me a hard shove from behind. I'd know his growly voice anywhere.

Still, my eyes stay glued to the exit for a few more seconds. I'd give anything for her to throw aside that overgrown canine and come back inside my bar, where I can keep an eye on her.

One more push from my friendly vampire hybrid, and I turn fast on my heel, only to jab my elbow hard into his side.

"Not in the mood," I grumble as I make my way back behind my bar. I know where this is going.

"Hmm..." he heckles, running a hand through his slick, black hair as he saunters to the bar. Hooking his boot to the barstool, he swerves the seat side-to-side. Humming something dark, yet strangely catchy, he keeps his gaze on me until I can no longer take the squeaky sound of the metal grinding against itself. "Oh, does this bother you?" he laughs, his eyes fading into the black veiny lines framing his face.

Reaching over the counter, I grab the back of the barstool, halting his motion. "Yes," I grit through my teeth.

"Well, that's strange." Cade slants his eyes toward me, his thin lips crowding to one side of his mouth. "You're bothered by the squeaky chime of a barstool but not bothered to see the one who holds your heart scatter out the door with yet another worthless soul."

A low growl rumbles through me, and a warm light emanates from my hand as the back of the stool steams.

"Ahh..." he continues, his chin now resting on his fist. "So this inanimate object is now the recipient of your ire, but not–"

"Stop it, Cade!" I bite back. "I know what you're doing."

"Oh, come off it, Sincade!" my assistant, Gypsy, chimes in as she comes to my side. "You're just making things worse," she says, patting my shoulder.

"Thank you, Gypsy," I smile, thankful to see my ever-faithful ally at my side.

Gypsy gives me a wink, showcasing her heavy pink and purple eyeshadow while blowing bubble gum through her glossy fuchsia lipstick. "Don't mention it, boss," she continues, leaning her arm on my shoulder. "You know I've got your back."

Cade's shoulders roll in amusement as he shakes his head. "And if by having his back, you mean standing aside as he lets his one true love stroll on through life with another, then that's not actually having his back, I'm afraid."

Snarling, Gypsy's fangs protrude as she leans into the bar with nothing but my arm stopping her from lunging at Cade.

"Watch your words, Sincade DeLuca!" she sneers, gnashing her teeth.

Cade's eyes darken as he lets out a dark chortle, his own fangs hanging lower. "There, there, young one," he warns in a stern yet calm tone. "We both want the same thing for our friend."

"I doubt that!" she hisses in return, swatting her bar towel at him.

"Oh, I assure you, we both want him safe and happy with his one true love," Cade answers warmly, keeping his eyes set on me.

Pushing back and leaning against the sink, Gypsy huffs. "Well, speak for yourself. I, for one, have no interest in seeing my best friend turn into stone. He's a Bulwark, remember?"

Cade's shoulders roll in amusement. "I am quite aware. But–"

"Enough!" I bark, tired of the back and forth. These two could go on like this for hours if I don't stop them. "Look, I know who and what I am. I don't need either of you to cement that any further. Anyway, Gypsy, can you ring the bell? Time to wrap things up. Dawn will be upon us soon," I say, nodding toward the transom. The moon is still aglow, but I know sunrise is near.

"Got it, boss," Gypsy replies, smacking her gum as she playfully swats her towel toward Cade.

He smiles in return, dodging her while shooting a quick wink. Those two might argue like alley cats, but they're the best of friends.

It was Cade who found Gypsy, a blood-thirsty vampire, wandering the streets almost twenty years ago. He trained her, right here in my bar, and taught her how to control her thirst. I gave her a job here with me. We've been an impenetrable duo ever since.

Cade, however, is still very much a wanderer himself. Although he's originally from Biloxi, he remains fairly mysterious, only popping into the bar in spurts then disappearing just as quickly as he came. Strange enough, he always seems to appear just when I need him most.

Pushing his shot glass across the counter, Cade gives me a nod. "You know I only want the best for you, right?"

"I know," I sigh, filling up his glass with whiskey and adding one for myself.

"Last call!" Gypsy shouts as she rings the cowbell.

Vampires, wolves, and all manner of other creatures crowd the bar as soon as the bell rings. Some reach for blood, while others whiskey, vodka, or whatever cocktail sates their thirsts. Much like those surrounding my bar, I feel my throat go dry, as I too, thirst for something.

But I know I won't find what I long for in my bar.

Cade's daggered eyes bore into me, and I even sense Gypsy watching me from my periphery. As folk gather around the bar for one last round, my sights stay glued to the exit door.

It's now or never.

He's one handsy wolf.

We haven't even made it across the street, and he has his arm wrapped around my waist so tight, I can feel his belt buckle dig deep into my side, almost pinching my skin right through my dress.

"Whoa, hold on there, Devin," I say, pressing my hand against his chest to create a little distance.

He goes to nuzzle the nape of my neck once more. "Name's Derek," he growls playfully as he pulls me back into his side.

"Well, Derek, drop back a bit," I whisper, tugging his beard a little while I create some distance between us. "We don't need to give the neighbors a show," I add, whirling my free hand around.

Although I know most folks are still asleep, I don't want to bring any unwanted attention our way.

Derek turns his head, looking down the street and back at me. "I don't see anyone," he groans, gently gripping the back of my neck as a sly smile hovers at the side of his face.

"Let's keep it that way," I whisper, running my finger through his beard and down to his chest.

His chest rumbles a bit, his sun-spun wolfen eyes glowing as he gazes at me. He's a stunning creature. Perfect jawline. A great smile. Hard muscles that would make carved stone jealous. Yet, I feel nothing, not an air of excitement nor an ounce of whimsy.

Perhaps it's because I don't know him.

But I don't have the luxury of formalities. Right now, all I need to know is that he can sustain mating me. If so, we can work out all the rest, just like my parents did.

My father searched high and low to find the one person capable of holding her own within the shadow of his mating call. Although she hated him at first, only my mother, Persephone, was able to withstand the power of Hades.

And so shall it be with me.

I just need a mate strong enough not to burn to ash when he lies with me. That's not so hard, right?

Besides, wolves are known for their mating prowess. In fact, their mating rituals rival any creature on this earthbound plane. Though most wolves are sticklers for keeping to their own kind, Derek seems more than willing to indulge otherwise.

And so he shall.

Swallowing down any remnants of angst, I tug Derek's beard gently, bringing his mouth to mine.

His lips are softer than I thought they'd be, but his tongue is demanding as he tries to pry my mouth open. For his own sake, I keep my lips pressed tight. Sometimes, my kiss has proven dangerous to unequally yoked suitors. I'd hate to destroy our evening before it starts.

"So you're shy, huh?" he breathes against my mouth. The hard smell of garlic and bourbon hits my nose, and my throat clenches at the odor.

I take a small step back to catch some fresh air. If we are to go any further, he'll have to freshen up. Any act of repulsion from me could prove lethal for Derek. We have to be in sync—as much as possible—if this is to work.

"Not shy," I whisper, twirling my fingers through his beard, locking my eyes with his. "I just want to do this right," I add, working hard to peer into his soul.

After three millennia, you'd think I'd have this down by now, but I don't. I've worked hard to hone my craft at soul searching, but it's not as easy as my mom makes it out to be. She told me I should be able to see into any soul, discern good from evil and even a few things in between.

While there have been times when a pure evil soul has caught my gaze in a matter of minutes, I've even caught good souls, although those are rarer. Usually, it's children or very old humans. The worst are babies. I stay away from them at all costs. Their souls are murky at best, but every now and again, you find one evil soul from the start. Even then, it happens when I'm not trying.

Here I am, trying to see into Derek's soul, just to parse the good from the bad, to see if he's even worth the trouble, and I can't get a read on him.

I'm not sure if it's his cloaking abilities as a wolf or if I'm just really bad at this soul searching thing, but I'm coming up empty here.

"Which one's your place?" Derek asks, pointing to the row of townhomes in front of us.

"The pink one," I say, pointing to my rose-pink building nestled between two brownstones.

Derek's shoulders roll in amusement as he lets out a small laugh. "The flower shop? *Petals*," he scoffs.

My nose scrunches some at his off-putting tone. "Well, the flower shop is my business. I live above it."

As he shrugs his shoulders, his mouth curves to one side. "Makes sense, I guess."

I take another step back. "You guess? What's that supposed to mean?" Cocking my head to one side, I push my hair behind my ear.

Lifting a hand in caution, Derek offers a small smile. "Practical, that's all. I meant no offense."

I keep staring at him, still trying to get a read, but nothing. All I know is my mood is ruined. He needs to go.

"You know what, Derek? This was a mistake. I think I'll call it a night."

Derek steps in front of me before I have a chance to step up on the curb.

"Please, come on. We were just getting acquainted," he says with a broad smile. Gently cupping my chin, he lifts my face to meet his. "Besides, we can't let all these pretty petals go to waste," he adds, leaning his head over his shoulder.

My eyes grow wide in horror as I look at the ground behind him. A mixture of pink and purple rose petals adorn the cobblestone pathway to the door of my shop.

That can only mean one thing.

Mother is here.

"You should go!" I snap, side-stepping until I make my way in front of him. "Now!"

"Oh, come on, princess!" Derek says, grabbing my wrist. "You didn't drag me out of that bar just to end things so suddenly."

Shaking myself free, a small growl rumbles through me. My skin warms to the touch, and I feel my sight darken.

"Shit!" he shrieks, stepping away from me. "What the hell is wrong with your face?" he shouts, scattering back towards the pathway leading to my door. "Fuck! What in the hell—" he roars as his canines grow longer and his eyes flash to gold as steam rises from his boots.

Scurrying around, his feet trample over the rose petals as they burst into flames on his feet.

"What are you?" he howls, roaring aloud as he drops to all fours, his fear forcing his shift.

Darkness cloaks my vision as he turns into his wolfen form, and I see him for who he is: a lone wolf, derelict and exiled. His soul cries to me of the wrongdoings and the reasons his pack exiled him. He had sex with his brother's wife, a most egregious sin. There is no honor in this man. The burning roses are even more evidence of his duplicity. They only burn the damned.

Lunging toward me, Derek's wide jaw flexes with spital dripping from his canines as he nears my jugular, but I am not afraid. If he takes one bite, it will be his last. He'll burst into flames, his soul damned to the Underworld for my father's taking. The Great Hades will delight in devouring the soul of one who set his ways against me.

Yet, I don't have time to relish in Derek's finality when I'm pushed to the side. My eyes flash to their normal state just in time for me to see Arius holding Derek's mouth open as he rips him apart.

Arius throws Derek's torn body to the ground, and he bursts into flames as the roses consume him whole. Turning to face me, Arius blares a wickedly charming smile, and I know I'm doomed.

CHAPTER 4
Arius

Looks like I got here right on time.

I knew something was off about that wolf, but I just couldn't place it. I'm just thankful I stopped him from hurting Des. The thought of his teeth gnawing into her flesh drives me to near madness. I've never let anyone hurt her before, and I won't start now.

"Ari?" Desephone's voice is quiet as her raised brow tells me she's surprised to see me. "What are you doing here?"

I could stand here and watch her like this for hours. I don't know if it's the way the wind blows her hair against her small oval face or the way the streetlights shimmer against her beautifully bronzed skin, but everything about the Daughter of Hades drives me to the brink of insanity.

"Protecting my territory." I rush my words. I need to make this encounter less weird. Who knows how long I've stood here, ogling her like a fucking statue?

She lets out a hard sigh as she rummages through her purse for her keys. "You Bulwarks are so territorial. I can handle myself, you know."

I want to tell her that *she is my territory*, but I'll save that for another time. I force a laugh. "Yeah, because you looked like you had everything under control with the big, bad wolf."

Sucking her teeth, she gives me a haughty eye roll as she saunters by me, waving her key in the air. Her round hazel eyes travel the full length of me, like she's examining something, but her attention remains glued to my feet for a minute before looking back up at my face. "Why aren't your feet burning?"

Hunching my shoulders, I shake my head. "Why would they be?" I rock on my heel, twisting the ball of my foot against the crushed rose petals. "The wolf burned quick enough. He's not a vampire, so the flames shouldn't be that high."

"Yeah, but–"

"But what? Look, I don't think anyone saw anything. I was moving too fast for mortal eyes to see anyway. It would just appear as a flash of lightning. I think you're good."

Biting her lip in that cute way she always does when she's over-thinking things, she huffs as she puts her key in the door.

"Well, I'm good, Ari. Thanks–"

"Wait!" I nearly bark, taking her wrist between my fingers. She's shivering. Perhaps that wolf freaked her out more than I realized. "Des, please–"

Pulling herself from my grip, she turns back to the door. "No, Ari. I really think you should go! I mean it!"

"Not before I tell you something—"

"Ari, please, whatever it is will have to wait. Now isn't a good time."

Cupping her elbow, I give it a little squeeze. "Des, did he do something to you? Whatever he did–"

Desephone's big, round eyes look up to mine. I wish I could dive into those misty ponds that have my soul in a chokehold. I'd drown in her if she'd let me.

Her gaze softens some as she offers a small smile. "He didn't do anything, Ari. Really. Look, I appreciate you coming out here to check on me. You're a good friend. I know I got a little huffy with you earlier, but that's because you're like a big brother to me, and aren't siblings supposed to go tit for tat with each other?" She lets out a little laugh as she twirls her hair behind her ear.

"Brother?" I repeat, my voice cracking like a teenage frog.

"Okay, yeah, everyone thinks we're cousins, so there's that."

I gulp. "They do?"

Shit. Is this how she thinks of me? Like a brother? A cousin? I don't care how everyone else sees us. I just need *her* to see us.

Des gives my shoulder a small squeeze before turning back around to open her door. "Look, Ari, it's late, and you should get going."

"But I—"

"Well, if he's family, dearest, let him in," a dark, melodious voice calls from inside.

Blood drains from Desephone's face as she sucks in a breath while her hand trembles against the doorframe.

"Des? Is someone here?" I ask, patting her shoulder. She's cold as ice as her pensive gaze meets mine.

"Come on in, dearest. I won't bite," the lush voice calls to us. Des purses her lips tightly as her eyes close briefly. "And bring your friend," the same voice continues as the door swings open.

Des gives me a wary glance before nodding her head slightly. "Coming, Mother!"

Mother?

Shit. Am I about to meet the fucking Queen of the Underworld?

Rolling her eyes, Des tips her head forward. "Well, come on, Ari. You wanted to stick around for the fun, so here goes—"

Desephone steps over the threshold, her hand nervously reaching for mine, pulling me behind her. I tighten my grip, threading our fingers together until I feel her relax. She lets out a little sigh as we make our way inside the darkened space, and I relish the feel of her hand in mine.

I could get used to this.

"Come closer," her mother's voice bounces around us, making it hard for me to place where she could be.

A thunderous clap turns our attention to the right, and the lights in the foyer of Desephone's storefront blare brightly.

"Damn it!" Des shrieks, holding her arm over her eyes, shielding herself from the brightness. "What gives?"

"Aw, I thought this place could use a little light, dear," Persephone says, now appearing in front of us. Her brilliant, sea-blue eyes shimmer like sapphires as her dazzling white smile gleams from ear to ear.

Sighing, Des throws her purse down on a small table. "Happy to see you too, Mother," she mumbles, tightening her hand in mine. I feel my heart thump, thankful she hasn't let my hand go.

"Ah, yes, dear you seem ecstatic," Persephone continues dryly. Her eyes drift warmly over her daughter as she lifts Des' chin to meet her gaze.

Her skin is like porcelain in contrast to Desephone's bronzed brown. Legends say Hades formed his daughter in the fire with his own hands, but Des always said she was the spitting image of her mother. I suppose both can be true.

Even still, despite their skin tone, it doesn't take a genius to see the imprint of the Queen of the Underworld all over the Desephone. From the way her lips draw together to the fluttering of her eyes as the two women stare at one another, their connection is easy to see.

"You surprised me is all," Des says softly, now resting her face in her mother's palm.

"And you me," Persephone answers, but this time, her gaze travels to me. "Here I was, prepared to give you a tongue lashing about not having found a suitor, and you arrive hand-in-hand with this impressive stallion!" she lauds her praise appreciatively.

"Stallion!" Des shrieks, quickly pulling her hand from mine. "This is no stallion, Mother! This is Arius Knight, resident Bulwark. He's no suitor. He's my friend."

Ouch. I don't know what hurts worse: her hand falling from mine, or being put in the friend zone.

But I'll let it go for now. Soon enough, more than her hand will cling to me.

CHAPTER 5

Desephone

S hit.

I didn't mean for that to come out the way it did.

But the last thing I need is to get Ari tangled up in the mess I've made of my life. Even if I thought someone like Arius, who could have any woman he wants, was even interested in me in that way, I know it's impossible.

Bulwarks can't marry.

That's the rule, an impossible one to break.

Sure, they can fuck and frolic to their heart's content, but bonding in marriage is non-negotiable. Their sole purpose in life is to protect the peace and balance of the supernatural. Everything else is secondary. Bulwarks like Arius can never be put in a position to choose love over peace. It's forbidden.

I know this, and so does he.

So even if I've let my hand wander my body to thoughts of him at night, that's a secret I'll keep forever. For now, and as far as Mother, Ari, or anyone else needs to know, he is just my friend.

"My, my, dearest," Mother breathes, stepping back with one hand over her chest. "Even a large tree makes a sound when it falls in the forest. And by goodness, I swear I heard his heart tumble when you threw him aside with no regard. I thought I taught you better than that."

Looking over my shoulder at Ari, I'm thankful he doesn't seem as jilted as Mother claims. His jaw does seem a little tight, but he has also been acting strange all day.

Giving him a gentle shove, I throw him a wink. "Oh, Mother, Ari knows what I meant. Don't you, Ari?"

His eyes narrow a bit, his jaw flexing until he comes up with a rigid smile that barely reaches his eyes. Turning from me, he offers a hand to my mother.

"A pleasure to meet you, Great Queen," he says, bowing at the waist.

Grinning like a schoolgirl, Mother shoots me a silly smile as he adds a small kiss to her wrist. "The pleasure is all mine, Mr. Knight. A Bulwark?" She raises a brow toward me. "Well, you are quite the specimen. I've never known those of your species to be so..." Her eyes scan the entirety of Arius, hovering a bit at his waist before traveling back up to his face. "Well-sculpted," she finishes, gliding her tongue over her teeth.

Although Mother knows Ari isn't my mate, she has always appreciated the company of a well-groomed man. With his taut, athletic frame, and the way his fitted trousers and polo show off his musculature, there's no question Mother is quite pleased I take company with such a handsome specimen like Arius Knight.

A slight rosy tint rises to his cheekbones as he takes a gracious step away from Mother's lingering gaze.

"Well, I should let you two get reacquainted," Arius says politely as he glances over his shoulder at me.

"Ari," I say, stepping in front of him before he can turn toward the door. "You don't have to leave right this second." The longer Mother spends ogling Ari, the less time she'll spend lecturing me on claiming a mate.

"You want me to stay?" he asks, his brows raised in surprise.

His searing stare locks me in place, as though he's trying to read my soul. Although I know it's impossible for him to do so, Arius is the only one who can read me like a book. I have no poker face with him.

"No," Mother answers for me, breaking the tension between us. "She wants you to keep me occupied so she can further neglect her duties as the next ruler of the Underworld. Isn't that correct, Desephone?"

Blowing out a breath, my long bangs sweep against my forehead.

"Is that so, Des? Am I just a convenient distraction?" Ari laughs, throwing me a jaunty grin. He knows Mother is right, but him making light of it tells me he's willing to play along.

Shaking my head, I laugh with him, maintaining the pretense. "A most convenient one, I might add," I reply with a wink.

"Very well. Have it your way," Mother groans, sauntering across the foyer into the floral shop. Her long, red cape dusts the floor as she moves along. Making her way to a small white wicker bench near my office, she takes a seat, waving her hand for Arius and me to follow suit.

Our eyes drift to one another, but Arius gestures for me to go ahead as he walks close behind. I'm so glad he decided to stay. It feels better having him here with me. Mother will likely proceed civilly just because he's here. My parents pride themselves on appearances.

There's no way she'll let Arius be present for her more grimly side, even more so because he's a Bulwark. By all rights, Bulwarks should exile anyone from the Netherworld, including me, but he has made no move to out me to the powers-that-be all this time. I highly doubt he'll do so now.

"So, I suppose you know why I'm here," Mother begins, keeping her gaze fixed on me.

"Whether I do or not, I'm sure you'll inform me," I sneer, rolling my eyes.

Mother takes a deep breath, lifting her chin high as she raises an appreciative brow. Turning slightly to Arius, she blares another bright smile. "It appears my daughter is rather cheeky today. Tell me, Master Bulwark, is she always so snippy? Or is it me?"

Ari lets out a small chuckle, looking at me briefly over his shoulder before returning his attention to my mother.

"I'm afraid I can't call it, Great Queen. Then again, the hour is quite late. Perhaps she—"

"Can speak for herself?" I wistfully bite back, surprised at my friend's ill-fitted alliance with my mother. I kept him here for my comfort, not hers.

"Well, by all means, please do so," Mother charges, gesturing her hand toward me as though she's allowing me to speak.

Studying her face, I can tell Mother is hardly bothered. In fact, this is what she wants to see. That I am tough. Not a pushover, can hold my own. More than finding a suitor, Mother told me if the barbarity of the earthbound plane didn't toughen me, nothing would.

She was right.

Mother's posture shifts a bit, and I watch her closely, parrying her movements until my leg crosses the other just as she does the same. Her eyes share a smile her lips can't tell, but with the sparkle I now see reflected in her shimmering gaze, I know I've impressed the reigning Queen of the Underworld.

Exhaling a small breath, I smile, curling my hair around my finger and placing the loose tendril behind my ear. "You want to know if I've found a suitor. Am I correct, Mother?"

"Presuming you know the answer to that question, I'll ask plainly: have you, in fact, found a suitor, my dear?" Mother's stare narrows a bit, and I know she's trying to read me. Although she has always been content to let me tell her the truth rather than search my soul, I know her patience with me is waning.

Quickly, I reach for Ari's hand, squeezing it tight and resting it on my lap. My nervous glance over my shoulder betrays me as Ari's eyes search mine with confusion. I flit my eyes back to Mother before the sight of the curl of Ari's mustache against his full, raspberry-colored lips lulls me into thoughts best left to my own secret lusts.

"As I mentioned before, Arius is the resident Bulwark of this region."

Mother lets out an exasperated sigh coupled with a hearty eye roll. "Yes, and?"

Squeezing Ari's hand harder, I shoot him a knowing glance, hopeful he'll play along. He grips my hand tighter, his thumb lightly grazing my knuckles, making prickly goosebumps erupt up my arm.

"Well," I choke out, working hard to ignore the feel of Ari's hand in mine. "He also runs a very successful bar, Dram Deaux, just across the street," I say, pointing out the window. Mother's eyes drift toward the window just long enough to see Ari's place before turning back to me. Rushing to speak before she asks more, I continue, "All types of creatures, vampires, wolves, and others, make their way through. And Ari has agreed to host a speed dating slash Culling type of function there this week to help me select a suitor. We were just on our way here to discuss the particulars when you arrived."

Ari's hand falls from mine, and I feel his body tense like stone. Mother's speculative stare shoots like daggers toward me. Yet, losing Ari's touch is the only thing stabbing my heart.

CHAPTER 6

Arius

W*hat the actual fuck?*

As much as I want to help Des out right now, I'm finding it hard to muster the will to keep a straight face.

Does she think I want to help her find a man?

The hell I do.

It's a wonder how I put up with her corralling all these years. Sure, I dug this damn hole, lying to myself that there was no future for us, but who am I fooling? The only future I see is her. She is my future. My present. My everything.

31

"Marvelous!" Persephone squeals, surprising both me and Des.

Des is shocked, her eyes traveling fast between me and her mother before placing a fretful palm on my shoulder. "See, Ari?" Her piercing eyes hold me still, hopeful I'll fall in line. "Mother thinks it's a grand idea," she whispers, her eyes pleading with me to stay the course.

Persephone jumps up, clapping her hands as she rushes toward the window, pulling the curtains aside to take a look at my bar.

"Ari, please," Desephone mouths with her pretty, pouty lips. Her round, glassy eyes are making promises she has no idea she'll one day fulfill.

Everything in me says hell no. There's no way I should agree to anything remotely as ridiculous as hosting a tribute of suitors for the woman I'm in love with.

But damn it, I can't deny her.

"Great!" I swallow hard as I give her knee a small squeeze. She needs to know I'm not cool with this idea, but I'm going along with it for her sake.

"Thank you," Des mouths once more, and her mouth stays puckered long enough for my mind to wander into thoughts of a better place for those lovely lips.

"You will." The dark promise leaves my mouth the moment it enters my mind. Desephone's eyes grow wide, and her breath hitches as her cheeks blush red.

"Perfect!" Persephone continues, making her way back to us. Des turns away from me, swallowing hard as she slides away from me on the bench. "I am so glad you've maintained a sense of propriety after all these long years, my daughter. I know it hasn't been an easy task, but the time has come."

Clearing her throat, Des looks up to her mother. "Is this about Father? Is he—"

"Oh, Nethers no, dearest!" Persephone exclaims, taking her daughter by the hand, pulling on her until she stands. "Hades isn't the issue here. We just don't have the luxury to drag this on any longer. The Culling—or speed dating, as you call it—needs to err on the expeditious side."

"But Mother, we–"

"I know, I know, dearest. You were likely hoping to procure a sizable lot for this Culling, but we can't waste the week on such a venture. You'll need to commence with mating, then the nuptials, and then—"

"Wait! Wait!" I jump up from my seat. "Did you say mating?" I can almost feel the intensity of my thick brow nearly lifting from my forehead as I lean toward Desephone.

Her eyes widen in just as much shock, but she bites her lip and turns her attention back to Persephone.

"Mother, please." She lifts a cautionary palm toward me. "Let's not get ahead of ourselves. One thing at a time, please."

Sighing, the Queen of the Underworld sways side-to-side, trying to rein in her zeal. "It's just that we don't have time for a drawn-out Culling. A quick and dirty bout of wits and strength should suffice."

Desephone shoots a look at me, likely still hoping I'm good with this idea. I'm not, but the train has left the station as far as Persephone is concerned.

"I suppose Ari and I can put something together, but—"

"Splendid!" Persephone issues a thunderous clap at her thin waist. "You two discuss the particulars of sport, and I'll make a quick call to an old friend. I'm sure they can get a full-bodied brood to make their way to the Dram Deaux later tonight. Do you still have that jade mirror?"

Des lowers her head, pointing toward the staircase. "Yes, Mother. Upstairs on the mantle."

Pulling Des' face into her frightfully pale palms, Persephone kisses her daughter's cheek, lingering for a moment before disappearing like a flash of lightning before my eyes.

"Des, I—"

"Look, Ari, I'm sorry you got dragged into this. I know I panicked. But I can straighten it out if you need me to."

My better judgment tells me to shut this shit down now. Everything inside me is screaming to tell Des how I feel, but my better judgment is no match for the stunning creature staring back at me. Besides, her mother might possibly object to the mere notion of us together just by nature of what I am.

Bulwarks and Netherfolk have a sordid history. Long ago, when the earthbound plane was separated from the Netherworld, it was my ancestors, the Bulwarks, who drove those like Persephone and Hades into the darkness.

Since that time, Netherfolk have been at war with my wicked distant kin, the Changelings. Not only have the Changelings, the dark fae of both worlds, been at odds with every supernatural creature since the beginning of time, but even now, they work hard to strip Hades of his power, hopeful to one day rule the Underworld.

The ruler of the Underworld keeps the power of the dead and the damned. If the Changelings were to come into such power, they'd be unstoppable. That's why Desephone was sent away all those years ago. Once she claims rulership of the Underworld, the power belonging to Hades will become hers. She will be impenetrable. For thousands of years, Hades has held off the Changelings. Now, it's her turn. Coupled with her father's power, Desephone will be a force.

And it's for this reason, I'll once more acquiesce to this lovely woman before me, who has my heart locked in the palm of her hands. She is the force that keeps the wind beneath my feet.

"I've got you, Des," I whisper, offering my hand. She places her palm in mine, and I pull her close.

"Oof!" she squeals as she stumbles, landing square on my chest. "You caught me off guard with that one, Ari. I almost fell."

"You fell right where you belong," I say, brushing her hair from her face. Her round eyes stare up at me, and it's taking all my willpower not to crush my mouth to hers. "Like I said, I've got you."

Resting her head on my chest, Des sighs, the feel of her body pressed into mine driving me insane. Every soft curve of hers molds perfectly into every hard ridge of mine, making me think of how perfect this moment would be if we were alone. In fact, I have no doubt that if her mother, the Queen of the fucking Underworld, wasn't right upstairs, this could be far beyond a fantasy.

"Thank you, Ari," Des whispers as her petite fingers circle the buttons on my shirt. "I don't think I could've done this without you."

Against my better judgment, I plant a small kiss on the crown of her head. I know unrequited intimacy with a daughter of death could be my end, but I don't give a damn. My soul could burn, fall into a heap of ash, and be swept into the sea, but she'll always remember being in my arms.

"Don't worry, baby. You'll never have to do another thing without me. I promise you."

Baby? Shit. Did I say that out loud?

Des pulls back some, her lovely lashes sweeping upward until her eyes meet with mine. Just one look, and I know she heard me clearly. And yet, I see no objection in her eyes.

CHAPTER 7

Desephone

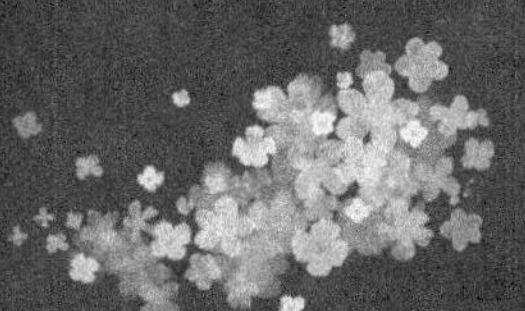

Arius Knight just called me *baby*. I must still be tipsy. That's the only explanation for bringing home a wolf I barely know and clumsily falling into Arius' strong and waiting arms like a silly schoolgirl. Then again, I don't know how much of that was me being tipsy, or me wanting to be in his arms.

Over the years, he has never shied away from hugging me or holding my hand. I assumed this was more of his big brotherly antics.

Then again...

"It's all settled," my mother chimes as she flashes into the room like a bolt of lightning. Arius and I take a generous, albeit awkward, step away from one another. Mother doesn't seem to notice as she casually saunters between us, her clasped hand resting beneath her chin. "I just spoke to my contact, and they assured me there'll be a fitting assortment for the future queen."

"Mother!" I shriek, turning toward her. "Please tell me you didn't tell them who I was. We're Nether. By rights, we're not even supposed to be on the earthbound plane. I've worked hard at keeping a low profile for a reason. Besides, I hardly want to bring any undue attention Ari's way."

She swipes a dismissive hand through the air. "Oh, rubbish! News of your Culling will hardly make it outside of the city. Only the best-suited will be sent. Of those, only someone comparable to your own soul will make it through the Culling. All others, well, they—they can die knowing they were given such an opportunity."

"Mother, please. You could show some measure of empathy. We're literally asking folk to possibly give up their lives for me."

"You're worth it," Arius interjects, his tone flat and hard as his pointed gaze sears into me from the other side of the room.

Mother briefly casts her gaze between us before turning back to me. "The Bulwark is absolutely right, my dear. Besides, their meaningless lives won't be for naught. Hades will procure their souls once they reach the Underworld."

Sighing, I plop down on the bench, resting my forehead in my palm. "You do realize calling their lives meaningless hardly makes me feel good about this, right, Mother?"

Sitting down beside me, Mother wraps her arm around me, squeezing me so I'm deep into the crook of her neck. "Oh, dearest, you've been earthbound too long. You're beginning to sound like them. Listen," she continues softly, lifting my chin with her ghostly pale forefinger. "I know this isn't how you wanted things to go, but it's what must be done, especially since you haven't found a suitor. That's why I was glad to hear you were working with your friend here to put a Culling together."

"Yes, Mother, I know what has to be done. But why does it have to be an old-fashioned Culling? I don't want anyone dying for me.

Maybe some arm wrestling, blade-wielding, or jousting, but to be culled within an inch of their life, all for me? It's not worth it!"

"You're worth it and then some!" Ari grouses once more.

"Ari?" I groan, surprised by his stance.

Mother's face brightens as she pushes up in her seat, looking up at Arius. "Do tell, Bulwark."

"Why shouldn't someone put it all on the line for you, give their all for you? I know I would."

Silence fills the space between us as my mother's eyes toggle from me to Ari. Perhaps even she thinks he has taken his role as a protective Bulwark too far.

My mouth cracks open just as Mother raises her hand, halting my protest. "I understand, dear, that you don't want anyone dying, but perhaps we can set up a *tour de force* of sorts."

Nodding in agreement, Arius chimes in. "We can arrange the bar where there are various skill levels. The weakest are sent home, per Des' aversion to seeing their demise."

"And the strong?" I ask.

"The strong continue forward, leaving one champion behind to commence with the mating," Mother answers brusquely.

Both Arius and I trade awkward glances as Mother rises from her seat.

"Bulwark, do you think you can work with my daughter to put together a selection of skills?"

With a slight bow, Ari dips his head with a hand pledged over his heart. "Yes, Great Queen. It would be my honor."

Smiling over her shoulder at me, Mother throws me a wink. "I really like this one."

"He has his moments," I grumble, gnawing at my fingernails.

Lightly swatting my hand from my mouth, Mother shakes her head in disapproval. "As I said before, I've left you here too long, dearest. You've even picked up some of the mortals' disgusting habits."

Ignoring her rebuke, I fold my arms and lean back into my seat. "And what will the Queen of the Underworld be doing while we're busy at work?"

Her shoulders roll forward as she chuckles, sauntering past me to the display of flowers. Gracefully, she trails her petite fingers over the petals. Each one withers, crisp petals falling to the ground as she makes her way around the store.

"Well, someone ought to see to the beautification of this place in preparation for the prenuptial mating. Would be a shame to go through the whole trouble of a Culling only for your mating to fail due to an improper setting. Then, we'd have to do it all over again, and I promise you, it will not be this weak-kneed *tour de force* or speed dating, but a full-fledged Culling."

"What exactly does a full-fledged Culling look like, Your Highness? I'd like to get the selection as close as possible," Arius says, rubbing the stubble on his jaw.

"Arius, please—we don't need to get into that right now," I plead, but Mother shoots me a cross look.

"The Bulwark is curious, so I'll give him the condensed version. In a proper Culling, the potentials would vie for Desephone's attention through a series of strength competitions and wits battles. Those who don't catch her eye die. Those who do progress to the next round until there's only one left standing."

"Ah, I see," Arius says, pursing his lips tight like his mind was somewhere else. "And then you move onto the mating."

Mother gestures her hands toward Arius and smiles. "Precisely!"

"No, you don't, Ari!" I snap as his eyes flit to mine. "What Mother is leaving out is that the mating is even more perilous."

Arius keeps his eyes pinned on me. "How so?"

Mother steps in front of Arius, blocking my view. "I believe that is a matter best left for her and her intended."

"No, Mother!" I shout, jumping up from my seat. "He should

know. I mean, since he's being dragged into this. Since he'll be partly responsible for leading *meaningless souls* to their demise!"

"Des, please," Ari begins with a soft smile that reaches his eyes. "I'm not being dragged into anything."

Mother turns me away from Arius. "This doesn't concern the Bulwark, my dear," she warns, narrowing her eyes tight as she looks at me. "Right now, your focus should be on the Culling. I'll stay back and take care of things here." With a firm grip on my wrist, she adds a little squeeze as her blue eyes flash like lightning. "Should he withstand the Culling, the champion of your heart will acquiesce to the rules of the mating if it is truly meant to be. You, my dear, should keep an open mind, for even the stoniest of hearts can be molded into a beautiful flower in the right hands."

Her gaze briefly travels over my shoulder to Arius and then back at me as her mouth curls into a soft smile.

I offer a slight nod, knowing both Arius and Mother mean well. This is my lot. "Yes, Mother."

CHAPTER 8

Arius

Queen Persephone wasted no time sending us on our way. She seemed rather eager to transform Des' place into whatever she considers a place conducive to proper mating—whatever that means.

After I ran to the bar to change and grab my keys while Des changed her clothes, we were alone in my car. I do my best not to notice how adorably fuckable Des looks in her yoga pants and crop top with her hair upswept in a ponytail. If she didn't look like she was going to pass out from exhaustion, I might consider taking her somewhere private and finally share how I feel.

But I'd rather she take some time to rest, if that's what she needs right now.

Neither one of us *requires* sleep but sometimes it helps to sleep off a bout of frustration or simply to pass the time. Sure, we do it to maintain appearances, but we can go days or weeks at a time without it. Still, Des is far too quiet for my liking. It's not like her.

She's not even looking at me. Instead, her head is pressed against the cool glass as her arms fold around her.

I've never seen her so dejected. The sight of it is tearing me up inside.

Desephone is always so sure of herself, so strong. Yet, in just a few short minutes with her mother, she has withered just as quickly as the flowers in her shop. I suppose her mother does have that effect on everything she touches–even her daughter.

Although a part of me believes the Queen only wants the best for her daughter, her old-world, Netherworld approach to Des is a bit off-putting.

So, I guess it's up to me to take care of her. We'll get to the business of the Culling soon enough. First, I need to cheer her up. If this is to be my last day with her, I'll be sure it's one to remember.

Pulling out of the parking lot, Des continues leaning into the window. Now, however, her eyes are closed. I'm not sure if she's asleep, but she seems content to let me take her wherever.

Knowing how much she fancies soundscapes, I turn on the nature playlist she added to my phone some time ago.

Once, a few wolves got into a scuffle at the bar and the place was a mess. After everyone was gone, she downloaded a bunch of nature tunes to the playlist and connected it to the bar Bluetooth so it could play while we cleaned up.

Until then, I'd never been much on soundscapes, but it seemed to settle the negative energy in the bar—so much so, not even Gypsy or Cade got into an argument. We just picked up merrily as the soothing sound of waterfalls and birds chirping lulled us into a state of serenity.

I'm pleased to see her arms fall into her lap and her head shift onto the headrest as the music plays and we continue down the road. Her eyes stay closed, and that's fine with me. She might not need sleep, but she needs to rest.

"Wake up, Sleeping Beauty," I whisper with a light pat to her shoulder.

Her eyes pop open in a dreamy haze before she focuses on me. "I wasn't asleep," she mumbles with a cute little yawn. "Where are we?" she adds, stretching her arms in front of her, her hands clasped together, cracking her knuckles.

"If you were awake, you'd know. Now, come on," I say, pushing the button of her seatbelt and hopping out of the car.

"Bessie's!" I hear Des shriek as I round the front of the car, making my way to the passenger side. I open the door, and she looks up at me. "Ari, we don't have time for this," she protests, climbing out of the car. "Mother will–"

"What was that?" I laugh, leaning toward her with my hand cupped at my ear. "Was that a grumble?"

"No, Ari! It was a disagreement! I am disagreeing with you!" she fusses, poking my arm hard.

Still laughing, I lean into her once more. "Nope, I distinctly heard a rumble. At least, that's what I heard on the drive over here —your tummy doing somersaults over the sound of ocean waves. Oh, and is that bacon I smell?" I continue, waving my hand toward her.

Looking around, Desephone's eyes wander. She has always been enamored by the lure of New Orleans. Her eyes roam to the festively decorated buildings in yellow, pink, and green. It's nowhere near the season for Mardi Gras, but you couldn't tell by the looks of things. Even though it's more than ninety minutes from where we live in Biloxi, I also know it's one of her favorite places to visit. My goal today is to lift her spirits, and this is just the beginning.

Des lifts her chin, inhaling the alluring smell of bacon seeping out of Bessie's Tavern. Her stomach growls, and she folds in at the waist, embarrassed. "Damn it!"

Looping our arms together, I close the car door with my foot and hit the car alarm. "Good thing I brought you to your favorite place for breakfast. You know, the one with the fluffy, stuffed French toast and endless helpings of—"

"Brown sugar bacon!" she squeals, tightening her hold around my arm as she bounces up and down at my side. "You'll be the death of me, Arius Knight!"

"I should hope not," I laugh, leading us inside.

"That's if Mother doesn't get to you first. I mean, you *did* take us over the friggin' Pontchartrain into New Orleans. We're over an hour from home!"

I give a hard squeeze to her hand in mine when a hostess greets us. "How many?"

"Table for two, please," I reply before Des can answer. My gut tells me she was going to ask for food to go. There's no way she'll get off that easy. I'm soaking up every moment I have with her.

We're seated at our table, and Des quickly throws the menu up to her face. "I don't know why I'm even looking at this menu," she chuckles, peering over the bifold.

I laugh with her, pushing my menu to the edge of the table. "Yep. We get the same thing every time."

Sighing, she shakes her head. "Yeah, well, it's a long way to come for steel-cut oatmeal, Ari."

"Perhaps." I shrug my shoulders and take a sip of the lemon water the hostess gave us when we were seated. "But it's the best oatmeal. You should try it."

"With the crumbled bacon in it? That's gross, Ari! I don't know how you do it."

"Don't knock it 'till you try it," I laugh, happy to see her spirits lifted.

A hearty chuckle from behind startles me. "Well, well, look what the cat dragged in!"

I don't have a chance to turn around when Des jumps up from her seat. "Miss Mel!" she shrieks, throwing her small arms around Miss Melvina.

I'm on my feet in a flash, waiting for my chance to hug one of Louisiana's finest and resident Grandmère Bulwark. "Miss Melvina! So good to see you!"

Opening her arms, Des nestles on the other side of Miss Mel, just enough for me to get a hug in.

She's still laughing, her round, soft frame shaking merrily as she holds us tight. "Always a pleasure to see my babies. What brings y'all 'round these parts?" she asks, finally letting us out of her hold.

"Oh, you know, we just love seeing our favorite Bulwark!" Des grins, still holding Miss Mel's arm.

Miss Mel smiles down at Des. She's almost as tall as me, making Des look like a child in her embrace. I marvel at how she has barely aged since I met her over seventy years ago. She was the one to set me up in Biloxi. None of the other Bulwarks wanted much to do with a halfling like me, but Miss Mel has been like a maternal figure in my life.

Desephone has been chummy with Melvina since we first came to the tavern. I was surprised the two had known each other. Neither has ever said how they met exactly, and I've never asked. I always assumed if Miss Melvina, being such a high-ranking Bulwark, didn't see any problems with Desephone being here, no one else could have room to talk.

"Ha!" Miss Melvina belts out, a hand on her hip. "Tell me

anything while I'm looking at ya. Well, you two have a sit-down, and I'll get your orders for you."

"But we haven't ordered yet," I frown, taking Miss Melvina's hand before she walks away.

Laughing once more, Miss Melvina leans toward my ear. "The minute I seen y'all pull up, I put your order in. I know my babies," she says before flashing a wink to Des.

She doesn't waste time with small talk. Instead, Miss Melvina sloths her feet across the dusty tile floor until she reaches the pastry bar. Pointing at us, she whispers something to the blonde hostess and disappears.

Resting her chin on her knuckles, Desephone sighs with a sweet smile. "It's always good to see Miss Mel. She's such a sweetheart."

"That she is," I agree. "You never told me how you two met."

Desephone's smile fades, and she quickly grabs her glass of lemon water. "I'm pretty sure I've told you that story," she says, taking a sip of water.

Pursing my lips, I shake my head. "I think I would've remembered."

She waves a dismissive hand. "Oh, you probably just forgot."

"You should know by now. I don't forget a thing when it comes to you, baby."

Damn it. I've said it again.

CHAPTER 9

Desephone

This is not a topic I want to discuss right now.

In all our years together, Arius Knight has dug very little into my past.

Besides knowing I'm the daughter of Hades sent here to find a forever mate, Arius always seemed fine to let me share at my own pace, and that always worked well for me.

He's always been the one to take me as I am and let the chips fall where they may.

So why is he so curious suddenly?

But if he wants to know, here goes.

"When we first met, I had just awakened after nearly five hundred years in repose."

"Whoa!" Ari quietly shrieks, surprised by my admission. "I had no idea."

An uneasy smile crosses my face, but I continue. "Yes. When my eyes closed, I had just escaped being burned at the stake for witchcraft in a small town called Tivoli near Rome."

"I don't understand. Supernaturals were known during that period. Why would anyone think—"

"His name was Cecil, and we were in love. In fact, we were just married. In a small church–we had a priest and everything."

Ari's eyes grow distant, and the color seems to pale his tawny brown skin. While his reaction is surprising, his eyes tell me to continue.

"As I said, we were in love, and we wanted to do things traditionally–so we waited." I nod, pausing to ensure he understands. He nods in the affirmative, so I press my eyes tight, opening them quickly to resume after a hard sigh. "I was sure he was the one. It had been over fifteen hundred years of trial and error, but Cecil, a kind and gentle farmer, seemed to be the one. But he wasn't." Sighing once more, I take another swig of water.

"Des," Arius says, reaching across the table to grab my free hand. "You can tell me. Or not. It's up to you." He offers a reassuring smile that doesn't quite reach his eyes, but I know he's being sincere.

My eyes sting with tears as the painful memory drags through my mind. It's the first time I've said this to anyone, and if there was anyone I could share this with, it would be Ari.

I take another sip of water, letting the cool refreshment ease me back into the conversation. "He didn't make it past the honeymoon. His body burst into flames and shot through the roof of our dwelling, far into the night sky. It could be seen for miles. His family, whose home we were in, came upstairs, saw me in the bed holding his ashen husk, and accused me of witchcraft."

Arius firms his hold around my hand. "I'm so sorry, Des. I can't imagine how—"

A few tears race down my face, and I pull my hand away, grabbing the linen napkin to wipe my tears. Ari places his hand once more over mine, gently taking the napkin from me to dry my face.

"You know what? I'm sorry, Des. I shouldn't have made you relive something so painful," he whispers as his thumb lightly strums my cheek.

His touch is soothing, and I press my face into his palm. He has never touched me like this, but it feels so good—*too good*.

I gently pull away, sucking in a breath to gather my thoughts. "Well, you asked about Miss Melvina, so... "

Arius's eyes narrow a bit, like he's searching my soul, but he resigns, drawing his mouth into a tight smile. Placing the napkin on the table, he sits back in his chair. "Yeah, I'm still trying to get the connection."

A small chuckle escapes me as I wipe a tear from my chin. My eyes wander over Arius' shoulder, where I see Miss Melvina placing a tray of pastries into the glass shelf near the register. Her large, round frame mirrors the sun as her flowy yellow sundress hugs her curvaceous figure. She's everything mortals claim to love about grandmothers–strong yet cuddly, a giver of warm hugs and good advice. Miss Melvina is all those things.

And a little something more to me.

Ari clears his throat lightly, regaining my attention as I take a deep breath before I continue.

"Cecil's family attacked me and pronounced me a witch in front of the entire town. Although I could have just as easily declared them vampires before everyone, I could never destroy Cecil's family like that–even if they did revile me. So, I ran, hard and fast. Before long, I found myself in one of the last temples of Athena. There, a woman I first assumed was a statue, as she stood as still as stone, offered me consolation. She was seated on a large sarcophagus in the atrium, awaiting her next task, as the inhabitant of the coffin had recently risen."

"Miss Mel?" Arius breathes in shock. I only nod in return. "I'd always heard she kept watch of some of the most notorious vampires in history. I didn't know just how much she'd kept watch of the damned all these long years."

"Yes," I quietly agree, taking my last sip of water. "She offered me to stay in the coffin in repose until I was ready. Without hesitation, I took her up on her offer, and for five hundred years, I lay in repose. When I woke, I was in the Americas—here, in New Orleans."

With folded arms and an expression I can't place, Arius Knight stares at me like he's seeing me for the first time.

"Wow, Des! I had no idea."

I shrug a little. "How could you? Besides, one doesn't just go around telling folks you slept in the coffin of Decaux Marchand without starting a rumor."

His lips crinkle a bit before letting out a dry laugh. "Yeah, pretty sure said folks would get the wrong idea."

"Precisely!" I wave my hand around. "Funny enough, I've never met either of the Marchand brothers," I whisper. Both our eyes dart around a bit. Everyone knows both Dalcour and Decaux Marchand stay within earshot of Bessie's Tavern, frequenting here often— hence the reason why we only come here during the day.

After what Cecil's family put me through, I kept my distance from pure-blood vampires. Sure, I'd take a mortal-made vampire, a Scourge, or a hybrid, into my bed, but the aristocracy of purebloods sickens the bile in my gut.

I avoid them at all costs.

"And now you know," I sigh, pushing myself up in my seat. Mother would have my hide if she saw me slouched like a peasant without manners.

"Thanks for trusting me enough to share, Des," Ari whispers, his eyes still searching me as though he was mining for secrets.

Shaking off the nervous chill crawling up my spine, I snort, letting out my very unladylike giggle. If Mother could see me now. Wiggling my shoulders a bit, I run a hand through my hair.

"Thanks for caring enough to listen, Ari," I smile, tucking some hair behind my ear.

"I care more than you know, Desephone," Arius says darkly, his pointed gaze searing a hole in my chest.

"Hot plates!" the hostess from before calls out, breaking the intensity of the moment as she lowers a tray of food in front of us. "Here's your oatmeal and brown sugar bacon, sir," she offers to Arius with a polite nod as she places a large porcelain bowl in front of him. "And for you, miss," she shares a bright smile and a wink with me, "your stuffed French toast and bacon. Plates are hot, so be careful," she adds.

"Thank you," I say when I notice Arius still has his sights set on me. It's like neither the waitress nor the food is drawing his attention.

"Can I get you two anything else?" the hostess asks. "Miss Mel told me to treat her favorite customers right, so if there's anything on the menu you need–"

"We're good, thanks," Ari hastily replies, keeping his eyes on me as the hostess walks away. "Besides, what I want isn't on the menu."

Arius is staring at me like a hungry lion waiting to pounce, and a part of me wishes he would do just that.

CHAPTER 10

Arius

Breakfast was quick and quiet.

I'm not sure if I'm making Des uncomfortable or if bringing up such painful memories soured her mood. If I had to guess, I'd say it was a little bit of both.

Still, I resigned to stay quiet for the duration. I haven't overtly made my affections known, nor do I believe now is a good time to do so. Between her mother's arrival and the pressure to choose a suitor, throwing my hat into the ring would just make things much more complicated.

Seeing as Bulwarks like me are forbidden to marry and she'll soon return to the Netherworld, I'll likely wander the earthbound plane as do many of my kind: alone.

Maybe I'll just give my life to the Dram Deaux and live out my days as the caretaker of wayward wolves and lonely vampires needing a stiff drink and a listening ear. Perhaps this is my lot.

But it doesn't have to be so for Desephone. It's clear I need to do a little more to ease her mind.

We're back in my car before Miss Melvina can make her way back to us. The tavern picked up a bit after we got our food. After everything Des shared with me, I could tell she was eager to leave after she ate.

I didn't mind. The last thing I need is for Miss Melvina to get too suspicious about my intentions with Desephone. If other Bulwarks knew how I felt for Des, it could not only put both me and Des in jeopardy, but I could end up just like my father, and that's the last thing I want.

"Ari," Des says quietly as she stares out of the window.

"Yes?" I'm quick to answer, thankful for the interruption, lest my mind run away with me.

"Thanks for breakfast. It was sweet of you to bring me here." Reaching across the console, she places her palm on my shoulder.

"My pleasure," I answer with a dutiful nod.

"I mean, it's not every day a girl gets to eat her favorite food for the last time."

My eyes bounce to her face. Once more, the glassy pools I find there are begging me to jump in and swim deep. A soul as beautiful as Desephone belongs far from the Underworld and the entirety of the Netherworld itself!

Swallowing down my need to declare my heart to her and take her in my arms, I force the same strained smile I've plastered on my face since the first day we met.

It's the smile that means *I want what I cannot have and I need what isn't mine to take.* And yet, I hope she sees the earnest desire in me to be the best me I can be for her. She deserves that and more.

Holding back a need to sigh, I restrain the vexing of my own heart and press forward. "Well, what if that was only a means to an end?"

Her nose crinkles in that cute way it does when she realizes that even after three thousand years, she, Daughter of Hades, can still be surprised.

Giggling, Des squeezes my shoulder, shaking her head as she locks her seatbelt. "Okay, Mr. Knight. Whatever you say," she scoffs, throwing a generous eye roll my way. "All I know is, Mother won't be pleased if we don't curate Culling activities for the evening. I'm pretty sure you don't want to get on Persephone's bad side."

I give her a side eye of my own, throwing my mouth to one side. Queen of the Underworld or not, Persephone isn't the one who strikes fear in my heart the most. It's her daughter.

"Then I reckon *Mother* will be pleased with where I am taking you next." I smile as I begin backing out of the parking lot.

"Well, aren't you full of surprises today, Mr. Knight?"

"That I am." I smile as we head to our next destination.

We're on the west side of the Warehouse District when I pull into a seemingly vacant lot. Des wanders her gaze around a bit, her face frowning some as she turns to me.

"Where are we, Ari?" she mumbles, her adorable boujee ways shining through.

I don't respond; I just smile and hop out of the car, making my way to open her door.

"Do you trust me?" I whisper, leaning into the car so my forehead is touching hers. Des offers me her soft, sweet smile that makes me melt every time I see her. Offering my hand, I add a small kiss to the top of her head.

"Of course I do," she breathes back as her wide eyes lock with mine. Des places her small palm in my hand, and I help her out of the car. "Are you going to tell me where we are?" she asks, nervously staring around as I close the door and lead us around a tall brick building.

"Trust, remember?" I merrily reply, locking our arms together as we make our way to a small lead door.

Desephone stares around, frowning as she takes in the rickety metal steps leading to the doorway. She pulls a loose piece of chipped paint from the side of the building, her lips curled in disgust as she stares at me.

"Oh, Mother will be so pleased with this place!" Des scoffs, rolling her eyes as she follows me up the stairs.

"I only aim to please, Your Highness." I shoot her a wink over my shoulder and bang hard on the door.

"We open at four!" a grumpy voice chimes in from the side speaker.

"Let me in, idiot!" I yell back, pressing the small red button beneath the speaker.

"Ari!" Des squeezes my hand, shaking her head in protest. "We should leave," she whispers, her eyes trailing around.

"Don't tell me the Daughter of Hades is scared?" I tease.

Huffing, she yanks her hand from my arm. "Absolutely not! We just don't have time for this, Ari! Besides, they're obviously not open."

"Oh, they'll open for me!" I haughtily smirk.

Banging on the door once more, I thrust my thumb onto the red button. "Hey, shitface! If you don't open the door this instant, I'll set your ass to stone. And I mean just your ass, just like I did to your brother Perry. You'll be shitting bricks for weeks!" I laugh.

"Fuck you!" the voice growls back.

"That's it—I'm leaving!" Des mumbles, turning away. Just then, a loud buzzing comes through the speaker, and the door clicks open.

"After you, my lady," I smile, holding the door open.

Desephone, with folded arms and still frowning, slowly turns back around. Shaking her head, she narrows her eyes at me. "I'm probably going to regret this," she grouses.

"Just trust me," I nod, gesturing with my arm for her to go through the door.

"Trust you?" Des groans, narrowing her eyes at me cautiously. "Why is it that I'm just now hearing you can turn someone into stone? I thought we were friends," she playfully bites back with a sly smile.

"Don't worry, Princess," I say, placing my hand just above the small of her back. Her breath hitches, and a rosy tint fills her cheeks as she looks at me. "We *are* friends, but we can be so much more. For now, just usher your pretty self inside."

Desephone bites her lip, her cheeks now bright red as she crosses the threshold. I'm not sure how much longer I can restrain myself, but it's getting harder every minute.

Taking a deep breath as I entered the building was like a tale of two cities all its own. On the one hand, I inhaled copious amounts of Ari's enchanting scent, that sits somewhere between the soothing smell of jasmine and hints of chocolate. On the other hand, the dank, sweaty, moldy air of this dilapidated building sours my stomach, making me want to hurl the strawberry French toast and bacon from earlier.

Thankfully, likely sensing my angst, Ari locks his arm with mine, and I turn my head into the nape of his neck as he leads us along. I'd much rather have his scent permeate my pores than whatever putrid scent lives within these walls.

Although Ari's last sentiment, *we can be so much more*, sends shivers up my spine, I don't let it get to my head. I'm sure Arius is just happy to see me finally opening up to him.

For over fifty years, our relationship has grown from neighbors to friends. We've gone out on double dates, exchanged awkward glances when said dates bored us, and have more than our share of inside jokes. And yet, in all this time, today was the first day I've mentioned Cecil. Memories of him have always haunted me. Until now, only Mother and Miss Melvina knew the reasons behind my five-hundred-year slumber. Thoughts of Cecil have always been too painful to ponder.

Strangely, for the first time, the sting wasn't as intense. Talking with Ari has always been so easy. Maybe it's because I'm leaving. Knowing I'm headed to the Underworld surely takes some of the pressure off me. I mean, having to look Ari in the eye for another century knowing he knows my darkest secret would be too much to bear. Telling him now feels more tolerable.

Yeah, that's it.

"What the actual fuck, bro?" an overly muscular, heavily inked, shirtless man says as he trots down a narrow staircase wearing nothing but gym shorts. Pulling a cut-off shirt over his head to conceal his chiseled physique, he tosses his long, wavy black hair to one side. "This better be urgent. I mean, I got my lady here and everything..." he grumbles, pointing over his shoulder toward the staircase.

I peek over his large frame and spy a woman wearing an over-sized jersey walking past the landing, sipping a cup of tea as a small, white and gray cat follows her. I can't make out much more of her than a voluptuous silhouette, but I have no doubt she's gorgeous.

"Your lady?" Ari laughs offering his hand. "What lies did you tell this poor woman?"

The two shake hands and go in for a quick hug, followed by pounding one another's backs like they're bricklayers.

"I could say the same to you, Bulwark," the man huffs, now

offering his hand to me. "How does a scum of a halfling like you have such a lovely creature on your arm?"

"Please," Ari scoffs, shoving the guy in the chest as he steps in front of me. I'm almost surprised at how easily Arius forces him back. The man is twice—if not three—times his size. Other than him ripping that wolf Derek apart and throwing his weight around here, you'd never think someone with his svelte frame could be just as dominating.

"Des," Ari continues, looking over his shoulder. "Let me introduce you to one of the Warehouse District's finest, Perry Bossier. He runs all you see here," Ari says, waving his arm around proudly. Perry's name sounds familiar. I vaguely remember Ari and Gypsy mentioning him from time to time.

I force a smile. I might not see the grandeur of this place, but I don't want to insult Ari or his friend, especially not after we so rudely barged in on his time with his lady.

"It's very nice to meet you, Perry. I'm sorry we interrupted your—"

"Oh, Des, don't worry about Perry. I'm sure he doesn't mind. Do you, Perry?" Arius says, playfully jabbing Perry's arm. Perry blocks Ari's next punch and throws one to his side while pulling his arm behind his back, restraining him.

Arius reaches up and over his shoulder with the opposite arm, making a mess of Perry's mane. Somehow, Ari manages to free himself from Perry's hold, shoving him away in a blink.

I inwardly chuckle watching how the two act more like brothers than friends.

"I'm sorry about Mr. Knight here, ma'am. It seems your boyfriend doesn't know how to properly introduce his lady." Bowing at the waist, Perry smiles, gesturing his arm toward me as he slowly rises.

Grunting, Arius shoves Perry again, but this time, it's not as playful. "She's not my lady," he says matter-of-factly. "Des is my friend. Isn't that right?" His tone is stiff as he turns his attention toward me. His nose twitches, and his eyes dance with something I can't understand.

A sharp pain stabs me right in the gut, and I wish I could disappear into a cloud of smoke. I never use my powers like I should, but now feels like the most opportune moment. I wish I could swallow down my own angst, but I cannot. My mouth is dry, my lips glued shut.

Silence stirs through the air as both men stare at me.

"Way to put her on the spot, guys!" a sharp feminine voice shoots from the top of the stairs. Looking up, I can still only make out a luxurious pair of legs as she leans against the wall.

"We're all good here, babe, thanks!" Perry calls back, laughing as he bumps his shoulder against Arius, who remains staring at me while standing like a statue. "Please forgive me. Des, is it? It's just that fart face here never brings a lady with him. I figure you've gotta be pretty special."

"Oh, no doubt, shithead." Arius forces a laugh as he pokes his elbow into Perry's side. "This one is pretty special. Des. My pretty special friend," he says, never taking his eyes off me.

Friend. Yeah, I think I hate that word right now.

"And where exactly is here, Perry?" I ask, sliding past Arius and closer to his friend.

A jaunty grin spreads over Perry's face as he looks over my shoulder to Arius. "Fuck, man. You didn't tell her what we do here?"

Arius lets out a wispy chuckle and leans against the wall. With one arm folded across his chest, he gestures for Perry to proceed. "I'll let you tell her," he says, shooting me a wink.

"Some kind of friend this one is," Perry scoffs, opening his arm for me to lock with him. "Hey, Ally Cat! I'll be right back. Gonna show these two around and get them a room," he yells up the stairs.

"Make it quick!" she answers cooly as she walks out of view.

A room?

Prickly sensations erupt all over me. Part of me hopes this is not what I think it is, but an almost greater part of me hopes it is. Then again, Perry said Arius never brought anyone here before, so what kind of room could this be?

Exhaling whatever is left of my indecision, I allow Perry to lead us through a pair of double doors. Arius follows so close behind, I can almost feel the heat of his body next to mine.

The doors open to a large, open warehouse. There are heavy bags, large tires, ropes, and dumbbells arrayed throughout.

"It's a gym!" I shriek, surprised. "So, what? Do you all train together? Circuit training or something like that?" I ask, pulling from Perry's side as I stare at them.

The two share a look and an awkward smile.

"Well, this is a gym. We get folks from all walks of life in here to —" He stops and looks at Arius, ensuring it's okay to continue.

"It's okay, Perry. She's cool," Arius says with an affirming nod.

Blowing out a sigh of relief, Perry runs a hand through his hair. "Mostly wolves come from all around to train here. While only the elite den leaders and alphas get to train at the Civility Center run by Dalcour Marchand, here, wolves from all walks of life come to train."

"Oh, that's nice," I breathe out, unsure why Arius wouldn't think I'd be interested in all he's done here.

"Nice?" Perry huffs with a small chuckle. "Yeah, more like Mr. Modest. While Dalcour Marchand takes all the credit for coordinating civility efforts between us monsters, it's Mr. Modest over here who makes sure no wolf, hybrid or otherwise gets left behind. He may be a shithead, but at least he gives a fuck. That's more than those pure blood vampires or den leaders have ever done for us *lesser* creatures."

I can't believe this is the first time I'm hearing about this side of Ari. Beyond the bar and being an ardent ladies' man, he doesn't talk much about himself. Now I'm starting to see him in a whole new light.

Circling Perry so he alone is in my view, Arius adds a faux cough as he curves his lips to one side. "But that's not why I brought you here, lovely," he says, flashing a quick wink. "Perry," he says over his shoulder, keeping his eyes on me. "It's time to take Des to my room. It's why I brought you here," he adds with a dashing grin that makes my heart thump.

CHAPTER 12
Arius

I'm an ice bucket of nerves right now.

I should be using this time to tell Des how I feel—how I've always felt about her. Instead, I've backed myself into this friend zone. With no end in sight or even a light at the end of the fucking tunnel, giving me even a glimpse that she'd be open to the idea of us, I have no choice but to cement my place as her friend.

And if I must be in the zone, I'll be the best fucking friend she'll ever have.

"Right this way, folks!" Perry says merrily over his shoulder. Des gives me a quick look before following Perry past a pair of heavy bags through another door. Perry leads us down a long, narrow hallway until we get to a red door. "You sure about this?" Perry's tone is heavy as he stares right past Des, his eyes locking with mine.

"Absolutely," I rush out as I feel Des's hesitation building. I won't give her a chance to renege before she even sees what I want to show her. Besides, she's been open to me; it's time I do the same.

"Wait!" Des shouts, holding a hand toward Perry. Turning to me, the worried glare on her face sends icy shivers up my spine. Still, I hold firm. "Arius, tell me–what's in there? What's in *your room*?"

"Well, you can either stand here–too chicken to open the door–or open it. Your choice," I answer pointedly.

Her lips curve into a frown, her eyes narrowing a bit as she marches past both me and Perry and turns the door handle, plunging her way inside.

"What the—" Des gasps, turning about, her eyes wandering from the floor to ceiling and back at me. "Ari?" she mumbles, her fingers fidgeting at her sides as she gazes around.

"Like it?" I smile, my hands in my pockets as I saunter inside.

"Yeah, Stoney here has made quite a beautiful mess of the place, don't ya think?" Perry laughs, as he flicks the light switch on, illuminating the room.

"Arius, what is this place?" Des asks, still turning about, her mouth gaping in wonder.

Perry chuckles, walking past us shaking his head as he opens a small closet door to our left. He shuffles around a bit before pulling out a large duffle bag.

Dropping it at my feet, Perry pats me on my shoulder. "Hey, I'll leave you two to it. I need to get back to Allyson."

Dapping me up, our fists pound together, and he gives a firm squeeze to my shoulder.

"She must be some girl to have you running back so fast," I tease as he begins to walk away.

His eyes circle playfully as he shakes his head, amused. "You have no idea. Anyway, you only have a little while. I have to drop her off at the airport soon so she can make it back to D.C."

"D.C., huh?" I chuckle. "Yeah, that sounds like a story I want to hear. Well, alright then. We won't be long. Just hit me up with my usual, please. Appreciate it…"

Perry raised a brow as he stands with the door ajar. "Your usual? Are you sure? For her first time?"

"Ari?" Des says my name through clenched teeth as her wary gaze drags the entirety of me.

Looking over my shoulder at Des, I offer her a reassuring wink before returning my attention to Perry. "Positive," I say, and Perry shuts the door hard.

Des rushes toward the door, lifting onto the balls of her feet and peering out the small peephole. "Arius," she groans over her shoulder. "Either you tell me what we're doing here this instant, or I'm out of here. I'm serious!" she shouts, spinning on her heel to face me.

"No need to get huffy, Your Highness," I laugh with my hands raised in surrender. "I suppose it's not entirely clear why I would bring you to such a charming little spot." Waving my hand from the ceiling to the floor, I know I'm being cheeky, but it's all I can think to do to ease the apprehension I sense brewing within her.

"Charming is not the word I'd use to describe this, this hovel!" Des groans while stepping over shards of glass on the floor. "I mean, look at this place, Ari. I thought you were taking me somewhere to get things for the Culling."

"We'll get to that," I answer quickly. Her eyes cut to mine, obviously not pleased with my tone. "But first, I thought you could blow off a little steam."

Tilting her head, she squints a little, her mouth scrunching sweetly to the side. "A little steam? I don't see any heavy bags or equipment in here, Ari. All I see is a rundown car and trashcans."

Laughing, I take a few steps toward her with my arms folded

over my chest, one hand on my chin. "I suppose it would seem that way, but even this rundown space has a purpose."

"What purpose?"

"Rage."

Desephone's gaze digs deep into mine, as though she's waiting for me to say something else. Slowly, her eyes wander a bit before returning to her daggered-eye stare.

I know she wants to say something, but I don't give her a chance to respond.

"That's right, Princess. This is a rage room."

"Arius, why would you bring me here? I thought you were taking me somewhere so we could get a few things for the culling tonight. Mother would want—"

"And that right there is why you need to rage, Des. Until a few hours ago, you lit up any room you entered. You commanded every stage. You even snarled at me when I objected to you coupling with that vagabond wolf—and then *Mother* arrived... "

"What?" she snips, her lips curling as her head tilts to one side. I'm pissing her off. Good.

"You heard me," I say, matching the darted stare she's giving me. "Just as the flowers wilted at your mother's touch, so have you shrunk since the moment she arrived."

Swallowing hard, she lifts her chin, turning her head away. "That's not true, Ari, and you know it."

Stepping to her side, I take her chin in my hand. She resists a little, but my firm grasp leads her attention back to me.

"I want to see you blossom like the fragrant flower you were always meant to be, Daughter of the Underworld." I pause, taking the time to simply enjoy the feel of her face resting in my hand. My eyes sweep over the entirety of her perfect face, and I marvel at just how lovely she is. "But first, you need to release your rage. You know, sharpen the thorn around the rose a little bit."

Rolling her eyes, she lets out a little chuckle. My jokes have always been dreadful, yet she laughs every time.

"Sharpen the thorn? Really, Arius?"

My shoulders bounce in amusement. "You know what I mean, love," I smile, taking her hand in mine. Her eyes settle for a minute on me, her lips softening into that sweet smile that turns my heart from stone to flesh.

"I–I don't know, Ari. I mean Mother may be a bit much at times, but that's hardly a reason to rage, as you say," she whispers, slowly slipping her hand from mine. The loss of her touch stings more than I can admit, but I need her to know I'm doing this for her.

"Oh, I'd say you have plenty of reasons to rage, Princess. Your mother. The Culling. Even what you shared about Cecil–" Desephone's now darkened eyes cut to mine. I know I hit a soft spot. "You've carried that secret for five hundred years, the weight of it all crushing you from the inside out. And now, you're faced with an even greater weight still: to leave this earthbound plane, the only home you've ever truly known, with a suitor in tow—all because it is your duty as the Daughter of Hades. Oh, I'd wager you have an inferno of rage blazing within, as sure as I stand before you now."

Flaming embers spark behind Desephone's eyes, her nose scrunching as black veins course through her hardened face. It's at this moment, I know I've done what I've set out to do.

Release her rage.

CHAPTER 13

Desephone

Fists of fire burn at my sides as my blood boils within me. Still, Arius keeps his ground, shoulders squared, eyes narrowed, full of the arrogant charm I've come to adore so much.

Everything in me wants to pound my flaming fists into his face, but I'll never mar that chiseled chin that keeps my lady parts dancing in the dark watches of the night.

Damn you, Arius Knight. I groan within myself. How I hate and love him so much right now.

As I wail, my body erupts into a mix of fire and smoke as I whirl through the room like a flume of rage, just as Ari intended.

A powerful gale blows through my hand as my fist crashes through the window, and my body weaves like smoke through the driver's side door, yanking off a tall antenna on my exit. Whipping the metal through the air, it crashes into an adjacent mirror on the wall, and I hover in front of it, marveling at the sight of the dark ethereal creature staring back at me.

I haven't seen this side of myself since my chaotic teen years, when I couldn't control the dark tide within me. Over the years, I've subdued my dark nature so much, I've gotten accustomed to this overly-delicate earthbound flesh.

With fiery eyes and a misty chasm of fire and smoke that is my bodily form, I take notice of the shimmering embers of ash and soot shaping me from head to toe. I am death incarnate, woven from the far reaches of Night itself for one singular purpose: to house the dead and consume it whole.

Motioning my arms around, I watch as dark electricity threads through my veins like lightning, sending fiery bolts to the tips of my fingers in one fluid motion. Scorching fire blazes bright through my eyes like a volcanic eruption, while my hair singes with an iridescent array of shadow and soot.

It's all a marvelous sight to behold, and I take it all in, relishing in the beauty of my darkness and the burning pangs of rage coursing through the entirety of me. I've never felt so *me*, at least not in a very long time.

Looking over my shoulder through the mirror, I'm surprised to find Arius smiling, smugly as ever, proud, even, delighting at me in rare form, as though he molded me with his own hands. Oddly, even the hubris I detect from him from afar sends tingles up my spine, as though he awakened something in me long since lost. And for that, I am thankful.

"Beautiful," he breathes, taking a few cautious steps toward me. "Glad to see the real you came out to play," he smiles, shooting me a sly wink as his arrogant little smirk crowds the side of his face.

"Rage," I growl back, my tone harder and harsher than usual, but Arius doesn't seem to mind.

"Then rage we shall!" Arius chimes aloud with a thunderous clap of his hands. As he does, the sound of a loud guitar and drums blares through the room. I look up and notice there are speakers neatly placed within the walls that I hadn't noticed before. In fact, as my eyes travel about, I notice this room is actually ordered chaos. Sure, there is glass and debris all over, but it's meant to be this way.

The music picks up the pace, and a small smile wanders on my face. I feel my fleshly form take over, noticing my earthbound appearance in the mirror as small fissures of fire and smoke hover around me.

"You like this one?" Arius shouts over the music. His smile is wide, stretching from ear to ear as he stares at me with hope beaming across his face. I only nod, curling a loose piece of hair behind my ear. "Glad you like it. It's called *Vice Grip* by Parkway Drive."

"It's nice!" I yell back, feeling strangely uneasy to be back in my earthly form. "I didn't know you liked metal. You're always listening to my soundscapes and jazz."

Ari laughs as he reaches down and picks up the duffle bag Perry left for him. "Yeah, well, Perry knows my playlist when I come here. Besides, it's pretty hard to let off steam to the sound of waterfalls. But enough about me," he adds darkly, pulling out a large metal bat from the bag. "It's time for you to tear some shit up."

Ripping the bat from his hand, I instantly feel my otherworldly nature take over. "Let's rage!" I growl, raising the bat within my fiery grip.

"That's my baby," he mumbles, and I feel a cold shiver travel up my spine. As soon as he says it, his face pales some, and I fear the sight of me like this is a bit much for him to handle. But when he lets out a roar of his own, I watch in awe as he shifts into the most alluring creature I've ever seen.

Hardening like stone, rippling muscles tighten beneath his tee as his skin smooths like marble with an iridescent sheen just beneath the exterior. Ari's chest broadens, and his eyes darken like a storm.

I've seen Bulwarks in their full gargoyle form before, but Arius is something different entirely. Being part human, part Bulwark, he is a stunning amalgamation of both worlds.

We're always in our human form; it's not often we see one another like this. We should do this more often.

His gaze locks with mine for a moment, but he doesn't say anything. Offering just the slightest nod, Arius roars once more, and I notice his pointed tail whipping side to side at his bottom as he marches in front of me.

Charging forward, Arius plows his hand through two drywall boards while kicking his foot through a large television atop a metal trash can. Next to the waste can, I see an orange door on top of tires, and I smash the glass pane. I scream as I do, and the exhilarating feeling of the glass breaking beneath me sends a surge of energy through me as I look to find something else to smash.

An appreciative smile spreads across Ari's face as he watches me. He nods behind me, and I turn to find three copper busts of unknown men on a table. I share an awkward glance, knowing how many of his kind are now relics of stone, but the small smile he gives lets me know I'm free to proceed. There's no further provocation needed as I swing the bat through all three statues in one, fluid motion.

"Yeah, baby!" Arius shouts, waving his fist before punching a metal door so hard, nothing but the imprint of his knuckles is left behind.

We go on for a while, hurling objects like feathers in the wind throughout the room as more of Ari's metal playlist blares through the sound system.

My body transitions between its earthbound and Netherworld state seamlessly, giving me what I need when I need it while letting my more subdued nature take a literal turn at bat.

Just when I think I've taken my bat through everything, Arius taps my shoulder and points up. "I've been saving this one for you," he whispers in my ear.

Looking up, I'm surprised I hadn't noticed it before, but there it is, waiting for me. Suspended from the ceiling, icicles like diamonds hang from the chandelier. The light isn't on, but it still brightens the darkened space with a brilliant glow. It's beautiful.

"Well?" Arius says, his mouth so close to my ear, I fear if I turn to face him, we'll kiss—although it might not be such a bad thing if he did. "Or are you still a bit wilted, Your Highness?" he teases.

Once more, I feel my eyes burn with anger. Dropping the bat at my side, I reach into the bag without looking and pull out a heavy brick mallet. For any other person, this mallet might be too heavy to lift, but I fling it over my shoulder as I lift from the ground. Allowing my shadows and smoke to carry me to the top of the ceiling, I chuck the mallet through the crystal chandelier in one ceremonious hit so hard, it breaks from the gold chain.

"Fuck yeah!" Ari shouts from below as the crystals burst into fragments around him.

As I float back to the ground, I whip the mallet through the air, breaking any remaining crystal in sight. Thoughts of Cecil, Mother, and having to take up the Crown in the Underworld simmer within me. With each strike, I shatter the memory of my wedding night with Cecil and the condemning eye of Mother. Even though I miss my father, I crash through the crystals as he comes to mind. This is not the life I wanted.

I let out a shrieking cry so loud, the remaining crystals burst around me as I land in the center of the chandelier frame...right into Ari's arms.

Arius

I could hold her like this forever.

As Desephone cradles into my embrace, burying her head into the nape of my neck, I wish I could relieve the ache of her heart or lift the weight she bears. I might not be able to carry it, but I can carry her, and I'll hold her as long as she'll let me.

A steady, shimmery stream of crystal dust encapsulates us where we stand, and I wish I could freeze this moment in time, holding the woman I love as though there was no tomorrow. No Netherworld. No Underworld. No impending danger. No suitors. *Just us.*

Her small hand finally reaches to my chin as she lifts her face from my chest. Dark, tearful rivers race past her cheekbones, falling like diamonds as her watery gaze searches mine for consolation.

I wish I could tell her she didn't have to worry about anything. If only I had the power to keep her from all that awaits her in the Underworld. She'd never have to face the darkness alone—much less with someone she didn't love. We'd face every wicked thing as we've always done—together.

Yet, I can assure her of no such thing. All I can do is what I do now: be whatever it is she needs.

"I guess I'm still wilted, huh?" Des cracks a nervous smile, but she's not fooling me.

"Just the opposite, love. I've never seen you stronger."

She releases a slight gasp, her eyes pressing tight as a few loose tears race to her chin.

"You're just saying that, Ari," she protests, shaking her head.

Pursing my lips, I know I need to do my best to be as tender with her as possible, but truthful. "I'd never lie to you. You know that. Besides, it takes a lot of strength to do what you just did. You've been holding onto so much for so long. I just wanted you to know you had it in you to just be you, that strong, fearless hellcat who doesn't take shit from anyone. You're already a queen to me, Des. You're my fucking queen."

Her mouth parts as her hand trails my jaw. If only she knew I felt more in my hardened Bulwark form than I ever do in my fleshly state, she wouldn't touch me as she does now. Every touch of her hand sends a storm of desire through me she's not prepared to weather.

"How did I get you, Arius Knight?" The sweet breath of her words sweep over me like a feather, leaving me clinging to the wind. She has no idea the hold she has on me.

"Drew the short straw, huh?" I chuckle.

Patting my shoulder, she smiles. "Hardly. But everyone could use a friend like you."

And there it is. The fucking friend zone.

It's the one place I don't want to be, but the only place I can't seem to escape.

Slowly, I let her down and help her step over the chandelier. Releasing her from my hold is hard, but knowing she doesn't feel the same for me hardens the dark hole in my chest.

"Thanks for this, Arius," she continues as she wipes the diamond-like dust from her pant leg. "I wish I could say we should do this again, but–"

"Who said we were done?" I blurt out, not wanting to let this moment pass.

Des tilts her head to one side with a curious grin. "Ari?" she grouses like she suspects I'm up to something.

Offering my hand, she places her palm in mine, and I lead her through another door in the back of the room.

"I did promise the Great Queen we would get a few things for the culling, did I not?" I say over my shoulder.

"Ari, it's dark in here," she gripes with a tight hold around my arm.

"Says the future Queen of the Underworld," I huff in amusement. Des shoves my back hard, sucking her teeth. "No worries, Your Highness, I'll get the light going, but you'll have to take a step back."

"Huh?"

"Please, Des. I don't want to hurt you," I reply, using my arm to gently push her out of harm's way.

"Hey!" she whines as she stumbles back against the wall. "Future queen, remember?"

"Uh-huh," I laugh, turning my attention to her just enough to make sure she's okay.

Motioning my arms around, I stretch my arm back as though I'm holding a bow, touching my fingers together. As I do, a bright white light illuminates the small room as a large bow made of fire appears within my grasp.

Desephone gasps behind me. "Is that what I think it is?"

"Yes, Your Highness," I say, now taking the bow in one hand. Turning to face her, I present it to her. "This is the bow of Heracles."

"*Epirus*," Des whispers, taking a small step forward. Her eyes wander in amazement as her hand hovers over the bow, her small fingers carefully keeping from the fiery embers emanating from the bow. "I don't understand, Ari. What are you doing with this? And how can this help me with the culling?"

"Are you familiar with prisms?"

Des frowns a little, offering me a momentary glance before returning to the bow. Shrugging her shoulders, she continues. "You mean those training circuits the wolves and vampire guard use? I mean, I know of them. I haven't seen one in a long time."

"Well, thousands of years ago, and probably when you first arrived, wolves and vampires trained out in the open. These days, they train in secret, in civility centers for the supernatural or places like this. Usually, Bulwarks like me oversee the training."

Looking up at me, Des quirks a brow. "Makes sense, I guess. I mean, you and your kin are the only ones neutral enough to administer such a circuit. But aren't prisms dangerous? Like if they don't make it out of a prism, they can—"

"Die," I answer plainly.

Covering her mouth in shock, Des turns away, folding her arms.

"Look, Des," I say, taking her elbow in my grasp and pulling her attention back to me. "I can set the prisms so they just get hurt. The only thing that might get killed is their pride."

"You'd do that for me?"

I let out a small sigh and chuckle. "I thought you knew by now; I'd do anything for you." Our eyes lock, and I swallow down my desire to take her once more in my arms. "But don't get it twisted; I'll by no means make it easy for them."

Desephone laughs in return, shaking her head. "I expect nothing less from my resident Bulwark. So how does this work, precisely?"

Placing the bow in her hand, I turn her back to me, positioning her to steady the bow in her hold. "Well, only a descendent of the first great Bulwark himself can wield this bow."

"Wait!" she snaps, turning her head to her chin. The way she looks up at me is driving me mad. I want to kiss her so damn bad. "Are you telling me Heracles was a Bulwark?"

I nod in the affirmative. I'm not surprised she's not aware. Bulwark canon isn't shared much outside of our own circles. "One of the first. It was his bow that opened the chasm to the Netherworld before sending all dark forces into the void. But we don't have time for history lessons today. We've got to get you ready."

Firming my hand around hers, I steady her grip against the bow.

"And how does showing me how to shoot prepare me for tonight's festivities?"

Leaning into her neck, I place my mouth at the tip of her earlobe. "Just trust me... I'm preparing you for more than tonight."

CHAPTER 15

Desephone

Just when I thought I knew all there is to Arius Knight, he still finds new ways to surprise me.

We spend so much time together in our earthbound state, it's not often we get to have moments like this. It feels far more intimate than when we are covered in pounds of flesh. Sure, Ari's earthbound features are certainly easy on the eyes, but I feel even more comforted by his bulking frame as a Bulwark.

"You're doing great, Des!" Ari shouts from afar as I weave in and out of the prisms.

Although he gave me a glimpse into his world via target practice with the bow, he wanted me to try out the elemental prisms. As I dash through each one, Arius shoots his bow, igniting the prisms. Each one pulls on elemental magic like earth, wind, water, and fire.

89

If I am caught in a prism once his bow connects, the element assigned to that prism releases its power.

Circling the fire prism, I lift above the ground just in time for Arius to shoot another arrow, sending a strong windfall my way, knocking me against the wall. Another prism appears, glowing and shrouded in ash and soot. I feel most comfortable with this one, as it more resembles where I'm from in the Netherworld. Instead of running from this one, I use it to my advantage.

Turning back toward the fire, I summon my own gale to shield myself from the wind. Volcanic ash lifts from the prism, and I jump over it just in time.

"Well done, my queen, well done!" Ari salutes me from across the room.

I give him a nod, slightly impressed with my efforts for the first time. I'm sweating a little as I shift back into my earthbound form. "That was fun!" I merrily exclaim. "I think Mother will be pleased."

"Are you sure? I mean, we have some ax-wielding stuff in the back if you want to—"

"No." I lift my hands in surrender. "I'm actually pretty beat. The prisms are harder than they look." I wipe my forehead, feigning more exhaustion. Ari's mouth crowds to one side; he's not convinced, but he decides to remain quiet.

Shifting back to his mortal form, he grabs an ax from the side wall and turns on the light.

"Oh, so there was light in here all along!" I sigh, turning toward the broken mirror on the wall. There's a large enough piece of glass still there, allowing me all I need to primp my tousled mane.

"Yeah, but if I turned on the light, it would make it hard to see the light from the prisms," he gruffly shouts back over his shoulder as he throws a small ax toward the target.

He misses and I laugh. "Ha! You missed it!" I tease across the room. Ari only turns his head slightly, huffing a little as he does as he grabs another ax from the holster. Throwing once again, he misses his target to the far left of the bullseye. "This isn't your game, Ari. Give it up!" I laugh, raking my hair to one side. Ari doesn't respond. He just picks up another ax.

"The hell it isn't his game," Perry cackles, startling me from where he now stands at the door. "This whole place is his sporting grounds."

Narrowing my gaze a bit, I wait for Perry to burst into laughter, but he doesn't. Instead, he just stands there, watching Arius, his gaze beaming with admiration.

"Am I missing something here?" I ask, turning back to Arius to see if he's close to the bullseye. He hasn't gotten it yet, but he's grabbing the smaller axes from the target, preparing to throw again.

"Well, I can tell you this: Arius Knight never misses a target, so whatever he's doing over there is intentional," Perry continues.

I look again at Ari. He's a tad closer to the target, but not by much. "He's thrown four times already and hasn't gotten it yet. Besides, that's okay; he's great with the prisms and the bow and arrow."

"Of course he is!" Perry snorts. "I mean, he practically built this place himself. Everything in here was made to his specifications."

"Really!" I gasp, my hand covering my mouth. "That must've been expensive. So folk can have rooms personalized just for them?"

Shaking his head and waving his hands around, Perry steps inside the room. "Well yes, rooms can be personalized, but this place —this entire place—belongs to the big guy."

My eyes grow wide in shock. I turn to Arius as he throws another ax. It's closer than before, but not quite the target. "Wait! I thought Ari said this was your place?" I ask, turning back to Perry.

"*Ari*?" Perry repeats mockingly. "That's cute-yeah, whether either of you admit it, you're his lady alright. There's no way in hell he's letting anyone call him *Ari* unless he—"

"This place!" I have to stop Perry before he says too much,

although I've never really thought about it. I *am* the only one to call him Ari. "Explain!" I demand, stepping in front of Perry.

Perry takes a step back, creating a little distance. "It's simple. My name is on the lease. His name is on the deed. This building, and a few others in the District, all belong to Mr. Knight. I mean I think he uses some other name, *Pen–*"

Lifting a finger, I stop Perry before he goes further. I really don't care about the name of Ari's business; beyond the Dram Deaux, I didn't think he owned anything else. I'm still trying to wrap my head around the fact that Arius owns this place.

"So everything here is his?"

Perry tightens his smile, nodding slightly. "Yep. Well, a lot of the equipment is mine, of course. But we wouldn't have access to prisms and such without a resident Bulwark like Arius."

"I feel like there's so much I don't know about him," I whisper, mostly to myself, but Perry's face perks up.

"Oh, I wouldn't worry about that. We hybrids are used to keeping shit close to the vest. It's hard being a hybrid these days. Folk don't really see you as one or the other. I'm a wolf through and through, but folk in the pack see me differently because I'm half vampire. Unlike everyone else, I chose my wolf. That means something to me. Same for Arius. He might be half-human, but he has far outlived any human he's ever known, so it's hard to have any real relationships with humans. But the Bulwarks, they don't see him as one of them really, so he works twice—no, a thousand times— harder to prove his worth. He knows how prisms work inside out. And he's the only hybrid I've ever known with the ability to call upon Epirus."

My eyes well with tears, thinking of all Arius has likely endured being a hybrid. He has spoken of those woes before, but this is the first time I've ever considered just how weighty and lonely it must be for him.

It's no wonder he wants to spend this time with me. Sure, he'll still have Gypsy, Cade, and even Perry here when I'm gone, but we literally spend every day together. The two of us are as thick as thieves. Besides, Cade goes off for months at a time, and Gypsy isn't one to get too sentimental. Perry seems like the only other one Arius has shared himself with, so once I'm gone, his list of confidants and friends shrinks significantly.

Life for Bulwarks is a lonely existence. The thought of Arius alone in this world crushes me.

I turn my attention back to Arius as he rears his arm back and shifts his weight forward, releasing the ax. This time, it connects with the bullseye, nearly splitting the target in half. Roaring, Arius throws up his fist, pleased with his skill.

I don't mock him this time. Blowing out a loud whistle, I slap my hands together, clapping madly as I fight back my tears. I'll never know if Arius is as good as Perry claims. In fact, it doesn't even matter. All I know is that he has been more than a good friend to me.

Arius turns around, a boyish grin spread across his face as he offers a playful bow.

As much as I'm glad we've had this time together today, it's the smile on his face right now I'll carry with me always, even during the culling and when I find a suitor; hell, even when I mate. That's the smile I always want to see.

If I had it my way, I'd take that smile with me to hell.

CHAPTER 16

Arius

"Okay, so you want me to have this stuff sent over to the Dram?" Perry asks while he thumbs his fingers across his iPad.

"Yeah and include the tournaments for the ax and a few brick towers," I answer.

"Damn, dude! You really want to make this challenge hard for them tonight, huh?" Perry chuckles.

Looking over my shoulder as Desephone talks with Allyson in the foyer, I smile. "She deserves the best."

"Mmhmm..." Perry grumbles, narrowing his gaze at me. "Or you could just tell her how you feel, shithead."

Growling, I turn back to Perry. His tone was cheeky, but the deadpan look in his eyes tells me he's serious.

"I mean, I get it. She's a fucking primordial destined for hell and all, but why not lay it all on the line. What do you have to lose?"

"Seriously?" I huff as he passes the iPad to me to sign off on the transport.

"Fuck, Ari..." he teases, scrunching his face playfully. "She's headed for the Underworld anyway. You can either tell her and she tells you to fuck off, or she can leave without ever knowing how you feel, and you fuck yourself. Choice is yours."

I barely scribble my name on the screen before shoving the iPad into Perry's chest. A low snarl churns through me as I spit out a few expletives in the old tongue and march off.

"You're welcome, asshat!" Perry shouts behind me. I almost regret telling him who Desephone is and why we needed to send things over to my bar. But I had to, because I knew he'd keep asking questions until I did.

Perry is like a brother to me. He knows more about me than anyone. Not even Cade or Gypsy knows as much as he does. We bonded as hybrids, a brotherhood that will never die. He's like family to me, and I know everything he said was for my benefit.

Still, I'm not sure how I can even make that move when Desephone only sees me as a friend.

There was a time I thought she saw me as more. On occasion, I would watch outside her bedroom window in my full marbleized state. Once I swore I heard her call out my name while she slept. I couldn't see much because of the position of her bed, but the wispy sound of her voice didn't sound like she was having a bad dream. It sounded like a damn good dream.

The next day, she met a mortal-made vampire named Luke. The

two hit it off famously, and for a week, they were glued to the hip. And then one day, he was gone.

I never saw him again.

Another bites the dust, Cade chided in laughter, nudging me to finally make my move as Des shyly wandered into my bar, seeing as my competition was gone. But what do I do? Treat Des to an all-you-can-eat shrimp tower and a midnight movie marathon featuring all black and white films at The Grand D'iberville? We had a ball.

Today is different.

For the last few days, there has been a wrenching feeling in my gut that I needed to tell Des how I felt for her. The old ones used to say that we Bulwarks can feel a shift in the tide when the balance of the supernatural world is shifting. Although I was just as shocked as Desephone to find her mother waiting at her place, I had a feeling there'd been a disturbance in the balance, and there's no greater imbalance than someone from the Netherworld breaching the earthbound plane.

Such an arrival never comes without consequence, but losing the love of my life is not an effect I'll so easily turn aside. Still, I know I have to choose the most opportune moment. This isn't it.

"I hate to bother you ladies," I say, brightening my tone once I reach Desephone and Perry's new girl, Allyson. "We should really get going."

Des offers me a sweet smile before taking Allyson's hand in hers and gives it a squeeze. "It was so nice meeting you, Allyson."

Allyson shares a bright smile as a rosy tint blushes her soft brown face. Her long, thick hair is pulled up in a high ponytail. She leaves little to the imagination with a fitted white top and leggings that have Perry's gaze locked on her behind from across the room. But it's the way she ogles at Desephone like she's staring at a creature in the wild for the first time that has all my alarm bells going off.

"Nice meeting you too!" Allyson grins wide, her eyes beaming bright.

I nearly have to tug Desephone's arm to break the two apart, but Des locks in step with me as we make our way out of the warehouse.

The heavy steel door closes hard behind us as we head down the staircase.

"Woah!" Des gasps, holding the bottom of the metal railing, clenching her chest.

"Baby, are you okay?" I quickly circle her, pushing her hair away from her face. She rests her cheek in my palm like it's her resting place, and my heart nearly combusts wishing I could hold her like this forever. "Des, what's wrong?"

"You know that's like the third time you've called me baby today." She winces, slowly pulling out of my hold. My jaws clench as I reluctantly lower my hand to my side. Des watches me as I do, her mouth twisting to a cute, curious smirk. Her eyes dance with something I can't make out, but she purses her mouth tight, shutting her eyes, like she's shaking off whatever notion just ran through her brain. "Anyway..." She pauses, taking one final step onto the pavement. "I can't believe that just happened." Primping her posture, she turns back to the steel door and then back at me.

Confused, I hold out my hand to help her step over a grate sticking up from the ground. "I have no idea what you're talking about."

"Didn't you feel that? I mean it was—electric!" she squeals, raising a fist over her chest.

My brows raise.

Maybe she does sense the connection between us after all.

This could finally be my moment to tell her how I feel for her.

"Yeah, baby, I felt it too," I breathe, firming my grip as I pull her close.

"See, you said it again," Des whispers, her eyes glazing with something unfamiliar. "Why?"

"Why?" I repeat, and I almost hate the boyish lilt in my tone, but damn it, who cares. This is my fucking moment. "Well, if you're finally feeling what I've been feeling this whole time, I think *baby* is appropriate. Unless you prefer something else like—"

Desephone's palm lays flat on my chest as I lean in, and she pulls back.

"Wait, Ari!" Her face scrunches in confusion. "That doesn't make any sense!"

I smile at Des despite the small frown lines now forming around her mouth.

"Well, didn't you just say you felt something electric?"

Desephone's face brightens some, her eyes hopeful rays of light. "Well yes, Ari, but I was referring to—wait, did you think I meant us?"

I step back, nearly tripping over the grate I just helped Des cross. "What?"

"Oh, I'm sorry if I confused you!" Des exclaims as she brushes past me to make her way to my car. "Believe me, Ari, I'd never want to put you in that position. You're my friend. I'd never dream of—-"

Forcing my eyes shut, I blink them open just as fast. "Fine! We're friends. I get it. So, who the hell made you feel electric all of a sudden? Don't tell me you've got your eyes on Perry. I mean, I know you've always had a thing for wolves, but Perry, he's my—"

"Whoa!" Des shrieks with both palms raised high. "I'm not talking about Perry at all! I'm talking about Allyson, Ari."

Well damn.

CHAPTER 17
Desephone

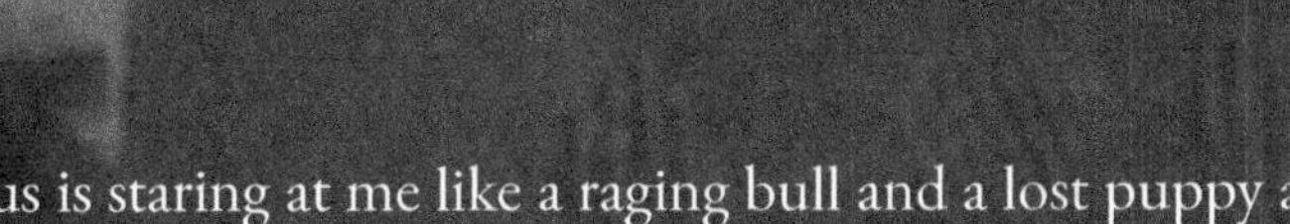

A rius is staring at me like a raging bull and a lost puppy all entangled as one.

I'm not sure what I've done to upset him or send him the wrong signal, but I need to get us back on track.

After all these years, I thought he knew I'd never sacrifice all we've shared on the altar of saving the Underworld. No matter how much I have pined for him in the darkest parts of my heart, I care too much for him to risk his life.

We can never be.

"Okay, let me get this straight," Ari begins, straining to speak through his clenched teeth. "After what, ten minutes or so, you like Perry's girl now? I mean, fuck, Des, do you know what kind of position this puts me in? You and Perry are like family to me. What did you two talk about that–"

My eyes grow wide in both frustration and pure annoyance. "Hey! What the hell, Ari? I never said anything about *liking* Allyson. Damn it! *Men!*" I snap before throwing my face into my palms.

I feel Arius grip his heavy hands around my wrist as he slowly lowers them to my sides until our eyes meet.

"Des, baby, what the actual fuck?" He laughs as his dark brows crowd together in confusion.

Shaking my head, I laugh with him. I'm trying hard to shrug off how comfortable he has become with calling me baby. Maybe it's a Bulwark thing. Melvina called us her babies earlier. Bulwarks are known for having nurturing and protective tendencies. That's probably why he seems more like an overbearing big brother most days.

Yeah, that's it.

"I mean, damn it, you're up here talking electric vibes and shit...
"

Shoving his shoulder, I give him a hard eye roll. "Okay, first, I never said anything about electric vibes. I just said electricity–anyway, I thought maybe you picked up on it. You know, since you're such an intuitive Bulwark and all. I read her, Ari. I frigging read her soul. I mean, I know she's a human, and they're pretty easy and all, but it's been so long since I've actually read someone. Well, then again, I read a little off Derek earlier, but that was only seconds before you ripped him in two, so—"

"Woah, slow down, little red corvette!" Ari exclaims, laughing as he takes my shoulders in his hands. "Well, fuck! That's awesome, Des!"

My shoulders shrug as I lean back against the car door. "It's nothing, really," I grumble, fumbling with my fingers.

"The hell it isn't, Des! That's why I brought you here today. You see what happens when you let off a little steam? Shit, baby, just think what will happen when you truly release everything you've got pinned up in there. The entire Underworld will bow before your crown."

Another eye roll followed with nervous laughter. "See, that's where you're wrong, Ari. The queen doesn't wear a crown in the Underworld."

"Crown or not, you'll forever be my queen, Des," Arius says as his fingers lightly lift my chin to meet his searing gaze. His eyes are darker now, like they were when he shifted to his Bulwark form. I know he won't shift in the daylight with so many mortals roaming about, but I can tell it's taking everything in him to hold himself firm.

"Arius Knight, you are just too good for me..." I breathe back as I feel him firm his hold on my chin. I want—no, I need to believe he's just the kind of friend who keeps you on your toes and boosts your confidence, but a part of me knows better.

"Your ego, perhaps," he chuckles, pinching my chin before stepping back. He lets out a small sigh as he presses the remote and unlocks the door. When he walks to the driver's side, I'm a tad surprised he doesn't open my door for me like he usually does. I guess I've become too comfortable with being his passenger princess. Now, he's doing his part to cut the cord.

"Yeah, I guess," I groan as I climb into the car.

"So?" Ari blurts as he settles into his seat.

I sigh. "So what?"

"So, what did you read about Miss Allyson? What did her soul say to you? Anything I need to warn Perry about?" He pushes the ignition button, but he keeps his attention on me.

As much as I want to share what I saw, I am no longer as excited about it as I was before. The thought of cutting the cord with Arius makes me sick to my stomach. Sure, I knew the minute I saw Mother that things would no longer be the same.

Despite breakfast and the amazing time I had with Arius at the rage room, once we pull off this parking lot, it officially marks my descent to hell.

Gone will be the days of sipping my cares away on the barstool, complaining about whoever bit the dust the night before. There'll be no more waiting to see Ari or Gypsy's raised thumb before taking up with a suitor. No, those days are over.

I can forget a midnight rendezvous at the Biloxi Lighthouse, watching the tide roll in as Arius takes his perch atop the tower. Sometimes, we'd watch until sunrise and then walk the boardwalk. If I had to do it all over, we'd have at least one more sunrise together.

Now, as I submerge in darkness, I'll never see the sun again.

"Nothing," I mutter, biting my nails.

"But—" His voice trails off as he takes my hand in his, hopeful to get my attention. But his touch stings too much. Knowing these are our last moments makes it harder than it should be. "You seemed so excited earlier."

I pull my hand away. "Yeah, it's nothing. Mother will hardly applaud me for reading a human. That's child's play."

"Well, I celebrate it, Des. I think it's—"

"It really doesn't matter, Arius. Anyway, we should be getting back. I'm sure Mother will be eager to get things going."

"Of course." Ari huffs as he backs out of the parking lot.

The remainder of our ride is quiet. No music. No small talk. Nothing.

I suppose I should get used to it, because from this day forward, there will be nothing between us.

We're back in front of my building. Neither Arius nor I have spoken since we left the warehouse. Even now, there's only dead space between us. Arius turned the car off, which is odd, because he normally parks in the garage behind his building, but I don't question him. I'm still not in the mood for small talk.

Everything in me wishes he'd break the ice and say something. *Anything.* But a bigger part of me is almost thankful he doesn't, for fear I'd beg him to stop me from going through with the Culling altogether. I remain silent and keep my eyes from his. Although I'm the soul reader, I don't have a poker face, and Arius Knight is the one person who can read me like the back of his hand.

The thought of it is frustrating enough, so after one lofty sigh, I rip off my seat belt and a bolt out of the car.

"Thanks for everything, Ari!" I squeak out as the door closes behind me.

Ari pops out of the driver's side, slamming the door behind him. "Please let Queen Persephone know everything will be set up by the time you arrive."

I'm still leaning against the passenger door when he breezes by me and makes his way across the street. He doesn't turn around or give me so much as a wink or stare as he reaches the other side. I don't even think he locked his car door, but he's back inside the bar before I can flag him down to let him know.

Fumbling through my purse, I pull out my key as I try to shrug off Ari's odd behavior. I knew cutting the cord between us would hurt. I just never thought it would be this painful.

CHAPTER 18

Arius

"FUCK!"

The loud crash of the door behind me makes the windows rattle as the wooden shutters shake against it.

A small metal chair is the first to feel the brunt of my ire as I ram my foot into it, sending it clear across the empty bar. The loud sound of glass breaking in the corner catches my attention. I see an empty glass fall to the ground as the chair slams into the side of the counter.

"Fucking Gypsy!" I roar. I don't know how many times I have

to remind her to make sure the rim of the glass is secured in the holster over the bar.

That thought alone makes me wonder why I've kept this bar so long. Most Bulwarks trade posts after a residency of twenty or so years. I've had this place for fifty. That's too damn long.

But I know why.

It's all because of Des. Being where she is is all I've wanted since the first day I laid my eyes on her. Even though I'm only half Bulwark, I could've petitioned the council years ago to give me a different post, but I've remained silent.

Easy enough, since no one wants to come to Biloxi. A place crawling with every supernatural reject imaginable, this isn't the most enviable of residencies for Bulwarks to take up post. But for me, there's no other place I'd rather be.

As I grab the small dustpan and broom from the side wall, I let out a little laugh, thinking how foolish I've been. I sweep the glass shards into the dustpan, shaking my head as I empty them into the wastebasket next to the bar.

"First fucks, then things crash, next comes laughter," I hear Gypsy whisper from the back steps. Her voice startles me as I turn around. Her shoulders roll in amusement as she blows the smoke from her cigarette over her shoulder. "Sounds pretty schizophrenic if you ask me," she huffs, exhaling a foggy cloud.

Usually, her sass snaps me right out of my funk, but not this time. "The sun is still high. Shouldn't you be in repose?"

"In repose?" Gypsy laughs, waving her hand through the smoke as she steps forward. "What are we, in the sixteen hundreds?"

"Whatever. Burn. But if you think I'm letting you drink a live one in my bar just to heal you—"

"Fuck you, Knight!" Gypsy snaps back, narrowly flicking her cigarette over my shoulder and into the sink. "And if I did get burned, it's only because I beat your ass in broad daylight one good time. Hopefully, it'll teach you a lesson on holding in your feelings until the last fucking minute. Unfortunately for me, I wouldn't be here to see the sick look on your face when you finally figured it all out."

Shit. "Gypsy, I'm sorry. I just—" I take a step forward, but she throws her hands up in protest.

"Look, I get it! You're a Bulwark, and this is all some elaborate exercise in forbidden passion or some shit like that. But maybe Cade is right. Although I'd never admit to his face, he's got a point. You should at least tell her how you feel. If nothing else, you can stop destroying the bar."

My gaze narrows at my friend's shimmering crimson eyes staring back at me. "How do you know I didn't tell her, and this is just what I look like after she rejected me?"

"Well, aside from the fact that I know better and that you probably spent the day fumbling over your feelings and clenching your jaws rather than admit the truth–I'm pretty sure you both want the same thing. There's no chance she'd outright reject you."

I let out a hard sigh as I fell back against the counter. "I highly doubt that. Des thinks of me as either a family member or friend and nothing more. She made that pretty clear."

"Was that before or after you made it clear how you felt?"

My eyes snap back to her searing stare.

"Yeah, that's what I thought. You're full of shit, Knight."

I can't help nodding in agreement before folding my arms over my chest and leaning my head back. "You're not wrong. I am full of shit."

Gypsy stares at me for a beat before rolling her eyes and taking a few steps forward. She's careful to sidestep the beams of the light coming in from the transom as she backs against the freezer door.

"Well, it takes one to know one, I suppose," she says with a slight chuckle.

My brow lifts with interest. "Don't tell me. You and Stevie?"

Shrugging her shoulders, her mouth crowds to one side as she pops a wad of gum between her purple-painted lips. "Yep." Gypsy cuts her eyes to mine as she pulls at the fishnet lace of her gloves. "And tomorrow's the fucking full moon."

"Oh, wait—did Stevie choose the wolf?"

She lets out a sigh after popping a big pink bubble. "I–I don't know. I haven't called them back."

"Well, why the fuck not? I thought Stevie was *the one*." It feels good to have the focus off my own troubles for a minute.

"Yeah, but I don't want to be the deciding factor for whether Stevie chooses their wolf or the fang. I can't even comprehend having that weight. I'm just a lowly Scourge; a damn mortal-made vampire. I never had a choice, but Stevie does. I'm not going to stand in their way of making that decision for themselves."

Closing the distance between us, I make my way in front of Gypsy, ensuring my back blocks out any remnants of sunlight. "I suppose you were right about one thing."

Her eyes march up to mine. Glassy crimson pools etched in thick black mascara, eyeliner, and mounds of purple and pink eye shadow do little to hide the porcelain doll face of my most loyal, sharp-toothed ally and friend. While she indeed has no qualms with biting, her bark is still far worse. Gypsy wears a brawn armor of bravado to shield herself from the let-downs of life. Right now, though, I just see someone like me, fearful of rejection.

"What?"

"We are both full of shit."

Both Gypsy and I break out into laughter, and it feels like a balm to my soul. Our romantic situations are so fucked up right now, all we can do is laugh to ease ourselves of the pain.

"You're not wrong, Knight," Gypsy continues, still chuckling. "We really should get our act together. I sure as hell don't want to be sitting at this bar, looking at your ugly mug, fifty years from now."

I smile as I pull away from the wall. "I thought you liked working at the bar?"

"Yeah, the bar I like. The owner—eh, not so much," she teases, blowing another bubble. "But seriously, what are you going to do about Des? Are you really gonna just let her walk out of your life without a fight?"

"When have you ever known me to cower from a good fight?"

"Well, you did hem up Jesse's ass pretty good when he got too handsy with me last week. And I think Cade and I caught a glimpse of you tearing that wolf Des left with earlier in two, so there's that... Hmm... Maybe you're not a punk after all, Knight," she laughs.

My brows lift as I roll up on the balls of my feet. "Maybe," I agree. "And what about you?"

"Who knows? Maybe I'll get my shit together as well and tell Stevie how I feel. Besides, we have this Little Red Riding Hood fantasy I've been dying to try out—you know, if they become the big bad wolf and everything."

As I wave one hand in protest and the other clutching my stomach, my mouth curls with disgust. "Please, spare me the details."

We both burst into laughter again. As we do, inspiration strikes as my eyes drift around the bar. I don't know why I hadn't thought of it before now, but I think I have just the plan to once and for all make Desephone mine. If I was a more nefarious man, I would have thought of this sooner, but now that I have, there's no going back.

CHAPTER 19

Desephone

"Dearest," I hear my mother call to me from behind. Her voice is quiet, but I can feel her looming presence at the door of my office, her gaze searing into my back like heat rays.

"Yes, Mother," I whisper over my shoulder. I don't turn around, but I know she heard me.

"We really should get going, my dear. Besides, you don't want to get anything on that lovely dress I brought you. I had it hand-stitched at the Soleil. Oru and Gao both say they'll be more than delighted to present you with an entire wardrobe upon your arrival. We'll have to make a stop Purgia, of course, but—"

"Mother, please!" I turn around in my chair, halting her casual stroll along the hardwood floor.

Gliding her hand over her heart, she gasps, her eyes aglow like lightning. "Why, dearest, I was just–"

"I know exactly just what you're doing, Mother!" I jump up from my seat.

Her brow arches as her mouth curves to the side, and she drops her hand near her waist. "And what, pray tell, am I just doing? Short of trying to endear you to the thought of what awaits you when you return home to the Netherworld once you procure a suitor, I can't fathom how I have once again offended you."

"That's just it, Mother—you don't know. You don't know me. About my life here. How I spend my days. My business. Social life. Nothing. You just presume I'm ready to leave all I've built here behind for a world I do not know. For over three thousand years, I have been earthbound. And in that time, whether you choose to acknowledge it or not, I have, in fact, built quite a life. So forgive me if I want to take a moment to close out the business of my life before I am to be relegated to not only the Netherworld, but the rulership of the Underworld and all that comes with it. And let's be honest, Mother; there is quite a heaping that comes with it."

In an instant, I have stunned the Queen of the Underworld. The very one who invokes fear and trembling in all who dare step in her shadow stands frozen before me, muted by the very one she divined in her own likeness.

Little ol' me.

She releases a hearty sigh, once more placing a hand on her chest, taken aback by my words. "My dear, I–I'm so sorry. I didn't know you felt this way. Please know it was never my intent to–"

"I know, Mother," I breathe back, taking a step toward her. "You never mean to hurt me. But if for nothing more than posterity, allow me a moment to reconcile all I am leaving behind."

Offering me her frightfully pale hand, Mother's face softens as she allows a smile that strangely meets her eyes. "Then tell me about it, my dear. Your business. Social life. Everything. I want to hear it all."

"Really?" My voice cracks as my eyes well with tears. "But what about the Culling?"

Mother throws me a lofty wink, her wickedly beautiful smile matching the machinations brewing in her gaze as she looks at me now. "Now dearest, one thing we, the Daughters of Demeter, can do quite well is make a man wait. Like the great one herself, we gather men like wheat into our harvest, awaiting a culling only we can offer. Besides, what good is a man who hasn't the patience to pine for perfection? So let them wait!" she exclaims merrily, snapping her fingers like a thunderbolt of lightning. As she does, two chairs gather to our sides, and she guides us to our seats. Pulling my hand to her lap, she smiles wide. "Now, dearest, tell me all about it."

Talking with Mother was a balm to my soul.

I hadn't realized how much I shoved inside me over the years, but Mother was here for it all. She listened, asked questions. There was a genuine interest in everything I had to say that both shocked me and made me realize perhaps I've judged Mother too harshly over the years.

Although it was clear she relished in all I had to say, our time was well spent. Almost an hour of chatter felt like an eternity, but I wouldn't trade a minute. Still, I condensed much of what I wanted to really say, knowing we still had the matter of the Culling to get to at the Dram Deaux. Suitors would be waiting, as would Arius. Since this is likely the last day I have with him, I'm eager to be back at his side, if only for a little while.

"Well, I am impressed, Dearest," Mother begins, gently squeezing my hand in hers as it rests on her knee. "But not because I didn't think you could make something of your life, but because you are far more capable a woman than I ever imagined you could be. You make me proud."

My cheeks warm at her sentiment, and my eyes glisten as her sweet smile sweeps over my face. "Thank you, Mother."

"No, in this, you only have yourself to thank. I mean, look at this place!" She beams, waving her hand around. "Petals is a lovely flower shop you've created for yourself. And to think you're not only staying afloat, but maintaining regular business and top-notch service. At least that's what one of your customers, the Pinnacle, I believe they were called, said in a rave review."

My shoulders roll, my cheeks still blushing with my mother's newfound praise. "Wait, how did you hear about that?" I ask, curious.

"The internet." Mother's tone is nonchalant, as if she, Queen of the Underworld, was well acquainted with modern earthbound technology. "I may have looked your business up while you were away with the Bulwark. It's no small feat you have garnered such business savvy."

"Thanks," I rasp, still unsure how to handle such compliments from my mother. "Pinnacle is my top customer," I share, needing to get the topic off me. "Every week, they place an order for Hydrangeas or Juliet Rose flowers. Just those orders alone practically keep me in business," I squeal.

"My, this Pinnacle corporation must be quite wealthy. What is their trade?"

"That's the thing —I'm not sure. The flowers are sent to a medical facility. I haven't really dug too deep."

Mother stares at me for a moment before pursing her lips and taking a deep breath. I already know what's coming next.

"Again, Dearest," she begins, softly taking my shoulders in her hands. "I am proud of you. But for now, we must get to the business of the Culling. I think we've kept your suitors waiting long enough."

My chin falls a little, wishing I could spend more time alone with her. "Yes, Mother," I answer.

Her petite fingers lift my chin like the light stroke of a feather. "Not to worry, Desephone. This will not be our last talk." She smiles sweetly.

Without hesitation, I throw my arms around my mother's neck, yanking her into my embrace. The gesture startles her some, but she folds into me as her arms wrap around my waist.

For three thousand years, this is what I've needed, what I've longed for: just a moment with my Mother.

Slowly, she pulls from my hold yet, she keeps a firm grasp at my waist. "Before we go, I need you to answer something for me. Honestly, please... "

"Of course, Mother. Anything."

"The Bulwark, Arius Knight. Is there something more going on between you two beyond friendship? Have you two been intimate?"

"Mother!" I shriek, pulling away from her grasp.

"I am sorry, but I have to ask."

Shaking my head, my stomach tightens, and my throat swells shut. "Why would you even ask that? I–I told you we—we're just friends. Besides, he's a Bulwark. It's forbidden!"

"Dearest, true love can never be denied, no matter the consequences. I know that better than anyone. Even more, we are bound to the Underworld. If the love is true, whether it be forbidden or not, the sentence could only be your fate as ruler. So, if he is the one, you needn't worry with the Culling and lay aside your fears of senseless death, as you say."

Mother's words lock me in place. Everything in me wishes I could say yes, that Arius and I are a pair. But alas, we are not. He only sees me as another resident in his purview, not his woman-much less his mate. Even if he did, I love him too much to put his life at risk and condemn him to such a hellish union, which is why I can never tell him or Mother how I feel.

"No, Mother," my voice cracks, stinging tears burning my eyes. "We are just friends."

Arius

"Damn, Knight!" Gypsy yells from the door post. "The line is around the fucking corner!"

"Oh yes!" Cade chimes in, perched at his usual seat at the bar. "Queen Mother sent out quite the call for this one. Every eligible vampire, siren, and wolf from Biloxi to the edge of the Gulf is en route to make the delectable Desephone their betrothed." Cackling, Cade rears his head back, ensuring he makes eye contact with me before turning his attention back to Gypsy.

"Fuck you!" I growl back.

"Not my type, I'm afraid," he scoffs, tossing back a glass of Scotch.

"Well, when should I let them in, boss?" Gypsy shouts, shaking her head at Cade. I know she agrees with him, but she'll never let him know.

"No need to wait!" a commanding voice calls from behind me. Turning around, I'm surprised to find Desephone and Queen Persephone standing near my side street entrance.

"Your Highness!" I exclaim, bowing before both women. "I'm sorry you had to come in from the side." My heart races as my eyes catch Desephone standing eerily still behind her mother. She quickly averts her gaze, and I wonder what could be bothering her. I'm sure me being an ass earlier didn't help, but I will find a way to redeem myself.

"It's quite alright," Queen Persephone answers, stepping in front of my view of her daughter. "We saw the line out front, and my daughter showed me to the back entrance. She's quite familiar with your establishment, Mr. Knight," she adds with a cautious lift of her brow.

Sucking in a breath, I tighten my jaw. I'm not sure what the queen is implying, but I don't want to do anything to make this night any more uncomfortable. Still, this is my residency, and I have no desire to shrink before anyone, not the Queen of the Underworld or any bastard-would-be-suitor who walks through my door tonight.

It may not be much, but the Dram Deaux is my kingdom, and I'll not spend the evening cowering in my own place.

"Yes, Great Queen." I lift my chin, squaring my shoulders. "I've worked hard over the years to ensure the princess is afforded all the comforts someone of her esteem should receive."

The queen's lips curve to an appreciative smirk as she regards me, but it doesn't last as she saunters by. Des is on her mother's heel, but she doesn't look at me. Both women are in oversized, hooded black cloaks, likely to conceal their identity as they made their way here. Although I can't see what Desephone is wearing underneath, the shimmering glow of her face, soft, pink-painted lips, and the thick flutter of her long lashes let me know there's nothing but perfection brewing from head to toe.

"Mr. Knight," the queen interrupts my thoughts as she calls to me from the center of the bar.

"Yes, Your Highness?" I answer, but I can't take my eyes off Des. For as radiant as she looks, I wish she would look at me.

"Did you receive the baskets I sent over?"

"Baskets?" My mind is a muddled mess.

"The rose petals, Knight!" Gypsy snips from across the room, her eyes glaring at me. I need to get it together. Cade sits idly, shaking his head, quite amused at my expense.

"Ah, yes, Great Queen," I say, rocking forward on my heel. Rushing to the side of the bar, I point to the two large barrels. "We have them right here. Where would you like them?"

The queen shoots a lofty eye roll my way. "Why, at my daughter's feet, of course!"

"Mother, no!" Des shouts back, finally casting a stare between her mother and me. Her pensive gaze drifts between us, but it's clear she's not happy.

"Dearest, where do you think the tradition comes from? From the first day, the Great Mother, Demeter, ordered all brides to walk among the petals to their betrothed. It is tradition!"

"At a wedding, not a Culling!" Des protests, finally throwing off her hood. She shakes her lovely, long, raven-black hair to one side, and I can't help but want to fist a handful of her hair and pull her until her lips are locked with mine.

"You are confusing us with mundane, earthbound human traditions, Dearest. As a direct descendent of Demeter, it is your right to walk upon the petals. You know this."

Tightening her lips, Des looks up to me, her eyes pleading with me to intercede.

"Well, Bulwark," the Queen continues, once more stepping in front of her daughter. It's clear she's not fond of the way my eyes roam over Desephone's every curve. "You are the proprietor and host of our festivities tonight, so it's up to you."

Des steps to her mother's side, and her wide, hopeful eyes make my knees weak while her mother's threatening gaze reminds me to tread carefully. Even if I somehow convince Des to consider me as her suitor, I'll not make it through the Culling without the Great Queen's approval.

"While I don't want to impede your traditions, Great Queen, I'm sure we can make things more amenable for the bride-to-be."

Des lifts her face toward me, and the bright smile that lit up my life from the first day I met her spreads from ear to ear. "Thank you!" she whispers sweetly.

A small groan hurls through her mother as she folds her arms across her chest.

"Of course." I tip my head toward Des. "But make no mistake about it, you deserve flowers at your feet."

Desephone's breath hitches in surprise as she regards me while another appreciative smile folds over her mother's face.

"So how about a compromise?"

"What would you propose, Bulwark?" the queen asks, the lilt in her voice laced with approval.

"How about just a small layering of petals once the Princess is presented and then again as she chooses her suitor?"

This time, it's the queen who throws off her hood, shaking her equally long locks at her back. With a thunderous clap of her hands, she turns to her daughter, lifting her chin. "How does this sound, Dearest? Not too much, eh?"

Des darts a quick eye over her shoulder to me. She's not

completely pissed, but I know her well enough to know she's not overly fond of the idea.

Taking a deep breath, Des forces a smile. "Sure, Mother. It'll be fine."

"Splendid!" Queen Persephone exclaims, clapping her hands once more. Turning to Gypsy, she smiles wide. "Pretty One at the door, in a few minutes, you can start letting everyone in."

"Yes, Your Highness," Gypsy says, adding a faux courtesy as she glances my way, shrugging her shoulders as she does.

"Alright, pick up your feet everyone!" I shout to the remaining bar staff. Most have been perched against the wall for the last hour, awaiting instructions, while a few others I'm sure are itching for the chance to cast in their lot as suitors. They won't outright admit it to me, but as quick as they accepted the offer to work overtime, it doesn't take a genius to know their intentions. "Preset cocktails on the right, blood drams on the left. Keep everyone happy tonight, folks—especially our bride-to-be!"

"Thank you, Mr. Knight," the Queen adds, coming to my side. Her sparkling eyes flit across the room momentarily as she takes in the sight of the prisms placed throughout. "My daughter told me you'd have an impressive array set for the Culling tonight, but this is far beyond my expectation. Well done, good sir."

"Nothing but the best for the Princess," I answer, my eyes still fixed on Des.

"Indeed!" the queen agrees as she floats around the bar, looking at the prisms and ax wheels.

"Yes, thank you, Arius," Des finally adds. I'm not fond of her formal tone, but I'm happy she's even speaking to me. "I look forward to seeing the suitors make their way through the tournament you've arranged."

"May the best man win!" Cade jauntily offers, coming to my side.

Still, my eyes stay pinned to Des. "And so he shall."

CHAPTER 21

Desephone

Everyone is scurrying about as I'm relegated to a dark corner near the kitchen. My stomach turns in knots as I watch Mother and Arius order the staff around, seeing to the final touches before they let in our guests.

It's nauseating to see this circus of sorts thrown together all in the name of matchmaking. While I have little hope I'll find the man of my dreams tonight, knowing that when it's all said and done, my life will inevitably change is a hard pill to swallow.

Not because I'm so attached to this earthbound plane, but because I'm destined to rule the Underworld, hand-in-hand, with someone I do not love.

My parents weren't a love match when my mom left, literally kicking and screaming her way into the Underworld. In time, however, my father carved a path to her heart. Of all the women, my father said, only Persephone was fit to rule at his side. She, on the other hand, had no say in the matter. My mother always said she wanted better for me. She wanted me to have an opportunity to cull from the best of the crop, as she would say, and find a suitable match.

But it takes more than that. My intended must be intimately suitable, which means even if they make it through the prisms and the tournament Arius has put together, they will have to match me in the most intimate way. My kiss alone has sent some to their doom, while others have died during intercourse like Cecil. Who knows whether anyone here will fare any better?

So, I'll do my best not to peddle over the particulars. What will be will be, and I have to make peace with that. Besides, if my parents could find a way to one another, perhaps fate will be on my side.

A whiff of smoke blows my way, and I wave my hand through the foggy flume as I feel a small pat on my shoulder.

"Well, it's a clusterfuck, that's for sure," I make out Gypsy's voice on the other side of the smoke. She blows out another puff of clouds, this time waving her hand around as well. "I know this has got to be doing a mind job on you, Des," she continues.

"What?" I ask, a bit confused as I make out her blood-red eyes staring back at me.

"All of this!" She wags her arm around.

I shrug my shoulders as my eyes bounce around the bar. Taking in the sight of it all isn't lost on me. It's quite a spectacle. From the ax wheels to the large mystical prisms hovering about, to the brick stations Ari was cheeky enough to include, it feels like we're back in the medieval period, albeit otherworldly. The Dram Deaux is usually overrun with supernaturals needing a little liquid courage via blood or alcohol. Now, it's become an arena of expedition for my hand, and the thought of it all makes me sick.

"Yeah, it's something," I mumble, pulling the collar of the cloak to my chin. I don't normally feel cold, but there's a steady draft coming in from the open door, giving me the shivers.

"I don't envy you, that's for damn sure," Gypsy chuckles, pinching the cigarette to douse the flame before tossing it in the trash.

I smile, thankful for the concern I spy drifting between her brows as she looks at me. For as much bravado as she gives off, the endearing look she's giving me now lets me know she wishes I could get out of this more than anyone.

"I mean, isn't there somebody? *Anybody* you'd rather spend your eternal days with? Someone you could call right now and say hey, let's do this. I mean, I'd hate to have to live out my days with some stranger all because they finished some damn obstacle course and I was the consolation prize. Because that's what this is, you know. It looks like we're at a frigging state fair where you play rigged games to win some off-brand teddy bear or a fucking goldfish in a damn plastic bag."

I sigh, shaking my head, trying to laugh it off. "Wow, you've painted a rather drab picture."

"Because it is drab, Your Highness." Gypsy's tone is a bit flat, but she stares at me like she's hoping I'll jump up and stop everything before it gets started. "You're far from a goldfish."

She's right. I know it and she knows I know it, but this is where we are. "Yeah, well, since I can't phone in a friend for this one, I'll just have to endure it."

"Are you sure about that?" Gypsy's face brightens some, her eyes drifting over my shoulder to Arius directing his staff alongside Mother.

The door opens, and one of the attendants extends his arms as a host of men pour inside. Arius smiles, dutifully shaking their hands, offering introductions to my mother as they enter. If I didn't know better, it would seem as though Mother and Arius came up with this idea together. Who knows? Maybe they did, and they outsmarted me so much that I thought this was my own idea. But I know better. Ari is simply being a good sport, and Mother, well, she's being herself.

"I hope you don't actually think Arius wants to do this," Gypsy whispers as she wanders to my side.

"Of course he does," I mumble. "Look at him. He seems pretty eager to pawn me off to the most eligible bachelor in sight."

Her smile brightens. "Oh, I'm sure he wants you to have the best, but probably not who you think."

"Then who, because I haven't a clue?"

Growling into her fist, Gypsy throws me a generous eye roll before taking my hand in hers. "Okay, you two have to be the most nauseating pair of... Never mind that, but answer this: what if Arius is your happily, or better yet, in this case, your darkly ever after? How would you feel?"

Snatching my hand from hers, I feel my cheeks warm knocking off the earlier chill.

"Wait—are you saying?"

Nodding, Gypsy offers a small smile. "Look, this really isn't my place, but I'd hate for you to go through this if you don't have to."

"But he's never– We're just–"

"Friends?" Gypsy scoffs, shaking her head in amusement. "You can't believe that he spent all these years with you the way he has because you're friends."

I pull away, leaning back against the wall in disbelief. "Well, he's friends with you, Cade, and Perry. He's just a friendly guy."

"Yeah, well, I'm pretty sure his hands don't get clammy when he sees me or Cade, and definitely not that foul-smelling mutt, Perry," she chuckles.

No, she has this all wrong. I'm sure of it. "But then why would he help me put all this together? I mean, why go through all this if—"

"If he thought that's what *you wanted*? Because he loves you, perhaps? Because he'd rather put you first before his own heart and doing what he thinks you want is what makes him happy? I don't know–" Gypsy's pointed gaze digs a hole in my heart.

Could I have been blind all this time?

"I don't—"

"Yo, boss!" one of the attendants yells from the side hallway. "There's a call for you in the back."

Arius throws up his thumb and whispers something to my mother and one of the guests before walking to the side hall. He shoots me a quick wink as he saunters along, adding that smug little smirk he does that always makes him look so unbearably sexy.

"So do you believe me now, Princess?" Gypsy asks, using her cold fingertips to turn my face back to her. I hadn't even noticed I'd turned completely around to look at Arius. "Or do you drool when you look at all your friends? Because I don't recall you ever looking at me like that," she snickers, dropping her hand from my face.

I want to say something, but I can't. It's now or never. Maybe Gypsy's right. Although the thought of risking Ari's life just for the sake of loving him is gutting me from the inside, I can at least test the theory.

Throwing my cloak off, it falls to the floor as I make my way down the same side hall. I turn back, taking a look at Gypsy, who only offers a brief nod, encouraging me to carry onward. I catch my mother's eye, and she gives a cursory nod to the clock, letting me know it's time for us to officially get started. I nod back in affirmation before pushing the swing door open to find Arius.

As I continue down the hallway, my heart warms when I see the picture frames along the wall. It's like a shrine to notable supernaturals. I see several of the Marchand brothers, Miss Melvina, a few with Gypsy and Cade, and more than a fair share of my own face plastered along the wood panel wall.

I take note of how Arius is looking at me or how his hand is on me in every picture. How have I missed this all these years? I've always felt so comfortable with him. I thought it was just friendship, but how can something so familiar be so strange?

Heaving one gulp of air, I exhale just as I turn the knob into Ari's back office.

His back is to me as he holds the cordless phone to his ear. "Oh, it's no bother at all. I'll drop whatever I'm doing to talk to my favorite lady... "

Favorite lady?

Who?

"So, did you get the red one I sent you? Yeah, well, I can't wait to see you with it on. Ah, and the flowers... Did you like them?"

The flowers? He has never sent *me* flowers. And whoever he's sending these to, they didn't come from my shop.

My heart sinks to the floor, shattering into a thousand tiny pieces. How could I let Gypsy get into my head like that? I knew better. *I know better.* Arius has always been a ladies' man. There has always been a woman to occupy his bedside, that I'm sure of. And it has never been me.

Maybe I saw what I wanted to see in those pictures, but now, I see the truth. We are friends, nothing more.

The door squeaks as it closes behind me, and Arius turns around, shocked. His face doesn't pale when he sees me, and he doesn't look ashamed to be on his call. Because he has nothing to be ashamed of. We are friends, and it's not the first time I've heard him on the phone with one of his women. But after tonight, however, it will be my last.

I look over my shoulder, prepared to leave and give him privacy, but he holds up one finger, telling me to wait. I smile awkwardly, wishing with everything in me to get out of here, snatch the first willing suitor off the barroom floor, and whisk him away to the Underworld. Anything to break free of standing here in humiliation. I can only be thankful he hasn't a clue why I came.

"Okay, beautiful, I've got to run. But I—yes, yes, no worries. I'll see you tomorrow night. No, not tonight. I can't do tonight, but tomorrow... Yes, yes, you'll be the one in red. I know. Love you, okay, bye." Arius winks at me as he hangs up the phone, and I feel coldness sweep over me once more. The one man I've been too afraid to admit I love is in love with someone else.

If I could, I'd wish for death, but alas, I am death, and this by far stings greater than death itself.

CHAPTER 22
Arius

Damn. If I could freeze this moment in time, I would.

Here she is, the only woman to turn my heart of stone into beating flesh, standing before me now a breathtaking splendor of grace and beauty. I don't know if it's the way her pearl gown hangs wistfully over her shoulders, highlighting every perfected inch of her, or the iridescent glow of her high cheekbones from the pale moonlight shimmering through the window, but Desephone, daughter of Hades and Persephone, has set a snare for my soul, and I long for the trap.

"Des," I choke out, hopeful my lovesick gaze and puppy dog

eyes don't make her think I'm any less of a man than the would-be stallions darkening my door. "I'm glad you're here."

"Oh really?" she ponders with a raised brow. She doesn't look entirely happy to see me. Perhaps she's still mad at me from before.

"Yes. I wanted to apologize."

Her brows fold in as her slender fingers wrap around her elbows. I know it's drafty in the bar tonight, but she seems like she's freezing. If only I could wrap my arms around her right now and keep her warm. But not yet. I must continue as planned.

"For what?" Her face brightens some, her large, wishful gaze drawing me in.

"For earlier," I blurt, hopeful to douse her deepening stare. "When I dropped you off, I know I was a bit curt. I just wanted you to know it had nothing to do with you. You deserve better from me."

"I don't deserve any more from you than you've already given, Arius. Your friendship. After tonight, I'll expect nothing more."

Quickly, Des turns to leave, but I rush to her side, pushing the door closed before she has a chance to reach it.

"Arius, please. I need to go."

"Baby, I–"

"Stop calling me that!" she snaps, her eyes darkening to black. Dark veins crowd around her eyes, and her cheeks burn red. Her face is reminiscent of how she looked in the rage room as she crashed the chandelier into pieces.

Instinctively, my flesh hardens like stone, but I work hard to keep my otherworldly self in control.

"Des, I–I didn't mean to– What did I do?"

"Nothing, Arius!" Des shouts back, her face slowly fading back to her mortal form. "You've done nothing! But I..." She shakes her head, warning off her darker self before looking up at me. "I need us to be clear about who and what we are to one another, especially tonight. No crossed signals. No blurred lines."

"I couldn't agree more." I can't help the small smile now curving at the side of my face. Des, on the other hand, isn't as amused.

"Do you understand what I mean, Arius?" she barks, her eyes darkening like a stormy sea but not quite black.

"Straight, no chaser. I hear you loud and clear."

Des frowns, annoyed, shaking her head some as she looks away from me and turns the doorknob. Once more, I push the door shut.

"Ari, please," she breathes, still not looking at me as she keeps her sights on the door.

Slowly, I pull my hand away from the door, allowing her to crack it open.

I place myself in the crack of the door, repositioning myself so she has to look at me.

"Well, Princess, I promise you this: there'll be no blurred lines or cross signals between us from now on. From this point, I'll make every intention I have toward you as clear as a brilliant round cut diamond."

Desephone's eyes grow wide, her breath splintering in surprise as my gaze deepens into hers. She doesn't linger long in our face off when she whirls around me and begins making her way down the hall.

With her head raised high, her hard heels clank loudly against the wood floor as she marches forward. I keep my sights set on the sweet sway of her hips as she prances along, so regally sure of herself, her hands clasped tight at her waist.

"Des!" My voice reeks of desperation as I call to her.

Her gown flourishes off the ground as she turns around to me. "Yes, Ari," she answers with one heavy breath. Glassy eyes stare at me now, and my heart thumps. I would give anything to soothe whatever aches her heart. "What is it?"

"Why did you come to my office? Did you need something?" *Please say it's me.*

Drawing her mouth into a thin line, Des fires a darted eye my way. "I'm ready to find my match, Mr. Knight," she says pointedly. My jaws flex, and her brow raises as she takes some wicked pleasure in my frustration. "And as this is your residency, it is only appropriate that you begin the ceremonies. So, if you're done with your other matters, we'd like it if you could please commence the Culling."

I choke back the guttural groan lodged in my throat and force a strained smile. "Of course, Your Highness," I say, keeping with the formalities. "I just need to tend to a few more things, and I'll be right out."

I don't have shit to tend to, but if she thinks I'll rush out this damn door to help her pick some asshole to accompany her to hell, she'll just have to wait, especially with the attitude she's giving me right now.

"Well, don't keep us waiting long, Mr. Knight." Her snippy tone reminds me too much of her mother, and I don't like it.

"Be there in a moment," I rasp.

"Very well then, Mr. Knight," she wisps as she turns, allowing the hem of her gown to wistfully sweep in the wind she creates. "I'll be the one in white!" Des beckons over her shoulder.

Rushing back to my office, I grab my suit jacket off the wall hook. I turn to the mirror and am surprised to find my stonier features on display. Silver, marbleized flesh and darkened eyes stare back at me, and I can feel my muscles shift and contort beneath my clothes. There's no way I'll be able to get this blazer on if my true Bulwark form takes over.

I take a few deep breaths. I have to do what I can to hold back the monster brewing beneath the surface. Bulwarks may be the more peaceable of supernaturals, but I could easily level this whole damn building if need be.

That thought gives me a modicum of satisfaction. I'm in control. If even one vampire snares his fangs the wrong way, I'll ignite an orb brighter than the sun and burn them all. Same for the wolves. Just as I spared that lone wolf no mercy as I ripped him in half, I'll do the same to any of his kin should the need arise.

I watch as my fleshly form retakes shape while a small smirk escapes me. *You've got this.*

"Are you done ogling yourself?" I hear Gypsy's whiny tone from my door.

I don't look at her as I adjust my collar and wait for the remainder of my stony shift to subside. "Almost done." I smile over my shoulder.

"Yeah, well, while you're in here admiring yourself, your—well, Desephone is out there giving more than generous smiles to every Tom, Dick, and Harry–literally!" Gypsy hollers. "Hell, Knight, what did you do to her? One minute, I'm telling her she should come in here and see if there's a future for you two instead of dealing with all these dickwads at the door, and the next thing I know, she's storming out into the bar like a sultry siren. What gives?"

Turning sharply on my heel, I feel my skin tighten once more as I look at Gypsy. "You told her to do what?"

Gypsy jumps back at my thunderous shout, and it all becomes clear. Desephone heard my phone call, and she misunderstood it all. This could get messy.

Desephone

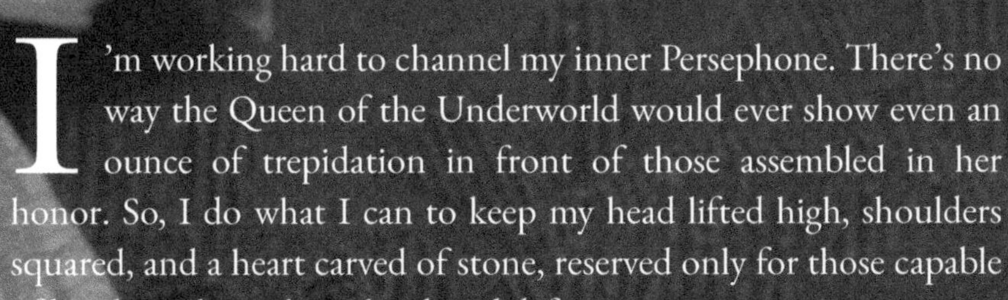

I'm working hard to channel my inner Persephone. There's no way the Queen of the Underworld would ever show even an ounce of trepidation in front of those assembled in her honor. So, I do what I can to keep my head lifted high, shoulders squared, and a heart carved of stone, reserved only for those capable of breaking through my hardened defenses.

"There are more here than I imagined," my mother whispers in my ear. She's quite pleased with her efforts. I still don't know who her earthbound connections are, but they certainly put on a concerted effort to get so many to the bar. "You'll have quite a harvest to cull, Dearest." She grins as her eyes wander to a few hand-some faces marching past us.

We're seated in the upper deck of the bar. Normally, Ari has two billiards tables and a few poker tables in the back for games. Tonight, however, there's just a luxe, velvety loveseat with potted plants on either side and a long linen-skirted table with golden Chiavari chairs. There's a floral garland hanging along the wooden railing, and I can't help smiling, realizing these came from my shop. I'm not sure when Ari and Mother connected, but the thought makes me happy.

Arius walks out from his back office. His stride is sure and just as confident as it always is, but tonight, it feels more pronounced. Gypsy ambles out behind him. Her arms are folded, and she hangs against the wall, eyes beaming red. I'm not sure if it's because I refused to speak to her when I came out of Ari's office earlier, or if something happened between her and Arius, but my heart sinks. Gypsy has been nothing but kind to me over the years. She has been a friend, and I was anything but friendly. Just because nothing will ever come of me and Ari doesn't mean she to blame. Before this night is over, I must be sure to tell her that.

Mother stands, her lovely black gown gracefully blowing from her shadowy wind, all eyes on her. With her long black hair now braided to one side, her radiant skin glows like a pale moon as her pomegranate-stained lips greet those gathered below with a bright smile.

Arius raises a fist, quieting our guests as all eyes turn to the Queen of the Underworld. I'm not sure if I should remain seated or stand, but my gut tells me to stay put. Mother is quite a ham for attention, and I'm sure she's pleased to have this moment to herself.

"Attention, everyone!" Arius calls out with a thunderous clap of his hands. "I give you, Queen Persephone!" Extending his hands toward Mother, Ari offers a small bow at the waist, as does everyone else.

"Thank you, Mr. Knight," Mother begins, offering a small wink to Arius. Looking back at the crowd, she continues, "Your presence tonight means you are not only well thought of in your factions and communities, but among those of the highest esteem. Whether your origins are vampiric, shifter, wolven, hybrid, or any others that remain–" She shoots another gaze back to Ari. He offers a small smile in return, but he keeps his sights trained on me, and for fear of being torn by his lure, I turn away. "We are very much welcomed by your presence. Of course, none of this would be possible without our resident Bulwark and proprietor of the Dram Deaux, Mr. Arius Knight."

The crowd gives Ari a dutiful round of handclaps and nods, just enough to acknowledge him. Every man here is quite intent on wearing their hubris with their whole chest tonight, and I'd expect nothing less.

My eyes scan around the bar, and I see a fair number of vampires, both pureblood and mortal-made Scourge. There's an ample array of wolves, including hybrid wolves mixed throughout, along with a fair number of other types of shifters, like bears and panthers. I am surprised to find a few Netherworld expats like me among those gathered. It's surprising that any would be willing to return to the Netherworld; although I suspect returning as a ruler of the Underworld has its perks.

I blow out a breath, doing my best to remain hopeful I'll find my suitor tonight. While I'm not averse to finding someone of good character, I, like anyone else, want to at least be attracted to them on some level. Many of the men are indeed handsome, but I can't say anyone is immediately catching my eye.

Perhaps it's because they're all standing beside Arius. It's quite impossible for anyone to draw my attention with Arius looking the way he does tonight. From the way the open collar of his lavender shirt splays open, revealing just a hint of his sculpted chest, to how his well-tailored suit accentuates his athletic build, it's hard to imagine anyone could stand next to him without feeling like a mere speck of dust. That's what they all are next to Arius: specks of dust.

My stomach churns in knots when Ari looks my way, his dazzling smile gleaming and his steely stare yanking me like a magnetic cord. Not that I thought tonight would be easy, but Arius Knight will make this damn right difficult.

What was I thinking dragging him into this?

Knowing our friendship will be my undoing burns a hole in my chest, and I have no one to blame but myself.

"Thank you, Great Queen!" Arius exclaims, lifting his clasped hands together, rallying everyone else to offer her a round of applause. The crowd echoes in kind. It's not lost on them to be on their best behavior before the bride of Hades. My father has been known to destroy kingdoms just because he thought it would please Persephone. Even more, they know supernatural does not mean immortal. Each of them will have to meet their end at the hands of my father. Better to chart the ferry to the Underworld on good terms than risk my father's wrath.

Or mine, in due time.

Mother indulges their ceremonious cheers for a few seconds before lifting her hands to quiet the crowd. She gives me a look, and a warm smile reaches her eyes as she regards me. Her head bobs just a little to let me know my time has come, and I adjust myself in my seat, pushing my hips to the edge of the chair.

"There is no greater treasure of a mother's heart than the jewel that is her child. Tonight, I present to you such a rare jewel: my daughter, Desephone!"

A loud chorus of admiration rings through the bar as I stand and make my way to Mother's side. Looking over the balcony, the gleaming white smiles, handsome grins, and puffed chests extend toward me, and it's clearer now than it has ever been: I feel like an antiquity on display.

Taking my hand in hers, Mother squeezes it, likely sensing my angst as she offers a reassuring smile.

"Now, know this, fair gentlemen: I do not offer my daughter as a mere prize. Quite the opposite. It is you, good sirs, who must not only showcase your strength, wit, and charm, but you must find a place in her heart. And while your time here tonight may be brief, please make the best of the time you have. This Culling has been not only curated for speed, but to ensure only one champion remains at the end of all things. Not only will you need to showcase mastery of your wit and skill, but you must, in doing so, catch her eye. Those who do will succeed to the next round, and those who do not will pass on. But be at ease; per my daughter's kind request, should you not meet her requirements, your life will not be forfeit. But be warned; our resident Bulwark, Mr. Knight, has ensured no matter how you fare tonight, you will not leave the same way you came."

I work hard not to gasp at this revelation. Although I am not sure what they are up to, it's clear Mother and Ari have accounted for every facet of tonight's festivities.

"So, without further ado, I present the Daughter of Hades, Princess Desephone!" Mother exclaims brightly while dropping a small kiss on my cheek.

Waving at the crowd like one of those Southern Belle debutantes, I lift a wide smile as I stare out into the bar. Nothing but charming smiles reflect at me, and for a brief moment, I feel a spark of electricity race through me. While faint, it's the adrenaline I need to continue onward.

Long strips of pink and white rose garland drape the banister, and I run my hand along the floral array until my fingers find a few thorns as I make my way down the stairs. A glutton for punishment, I dig a finger around until the sharp point of the thorn draws blood. As I do, I hear a faint hissing sound from below as the crimson eyes of a few vampires roam in my direction. Arius squares his shoulders, his jaw clenching, ready to take on any untoward aggression. My heart thumps wildly as I make my way down the long staircase, knowing he'll never let anyone hurt me. Even if I'm bound for hell, all I see is heaven in his eyes.

Arius gives a little nod to two attendants, and they pull a cord, allowing a rainfall of rose petals to fall at my feet. *You deserve flowers at your feet.* How Ari can feel so deeply for a *friend,* I'll never understand. Still, in this moment, I couldn't be happier.

CHAPTER 24

Arius

Damn, she is a lovely sight!

Perfect, in fact, adorned with an array of rose petals floating to her feet as she gracefully strides down the staircase, and I marvel at how beautiful she is.

And I'm not alone.

Every man has his sights glued to Desephone, pulled to her like a moth to a flame. Even the vampires who were just salivating with fangs-dripping bloodlust only minutes ago are now in awe of her.

Des smiles, her eyes bounce around the room and up to Queen Persephone, who remains perched at the top of the landing. Still,

Des stays in the middle of the staircase, watchful of the all-too-eager faces smiling back at her. For a moment, her gaze settles on mine, but she forces her eyes away from me, returning her sights to the crowd.

If I didn't know she was the Daughter of Hades, I'd swear she was an angel with the way the moonlight beams through the transom, making her face aglow with beauty. She waves, her bright smile as luminous as the sun as she stares around the bar.

"Thank you," she sweetly rasps, her cool tone sweeping over the room like a soothing balm. "There are so many of you!" she giggles, waving a quick hand around before covering her mouth.

"There should be a thousand more!" one man shouts just behind me.

"Two thousand!" another yells from the back corner.

A stabbing pain jabs my throat as I hold back the desire to roar like a fire-breathing dragon toward every man assembled here. For now, however, I'll play nice.

The ensemble of eligibles hikes their gleeful calls throughout the bar while Desephone's cheeks blush, likely a bit taken aback by so much interest hurled her way. Still, she smiles, waving her hands downward to simmer the crowd.

"Now, now, gentlemen," she calls out, quieting their jovial sounds. "There'll be ample time to enact your courtship." Desephone smiles, her gaze narrowing as she lifts her chin and squares her shoulders. She looks more like her mother now than ever before. Lifting a cautious finger, she deftly wags it side to side as she takes one step down the stairs. "But you've been warned, dear ones..." A beautifully haunting shadow seems to envelop her where she stands like a cocoon. Some of the men gasp, stepping back in sheer awe of her. Queen Persephone looks down, her chest heaving with pride at the sight of her daughter. The shadow recedes some, but her face remains ominous. "To court me is to court death." Her voice drops almost an octave, and her eyes darken to black as she reveals her more otherworldly features to the crowd.

The room stirs, and a wave of emotions wash over the bar. Still, Desephone takes it all in. Her gaze is calculating and precise. She wants them to understand what they are getting into.

The knot in my throat lifts a little as I pick up on the anxious and uncertain expressions of those assembled here. I'd be happier to see them all run. Although no one has made a go for the door, I'm certain if only one person took his leave, another five would follow.

It's not that anyone here, being monsters themselves, fears another monster. But Des is the Daughter of Hades, a representative of death itself. Even if they had only leisurely considered the consequences before, there is no avoiding them now.

"And death is what awaits all who dare court the Daughter of Hades with any but the truest intentions," a dark, shrill voice says from the doorway. All eyes turn in his direction, and nothing but a foreboding shadowy frame stalks the threshold.

My eyes shoot first to Desephone then her mother, all equally shocked by this stranger's outburst.

What the hell? I turn away from Des, my eyes darting to both Gypsy and Cade, who now stare with raised attention. Cade's nose crinkles as the stranger steps forward, and I snap my gaze back to the door. Lightning cracks across the darkened sky as thunder shakes the foundation of the bar. There was no indication of a storm brewing today, so I'm certain whatever is happening now is of supernatural origin.

Queen Persephone is at her daughter's side in an instant, and Des backs into her mother's more menacing demeanor. I give a quick nod to the queen, and she does so in return. Our allegiance is simple. Neither one of us will let anyone or anything hurt Desephone.

Cade also makes his way through the crowd, perching himself at my side. But when I see flecks of unease stirring in his eyes, I know something is wrong.

The lightning brightens the doorway once more, and the stranger's face is revealed in full.

It's Decaux Marchand.

Damn it.

Shock rolls through the room as the sight of one of the Leading Lord Vampires standing before us. His cruelty and treachery are widely known throughout the supernatural community. While Grandmère Melvina does an apt job of reining back both he and his brother Dalcour's machinations, even an esteemed Bulwark such as she is incapable of fully keeping him in check.

It's not lost on me that Decaux could easily place himself at the forefront of this Culling. I'm sure he'd like nothing more than to rule the Underworld. His darkened soul would surely delight in such a prize. Although I'm hardly a match for him by any stretch, I'd ripple the sky with the power of sun and burn his ashen husk to the ground repeatedly before I'd let him stand at Desephone's side.

"Who the hell invited you?" I shout, and the crowd parts like the Red Sea, leaving me alone in line with Decaux.

"My friend, no!" Cade hisses as his hand cups my elbow, hopeful to douse my ire, but it's too late.

"Ahh, I'm afraid I haven't an invitation," Decaux sneers, his thick, pointy fangs in full view. He taps his boot at the door, and a bright, golden light hits his foot. "Pretty sure this very thinly veiled Bulwark charm is meant to keep the likes of me out of tonight's festivities."

"Pity." I huff, standing my ground.

"Tread carefully," Cade whispers behind me.

I don't bother to look at Cade. Instead, I keep my attention on Decaux.

"And she seems to be such a beautiful girl, too," Decaux continues with a wicked lilt to his otherwise-charming tone. As he stretches his gloved hand toward Des, his crimson eyes bore into her like missiles locked on its target. Des doesn't flinch, but Queen Persephone steps down in front of her daughter, blocking Decaux's view. "Tsk, tsk," he says, shaking his head. I notice a red tint of blood staining his goatee against his brown skin.

"Why are you here, Lord Marchand?" Queen Persephone bites back, her displeasure of his arrival evident. "A man of your status is hardly seeking a mate. Last I heard, your most recent one met such a dire end."

A low snarl inches out of Decaux, and he takes a closer step toward the entrance. He knows he isn't permitted to enter, but still, he tests his boundaries. "And last I heard, when your daughter faced a similar fate, she could only find one place of solace: in my coffin."

"Bloody bastard!" Des shouts, her otherworldly form taking over. She's at my side before I can blink, her mother on her heels. The queen remains in her mortal form, but the lightning storm brewing in her gaze tells me she'll rip this place apart and drag Decaux to hell all in one breath if need be.

Postures stiffen while a mix of golden and crimson eyes illuminate the bar. Some of the men begin to slowly amble toward the door while a few others stare off weighing their options.

Rumblings and snarls permeate the air. *The little hellion has been with Decaux? I wonder how many others she's been with?.*

I'd gladly aid Persephone in delivering any of these ill-fated suitors into Hades' hands, but right now, only one person matters. Despite the flume of fire and smoke whirling around her, I know her well enough to see the makings of pain in the hollows of her darkened eyes.

Now, it's my job to erase that pain as best as I can.

CHAPTER 25

Desephone

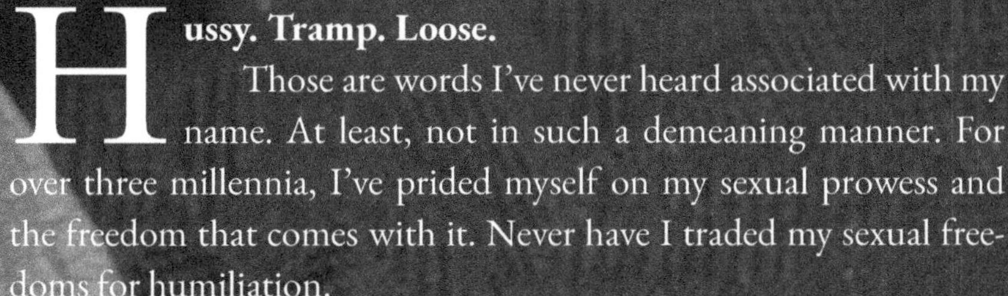

Hussy. Tramp. Loose.

Those are words I've never heard associated with my name. At least, not in such a demeaning manner. For over three millennia, I've prided myself on my sexual prowess and the freedom that comes with it. Never have I traded my sexual freedoms for humiliation.

I've enjoyed the company of men more than most, and on each occasion, I've held my head high. So, there's no way I'll let even Decaux Marchand mar my name for whatever sick purposes he might have.

The loud crashing of a chair being thrown across the room catches our attention. "And there's the fucking door!" Ari growls, turning toward the murmuring onlookers. "You got a problem with who's coffin she's in? Then fuck you! She owes you nothing. So if you're leaving—" he kicks another chair— "then there's the fucking door!"

"You heard him, morons!" Gypsy echoes in kind as she shoves two lanky wolves out of the bar. More shuffle behind them, shaking their heads, shooting both me and Ari a cross look on their way out.

Meanwhile, Decaux remains a fixture against the doorframe. With a cheeky grin, he waves farewell to everyone who walks out the door. About thirty or so men leave—some willingly, while others seem more fearful of Ari's fiery tone as he stands mid-shift, most of his Bulwark form in full view.

With hardened skin like marble and eyes as black as night, it's no wonder most are wary in his presence. Although Bulwarks are known to be peaceful creatures, everyone here is also aware of a Bulwark's powers. From compelling wolves to remain in their animal form to desiccating a vampire in an instant, Ari's anger is nothing to easily cast aside.

Only about twenty or so remain, and even they seem somewhat unsure.

"Are you happy with yourself, vampire?" my mother lashes out. Her gaze is still dark, but I'm surprised how she's restrained herself. "Now, my daughter's lost more than half her share of qualified suitors! Have you any idea how hard it was to curate such a grouping?"

Decaux laughs, rearing his head back against the doorframe. "Please tell me you're joking, Great Queen."

"Do you mock me, boy?" Mother growls, her eyes shining bright like fire.

Lifting his hands in surrender, Decaux shakes his head, feigning regret. "Please, Your Highness," he coos, slanting his gaze with a cool smirk tilted to one side of his face. "I mean no offense. I know it is not beneath the Queen of the Underworld to drag me, kicking and screaming to Hades, letting your husband rip me in two..."

"Oh, no, Vampire!" Mother bites back, taking one step in front of me. "It is surely I who'd do the ripping. And you wouldn't enjoy it, I assure you!"

Cackling, Decaux wags a finger in agreement. The gesture would seem mocking, but as he tightens his lips, it's evident he knows he's pushing his luck.

"I'm sure you would, Queen. However, for much as it would seem the opposite, I assure you, it was never my intention to sully your Culling, as it were."

"How can you say that?" Arius jumps in front of me and Mother. "Did you not just see them run from the bar?"

"Arius!" Cade warns, tugging on his friend's elbow.

Arius shakes Cade's hands from him, keeping his sight set on Decaux.

Adjusting the collar of his trench coat, Decaux lifts a brow, his crimson eyes aglow as he stares at Arius. "Well, Bulwark, I would think you of all people would be pleased. I suppose my good deeds remain unrequited by your kind. Pity..."

"Pity," Arius repeats, his tone flat.

"And why would Ari be pleased?" I groan, stepping closer to Ari's side.

Decaux stares between me and Arius for a beat, his eyes narrowing to a darker shade of red as he regards Arius then lifting to a softer hue as he looks over his shoulder at me. "Well, Princess, seeing as though I've rid you of the riff raff, you can now proceed with your evening without those who see a woman's past as a vitae of their own manhood. It's quite off putting, don't you think?" he quips, shaking his head in disgust.

"Honorable words from the man who threw her past in her face!" Gypsy bites back.

Decaux hisses in rebuttal, his eyes glowing into a threatening red alarm. His sharp fangs lengthen as he leans forward, likely wishing he could cross the barrier Arius added to the threshold.

"Mind your words, you venomous Scourge! Or don't you know who I am?" Decaux lashes toward Gypsy.

Both Cade and Arius quickly crowd in front of their friend, hopeful to keep her out of Decaux's sights.

"Oh, I know who you are, Lord Marchand," she snarls. "But Des wouldn't be in this situation if it wasn't for you, so your posturing to stand for a woman's sexual freedoms is a little lost on me, buddy!"

"Gypsy, that's enough!" Cade warns, his eyes staying glued to Decaux.

Drawing back, Decaux belts a wicked little laugh, clapping his hands in amusement as he does. "Not to worry, old friend, I think I like this one. She reminds me of another spitfire we know." He grins, his eyes glazing with a distant look.

"Yes, my lord," Cade hurriedly replies. "Our little Gypsy is certainly a spitfire, indeed."

Gypsy grouses, snarling and gritting her teeth as she stares at Cade, but Arius issues her a stern look, and she holds her tongue.

"None of that explains why you crashed my daughter's festivities!" Mother shouts, regaining Decaux's attention. "I certainly hope you don't wish to be invited in on some hopes that you've done us a favor."

"Not a chance!" Ari growls.

Decaux swipes his hand in the air. "Rubbish! I wouldn't dream of taking one step. Rather, consider this my wedding gift to the betrothed–whoever it may be," he continues with a sly grin. "And perhaps some good will shall befall me whenever I reach your gates in the Underworld, or even before, should circumstances necessitate it." With his shoulders squared and his stance still softened, if I didn't know better, I'd think Decaux Marchand sought a barter.

Mother casts me a wary glance, her mouth tightening like a button. She's not buying his plea.

"And why would we give you any allowance, vampire?" Mother grouses, her eyes narrowed.

"Because for those who remain, I want to be clear. Until now, I, Decaux Marchand, have never met the fair Princess Desephone. Our only mutual relation is that of the caretaker of my coffin and the Grand Watcher of New Orleans. She only loaned out my place of repose to the princess in her time of need, nothing more."

Gasps erupt through the room once more, and as I look around, I can see the pensive tone relax. Even those who chose to stay seem more at ease hearing the truth from Decaux.

Another sly smile spreads across Decaux's face as he stares around the bar, his sights landing on Mother. "As you can see, Great Queen, I meant no offense. In fact, had the others not been so hasty—"

"Fine, vampire!" Mother belts with a heavy sigh and dismissive swipe of her hand. "You've made your case. Now, go!"

"As you wish, Great Queen," Decaux replies softly with a slight bow of his head before bolting out of our sight.

Crashing my hands to my face, I work hard to muffle my screams. This Culling isn't going well.

Arius

Decaux is gone before I can blink. Both Gypsy and Cade rush to secure the door, ensuring there are no more surprise interruptions. I shoot one look at my attendants, and they also spring into action, engaging the guests who remain with drinks and appetizers.

The queen has her hand on her daughter's back, patting her lightly. She seems uncomfortable with consolation. With the way her eyes stay fixed on the door, I'm sure she's still thinking about Decaux. She isn't the only one. And while I'm curious as to his true intent, the only person I care about right now is Desephone.

"May I?" I whisper to Queen Persephone, gesturing she step aside and let me help Des. The queen's mouth is drawn tight, but her darkened eyes soften to her usual stormy gaze, and she tips her head, stepping back just enough to let me in front of Des.

Taking her wrists in my hand, my chest rumbles a bit as I close my eyes and unfurl my wings from my back. Even half-mast, it's a painful exercise I don't relish in, but this is what needs to be done. The pointed, hard tips of my dark wings tear through my shirt and suit jacket, and I feel them flapping at my back. My wings aren't as wide as most Bulwarks, but they're large enough to cover Des.

Slowly, she lifts her head as I pull her hands from her face. Her eyes drift to mine for a moment before staring in awe as she hovers beneath the shadow of my wings.

"Ari?" she squeaks in surprise. She knows I'm not a fan of revealing my form in front of others, and even more that I'm not a fan of my wings, so this is just as shocking for her.

"Just wanted to give you a little shade, baby, that's all," I whisper, tilting her chin so she's looking at me. "Besides, no one should see your tears but me."

"I can't keep doing this to you, Ari," she mumbles, looking up at how my wings arch over her.

"Doing what to me?"

Sucking her teeth, she rolls her eyes and shakes her head. "This! Making you responsible for me. That's not fair to you. Now we've got these folks here–and they probably think I'm—and not to mention Mother's disappointment–"

"Des. Stop." I take her head between my hands until I feel her relax. She blows out a few deep breaths, closing her eyes in between each. "That's it," I coax her, my hands now dropping to her shoulders. "Listen, the only thing that matters tonight is you. Do you understand me?" I pause, my pointed stare locked with hers. She nods, letting out a small breath. "Good. Now, if you say the word, I'll send everyone packing. Is that what you want?"

"But Mother will—"

"Is that what *you* want?" I repeat.

"But what about the ones who left after Decaux? Surely they'll run my name through the mud, and I—"

"No, they won't." I protest, shaking my head in disagreement.

"How can you be so sure?" she counters.

"Because I charmed this entire building. What happens within these walls stays within these walls. The moment they stepped over the threshold, all was forgotten. They'll have no memory of anything Decaux said or ever meeting you."

Covering her mouth, she gasps. "Ari, I–I had no idea you went through such lengths... *for me.*"

I smile, thankful to put her mind at ease. "I told you, it's my job to protect my territory." There's so much more I want to say, but I still sense the heavy weight she bears, holding her hostage.

Her eyes glaze over me for a few seconds before she blows out a heavy sigh. "I need to find a husband, Ari. Tonight. I can't put this off any longer." Her shoulders slump some, but I can see she is resigned to her fate. "I've got to go through with this."

"Then that settles it. If my baby needs to find a husband tonight, then a husband is what she'll get. I'll make sure of it." I can only hope the strained notes in my now-darkened tone don't give me away. It's taking all that I am not to fly us out of here and escape to an island made for us two so I can finally confess how I truly feel. But still, this isn't the time.

"You will?" Her voice cracks and her brows lift. "Why?"

"I'd do anything for you, Des. You should know that by now. Anything. Besides, it's kind of my thing."

Looking up at me with her big glassy eyes, Des lifts to the balls of her feet and pulls my face into her petite palms, planting a small peck on my cheek.

Shit.

She has never kissed me before. Just the feel of her mouth

pressed against the hard marble of my rigid jaw sends ripples through me and strength to my groin.

If only we were alone. But we're not. Pulling back, I offer her a small smile before I reluctantly withdraw my wings back into myself and shift into my mortal form.

"Thank you, Ari," Des says with a smile so gracious, it makes my heart melt. Before I can offer a reply, she turns, making her way to her mother's side.

As I look around, I'm surprised to see everyone is mingling with one another and the queen, as if nothing happened.

"I would've thought she'd announce the two of you a pair once you came out from under your wings," Cade slyly sneers with a cagey grin.

Turning to him, I grab him by his collar, pushing him against the corner wall. It's dark enough no one should see us, but even if they did, I wouldn't care.

His eyes narrow, but he cackles as I tighten my grip on his collar. "Go ahead, mate, unleash your rage on me. I care not!" Cade scoffs with a devilish snort.

"Then spit it out, damn it! I know you brought Decaux here!" I lash out.

He whimpers, still laughing. "Who, me?" He crowds his hands to his chest, feigning innocence.

"Well, he is your maker! And I'm no fool! So, tell me why you did it!"

Cade's eyes flash bright red, his fangs lengthening as he pushes himself out of my grip and away from the wall. "I could tell you I had nothing to do with his arrival, but seeing as you've made your mind up already, I'll just say this one last time: stop pussy-footing around and tell her the fuck how you feel. Besides, as far as I can tell, Decaux did you a favor," he snaps back, his eyes circling around the bar at the noticeable dip in guests.

However, what I see is Des. She's far more relaxed now than

before. She's laughing, mingling with the guests, and even Queen Persephone is enjoying the more intimate gathering. Perhaps Cade is right.

My eyes juts back to his daggered-eye glare, and beneath his annoyance with me, all I see is my friend. Still, it doesn't take away how it all upset Desephone.

"Favor or not, I have a plan. I know you and Gypsy want to help, but I've got this covered. I promise."

Cade blows out a hard sigh as he folds his arms over his chest. "Whatever you say, but with Father Time over there—" he points to a suave looking guy with his hair slicked back into a silver and black ponytail– "and Mr. Beach Blonde Baywatch on her left–" he points to an all-too-friendly yet strangely familiar man laughing with her, "it would seem you'd better leave me be and put whatever plan you have into action."

"And wear this!" I hear Gypsy huff behind me, holding up another blazer from my office. "Asshole!" she snips, adding a lofty eye roll.

Both Gypsy and Cade stare at me, and it pains me to know I've been far too hard on the ones who only want to see me happy. They are far better to me than I deserve.

"I'm sorry," I choke out, as I take the blazer from Gypsy. She only grunts with a little nod while Cade helps me out of my torn jacket and into the new one. "Thank you both." I smile at my friends.

They don't respond with words, because I already know: they'll always be in my corner. Until the very end.

CHAPTER 27

Desephone

"Arius!" I shout to the other side of the bar.

He looks over his shoulder at me and waves with his free arm as Cade helps him put on his blazer. It sucks knowing he had to ruin a perfectly good jacket just to shield me earlier, but I'm glad he has something else to wear.

"Be right there!" he chimes in with a luminous smile. He turns back to Cade and Gypsy and continues talking. I wish he was here with me now.

While Mother doesn't mind gaffing it up with everyone, I can't keep up the small talk. I know I'm supposed to spend this time getting to know the suitors, but I don't know how many rounds of, *I'm an expert at ice and spear fishing,* or *I enjoy long walks along the beach at night,* I can take. I'd rather burst their bubble and tell them there are no beaches or lakes in the Netherworld, but alas, I just keep this idiotic smile plastered on my face, waiting for Ari to get over here.

"Mr. Knight!" Mother croons merrily, waving Ari through the crowd.

All eyes are on him as he makes his stately march forward, owning every inch of every plank his foot touches. Bearing that smug smirk that always has me knots, I do my best not to seem too thrilled at his approach. I'd hate for the others to know he's the rubric by which all men are measured.

"Sorry to keep you waiting, Great Queen," Ari replies dutifully, primping his collar as he comes to our side. He gives me a brief look but keeps his gaze on Mother. I'm sure he's doing his best to stay on her good side, considering how things went so poorly with Decaux.

"Not to worry." She smiles, patting his shoulder. "But we can't start tonight's festivities without you lighting the prisms."

"Of course!" he exclaims merrily, sauntering forward to the center of the room. "With your shared permission, I'd be happy to get things started." Ari pauses, sharing another look between me and Mother. Mother and I nod in agreement, and Ari shoots us a quick wink and turns toward the guests. "Now that we're free of the —I forget, what did Lord Marchand call them?" He gestures his hand toward Cade in the rear.

Cade smiles knowingly, lifting a haughty chin and pointing back to Ari. "Riff-raff!" he shouts back.

"Ah yes, those vermin trolling Her Highness' hallowed grounds." Ari smiles brightly as all the other men chuckle at the dig at those who left. "Leaving behind clearly more suitable choices." He waves his hand around, esteeming each man with a dutiful nod. "We'll get on with the Culling. First, we'll start with some basics, like brick holstering and dismantle. Next, we'll move on to ax wielding, and from there, the prisms."

"Mr. Knight," a silver-haired man named Julian, steps forward, "how will each set be measured?"

"Yes," another dark-skinned man with curly hair, whose name I never got, calls out. "Who decides who moves to the next round?"

"I do!" I chime in, walking to Ari's side. "While you'll indeed be required to showcase your skill tonight, you'll be equally judged by your ability to keep my interest."

A light breeze of laughter stirs through the air, each man puffing his chest, assured in his odds.

Mother, too, steps forward. "Once our resident Bulwark here fires off Epirus, the flames of the bow will rest upon each of you. In order to proceed to the next round, you'll need to keep your flames lit. Should the flame fade, you'll not be permitted to the next round."

"While this will be a more fast-paced event, it will retain all of the appeal of the ethereal elements kept by the ancients," Ari adds. "Queen Persephone has charmed every element of this Culling to ensure all is fair in love and war."

"So, without further ado..." I say, extending my hand toward Arius.

Once more, just like when we were in the rage room, a bright flame shines through his hands as he lifts his arm, extending until Epirus appears between his hands. Bright, iridescent light sparkles around the room as Arius points the bow to an airy, diamond-shaped target now shining in the center of the room. Beams of light from each prism and fiery strands extend from the ax and brick stations, connecting to the light from the diamond target.

Arius releases the fiery bow, and we watch in awe as it arches through the sky like a shooting star. It lands perfectly in the center of the diamond, causing it to burst into tiny flames. Embers float through the sky, landing, lapel-like, on each guest. The small flames settle, breaking into three distinct orbs resting cooly against their chests.

Gasps erupt once more through the barroom as the flames make their way around. I'm not sure exactly how Epirus works, or how it knows to whom to fall, but I stand in just as much awe as everyone here.

Mother and I turn about happily as we find the welcoming smiles of each man.

"It's the Culling, Dearest," Mother croons in my ear. "Now that it's official, the testosterone in this place has shot up to the roof," she chuckles as we gaze out to the puffed-chest onlookers with flared nostrils and squared shoulders.

Most look at me as if I'm their next meal, or like they're ready to pounce– or a combination of both. Either way, it comes to reason that tonight's Culling will be quite an interesting one.

Squeezing my wrist, Mother leans into me once more. "Now, do try to thin the herd as quickly as possible. No need to lead anyone along if you're not interested. Understood?" Her eyes lock with mine as she pulls away, but her sentiment is clear. I acquiesce with a quick nod, and Mother smiles in return. Knowing Arius charmed the bar so anyone who leaves will forget everything altogether makes it easier for me to cut the cord.

"Shall we begin with the bricks?" Arius calls attention to the crowd.

Clapping her hands merrily, Mother lets out a girlish gasp. "Well look, Dearest! It appears our resident Bulwark has decided to play along!" she shrieks, clapping her hands wildly.

Pangs of fear churn like a saw inside me as I turn around, shocked to find the same fiery embers now resting on Arius.

Rushing to his side, I snatch him by the arm before he can lead the men to the first event.

"Ari, what in the hell are you trying to pull?" I grit through my teeth, hopeful the others can't hear me. Thankfully, most seem like they're trying to set up at the brick station.

Pulling himself from my grip, he looks over my shoulder at the brick station before returning his attention to me. "What are you doing, Des? We need to get started."

"Yes, we–not you!" I say with a sharp jab to his shoulder.

"And I'm part of the we, Des. How else do you presume I help you tonight? Just stand idly by while you–"

"Find a husband! Yes. That's exactly what I expect you to do, Arius."

He smirks. *Fucking smirks*, as if I just fell into a trap.

"Well, since you're not yet my wife, I don't have to do what you say. So, on that note–" He turns to leave.

I yank him back. "What do you mean *yet*?"

Once more that stupid fucking smirk. I would say sexy, but he's pissing me off.

"Oh, I think you heard me just fine, Princess. Now, if you'll excuse me–" He brushes past me.

Ari's dismissive tone infuriates me almost more than Lord Marchand's. What's worse is I thought we were finally back on good terms, but his moods today have me in a tailspin. One minute, we're good, and the next, we're this–whatever *this* is.

Rushing back to Ari's side as he makes his way back to the crowd, I round in front of him, halting his motion.

"What is it?" he groans, still smirking as he looks down at me.

"Look, Ari, I don't know what you're up to, but if I don't find a suitor tonight, I'll be ruined!"

His expression softens into a genuine smile. "Well, I wouldn't worry about that, Your Highness, because in case you haven't noticed, I'm the one who's ruined, but please, ruin me some more."

CHAPTER 28

Arius

The men waste no time showcasing their skill, and Des seems all too eager watching them vie for her eye.

The first task is simple: stacking bricks. The stacks can be ornate or simple. Whether the bricks are stacked like a windmill or a tower, the goal is to see them come down. At the end of this round, each participant will need to destroy the brick station of the man to his right. On the surface, it seems like an easy task, but Queen Persephone insisted on charming the bricks so neither destroying them nor building them will be as easy as it seems.

Although I'm working my ass off to put together a station I

hope she'll approve of, Des is intent on staying clear of my station on purpose. She's doing her damndest not to pay me any mind, but I know better. Or at least, I hope so.

"Well damn, Master Bulwark, you're clearly looking to throw this round," Mr. Beach Blonde says over my shoulder. "Everyone knows towers are the easiest to fall," he teases.

I don't turn around to see what I'm sure is an arrogant smirk I'd like nothing more than to knock off his face. Instead, I stay focused on finishing my station. Since this station is considered an easy entry, we don't have as much time to work.

"It seems rather impressive to me," Queen Persephone chimes in, surprising me from behind. "Wouldn't you say so, Dearest?"

I stack the last brick on. I don't even bother to smooth the putty when the sweet aroma of Des' floral scent prickles my pores.

"I highly doubt it!" Des groans, uninterested. I spin on my heel, annoyed to find the silver-haired gentleman flanking her rear. Mr. Beach Blonde also makes his way to her other side, plastering a bright white smile on his face meant just for her.

Mr. Beach Blonde laughs, pointing at my station. "Yeah, I told him towers are too easy to bring down."

Desephone's eyes widen as she rounds the corner, and my station comes into full view. Her lips quiver a little as her thick lashes flit back to me. "But–but–this isn't—"

"Oh, this damn thing will certainly come down!" another man shouts at my side. "All I have to do is huff and puff and blow this thing down!" he jeers, jamming his elbow into another man.

"And what are you? The damn Big Bad Wolf?" a crimson-eyed vampire with bright red hair fires back.

"Why don't you come closer and find out?" the first caller shouts back.

"There, there, gentlemen," the queen chides, waving her arms around. "Civil behavior, please," she says half-heartedly. If I had to guess, I'd say she's happy with their quips.

About five men gather, standing around my station, laughing with one another. The only one not laughing is Des. Her eyes are locked on my station, almost horror struck, and she remains frozen as her hand cups her mouth.

"Isn't what?" the queen asks, her questioning brow raised high as her glance travels between me and her daughter. "You were saying something earlier, dear."

I step in front of Persephone. It's clear Des is taken aback, and the last thing I need is everyone here gawking at her. "I think what the princess means is that this isn't a mere tower," I interject, shoving a hand in my pocket. Dashing a jaunty grin, I saunter proudly around my station, happy with the effect I'm having on Des. "Isn't that right, Your Highness?" I tip my head in her direction. "In fact," I continue, not waiting for a reply, "it should remind you of a place."

"It's the lighthouse," she mumbles.

"The what?" the queen quips, obviously annoyed with her daughter's response.

"The Biloxi Lighthouse, Great Queen," I answer. "It's one of her favorite places to watch the tide roll in along the bay and Deer Island. It's quite a sight at sunrise."

My eyes lock with Desephone, and the dark depths of her irises are like magnets, yanking me to her like a ripcord. I'd give her anything to have her in my arms right now.

"Sunrise?" my heckler from before, a vampire with deep, dark skin, groans lowly. His crimson eyes shoot up to me and over to Desephone. If I had to guess, even he senses the pull between us.

"Yeah, watching the sunrise is actually one of Her Highness' favorite pastimes," I wistfully add. He doesn't reply, but his now-pensive state tells me he's rethinking his reason for being here.

"Well, neither she nor her mate will have any more troublesome sunrises to contend with in the Netherworld," the queen cackles, rallying the crowd around us to join in laughter.

Still, Des stays quiet, her eyes continually drifting between me and the lighthouse.

"Great Queen." Mr. Beach Blonde offers his hand to Persephone, and she places her pale palm in his. "May I show you a better display? One quite impermeable, unlike a tower," he offers, throwing an eye roll toward my lighthouse.

"Splendid!" Queen Persephone says with a girlish lilt.

Some men follow close behind while others return to their own stations. Still, Des remains frozen, staring at the lighthouse.

"Do you like it?" I ask, coming closer to her side.

Desephone only bobs her head in return before her eyes bounce to mine. "How did you do this? So fast? I–I mean it's gorgeous. And a lighthouse? Ari, it's–"

I take her chin in my hand, tilting her face up. "It's for you. It's what I want to be for you: a strong, sturdy tower. I want to be that light in the darkness–a beacon just for you."

"What?" she gasps, stepping back. "Ari, I–I don't understand. Why are you talking like this?"

"Isn't it obvious?"

Desephone's eyes grow wide, glazing with water. She shakes her head in disbelief, pressing her eyes tight, holding back her tears.

I grab her hand, needing to steady the frenzy I sense brewing within her.

"I want out."

"Huh?" Her lips curl, and her posture stiffens, but she doesn't withdraw her hand.

"The friend zone. I want out, Des."

Once more, her eyes lock with mine as her luscious lips part, begging to be kissed.

Loud laughter bounces around us as the men corral together, likely giving the queen a lofty showing. Still, Des and I stay like this: in our own world, suspended out of time in our own reality. Or, at least that's how this feels to me.

"Dearest!" Queen Persephone calls, breaking our sweet standoff.

Des deepens her gaze for a few seconds longer but yanks her hand from mine, like she's afraid she'll fall off a cliff. "Yes, Mother?" she calls over her shoulder, keeping her gaze on me.

"Come see the other stations! They are quite impressive," her mother beckons.

"Coming, Mother!" Des replies, turning away from me.

Lunging forward, I take her wrist in my hand, halting her movement. "Des..." I pull her back and she stumbles into my chest again, like she did earlier today. "I meant it. I want out. And I have no intention of going back."

She doesn't immediately pull away, and I take a moment to enjoy the feel of her body pressed against mine. How in the hell have I gone so long without telling her how I feel?

Maybe it's because I've spent too long fearing my own shadow. But now, with the threat of her leaving, I'd resort to the comfort of her shadow if it meant I could have her in my life. But I want more than her shadow. I want this forever.

Before I have a minute to say anything else, Des rips from my hold, using her own power to take flight across the room to her mother's side. It pains me, letting her go, but I have every intention to bring her back into my arms where she belongs.

Des and the queen have spent the last half hour judging the various brick stations. Once more, she's doing all she can to stand clear of me. I know I threw her a curveball, but I had hoped, after the day we spent together, my actions wouldn't seem so surprising. Still, it would seem I caught her by surprise. Des has never been one for surprises of any kind. She's analytical. She likes to know exactly what she's getting into and isn't keen on diving deep without knowing the distance. I know this about her, and yet, here I am, playing my hand this way.

But I don't have a choice.

I'm not an idiot. I've done my homework. Once the queen pronounced the Culling, Des was obligated by Netherworld rites to proceed with it. *No matter what.* Being a Bulwark comes with some privileges. Not only are we the peacekeepers of the earthbound plane, but we are also the recordkeepers. I reached out to one of the ancients, Trieu, who also serves alongside Melvina in New Orleans. She gave me a few pointers about Nether culture while I waited for Des to make her way here tonight.

A thunderous clap and the clinking of glass from the bar pull my attention.

"Now that my daughter has apprised your stations, now comes the time for all you've built to come crashing down. As you know, your stations are symbolic of your ability to build something impenetrable, like the bond you wish to have with Princess Desephone. As ruler of the Underworld, it is imperative that the one who stands at her side is not only worthy to build a life with her but cement a bond that cannot be broken." Pausing, Queen Persephone's eyes travel around the room, ensuring every man understands the task at hand.

Nothing but proud, haughty looks stare back at her and Desephone. Desephone, however, keeps her eyes on her mother, taking in her every word, likely doing her best not to look my way. That's fine with me, just as long as she isn't looking at anyone else.

Lifting her hands, the queen gestures for us to take our place beside our stations. "Remember, dear ones, while there can only be one champion, only those whose stations are left standing are able to move to the next round." Persephone shares a dark glance with Des, and both women look at the crowd.

"Strike!" Both shout in unison, and an uproar lifts through the bar.

I keep my eyes on Des as I pummel through the igloo-like station on my right. With one kick and sharp blow with my fist, the bricks crash to the ground. My heckler from earlier hears the sound and turns toward me, gnashing his long fangs as his claws swipe near my face. He misses, but I don't as I thrust my hand through his chest, taking his soulless heart in my hand.

CHAPTER 29

Desephone

"**D**o it! I dare you!" the dark vampire scoffs as his feet dangle from the floor. He looks more like a ragdoll in Ari's hand than the brawn, sultry, creature-of-the night who walked through the doors only hours ago.

"Ari, no!" I shriek, my voice muted by my hands.

"Quiet, Dearest!" Mother protests with a wicked grin spread across her face. "They don't call it a Culling for nothing."

I press forward. "But, I thought you said no killing?"

"I did," Mother chides with a raised brow as she looks across the bar. "It would seem these gents have other ideas." Mother throws an arm in front of me, preventing me from going forward. "Stay here!" she warns me sharply. Just as she does, a chair flies right in front of my face. Mother pushes us back as bricks and beer bottles are thrown across the room. "It seems like we've gotten to this part a lot sooner than anticipated. Splendid!" She squeals with delight, tapping her fingers together beneath her chin.

I should have known. Mother seemed far too eager to get this Culling started. I wouldn't put it past her to have charmed this entire bar. There's no way this level of rage is normal.

"Shouldn't we stop them?" I ask, concerned by the hauntingly pleased grin plastered on Mother's face.

"Oh, they'll stop themselves," she coos with a patronizing pat on my shoulder. "Testosterone runs hot through the blood, but it fades fast."

My eyes drift across the room back to Arius just in time to see him rip the heart out of the vampire. His ashen husk falls to the ground at Ari's feet, but Ari doesn't have long to admire his feat when the blond guy, who introduced himself as Donovan, shoves Ari hard at the back.

Arius jabs him hard in the shoulder when he turns around. Donovan flails back some, his arm hanging loose like it's broken, but he snaps it back in his socket just in time to avoid another blow from Arius.

The two continue, making contact and dodging over and over again, but there's one thing that catches my eye: Ari's station. Despite everything happening around the lighthouse, it stands tall. I pay special attention to the ornate detail atop the lighthouse. A small smile crosses my face, knowing Ari found a way to carve the same ridges into the brick as that of the lighthouse. He even added iron railings to the top and a candle in the center to light the inside.

It's adorable!

As the battle in the bar rages on, my mind recounts memories of us taking flight to the lighthouse, side by side. Ari would normally shift into Bulwark form, resembling the gargoyles of old. With perfect stony skin and a wingspan that could almost rival a dragon, he always opted to perch atop the lighthouse, claiming the inside was too small for him.

Knowing how much I loved sunrises, he made sure we went often.

Why do you love sunrises so much? he once asked me.

Because one day, I'll never see them again, I told him.

That answer always seemed sufficient for Ari. He never made me elaborate, nor did he make a big deal about it, but I knew he took what I said to heart.

"Excuse me, Your Highness," a dark voice rings at my side, jolting me from my musing.

Startled, I'm surprised to find Julian, a gorgeous man with long, salt and pepper hair slicked into a neat ponytail, staring back at me. His luminous white smile catches my attention first. Although his fangs are eclipsed, they are reminiscent of Ari's friend, Perry and I wonder if he's also a hybrid wolf-vampire. He's dressed neat, in all black. His button-down shirt is open at the top, showcasing the makings of a sculpted, yet heavily inked chest beneath.

"How about a drink?" he offers, holding two stout glasses of cognac. Although I'm not a fan of straight cognac, I take the glass. "A little something to take the edge off while we let this show finish," he chuckles.

"Thank you, Julian," I smile, taking a sip. I choke back the taste and work hard to keep my smile. "So, you're not participating?" I ask.

Julian points an equally inked finger across the room to a small station on the side. He leans his head to the side and lets out a small laugh. "Well, the queen said you can only take out the station to your right. As you can see, my station is to the right of—well, no one!" He continues laughing.

Another chair wings by us, and Julian steps in front me and swats the chair away from my face.

"Oh!" I exclaim, rearing back in surprise. "Thank you, Julian!"

He smiles, and his dark amber eyes sparkle as deepened lines of maturity grace the sides of his face. "Well don't thank me, Princess. Thank the loophole." He smiles wide.

"Then to loopholes!" I smile as our glasses clank together.

"Loopholes!" he repeats with a hearty laugh.

"Ah-hem." A hard faux cough pulls our attention. I'm surprised to find Arius now standing in front of us.

The in-fighting has also settled some. I gaze around the room, and there are men nursing bruises and picking up one another from the floor. Along with the vampire Ari killed, there are other husks laying around, along with a few wolves who are either themselves dead or near death. Only about ten men remain standing, and of that, just six stations are left in-tact. Of those, only Ari and Julian's are untouched.

And with the darkened glare in Ari's eyes as he stares at Julian, there's no doubt in my mind that this is about to get interesting.

"Great Queen," Ari begins, gesturing a hand toward Mother. There's a small cut above his right eye, and some swelling on his bottom lip, but overall, he looks better than most of the others. "Are you ready to conclude this round?"

I hadn't noticed Cade now standing next to Mother. The two look like they were deep in conversation. Odd—I didn't know the two were familiar.

Mother gives a small wink to Cade, as though I didn't notice, before she steps toward Ari. "Yes, Mr. Knight," she quietly replies. "Let us proceed."

Ari claps his hands, summoning the attention of those who remain. Everyone turns to Mother as she bids them closer. "*Eu! Eu!*" Mother exclaims in a singsong tone. "You've all done remarkable—well, those who remain," she cuts shamelessly. "And while those of you who remain standing should be pleased with your success, we can only move forward with those who have retained the integrity of their stations. And to the others, *apage!*" she hollers, bidding them to get out in the old Latin.

Gypsy opens the door, waving the four men out of the door. As she does, I watch the vibrant orange glow along the doorpost. I'm sure it's the enchantment Arius placed at the door to ensure they have no memory of tonight.

The other attendants gather the remains and take them out of sight. I'm not sure where Ari has directed them to go, but the attendants move swiftly. As they do, other attendants move aside the bricks, cleaning the area as we make our way to the other side of the bar, where the ax posts are.

Mother pulls Julian to the side, and they continue talking with Cade, leaving Ari and I alone.

"What are you drinking?" He shoots me a stern look. I can tell he's still worked up from his brawl, but he sounds different from the man who just confessed what I believe had been affection just a short while ago.

"Julian got it for me," I say, taking a sip just to spite the scolding tone of his voice.

"Give me that!" Ari pulls the glass from my hand. He snaps his fingers over his shoulder, lifting his hand in the air. One of his attendants rushes to his side, and he whispers something and turns back to me. "I thought you hated cognac," he grumbles with a raised brow.

"Oh, I'm sorry, Your Highness," Julian says, resuming a place at my side. Mother and Cade continue talking, but she blares a cursory nod my way, letting me know she's watching. "I didn't know you didn't like the stuff. What can I get you?" He offers his hand, pointing at the bar.

Ari huffs, shaking his head. "That won't be necessary," he rasps with a cagey grin. Before I have a chance to chastise his attitude, one of his attendants brings me a whiskey sour.

My mouth crumples. Damn it, Ari! He knows this is my favorite drink.

I don't know what has gotten into him, but the arrogant look on his face says it all.

"This may be your bar, Arius Knight, but this is my Culling!" I grit through my teeth. Slamming the whiskey sour down on the table at my side, I snatch the cognac from Ari's hand and toss it back. Ari's eyes lift in surprise, but he maintains his staunch pretense. The last thing he'll do is let anyone here see him rattled, even if I know he's shaking in his boots. "Come along, Julian," I say, looping my arm through his. "Let's scope out the ax stations!" I mimic my mother's schoolgirl tone from earlier.

"Wherever you go, I go," Julian replies merrily.

Together, we amble through the crowd to the other side of the bar. I don't have to turn around to know Ari is staring at us. I can feel his daggered-eye glare like knives in my back.

Meanwhile, Julian takes the time to tell me about himself while showing me some of his skill with the axes. Though I want to give him my full attention, I can't. Between the face-off Ari and I share from across the room, I find my way back to Julian's voice. I hear a little about how he's a widow and how he has lived just outside Biloxi for about five years. Something about relocating and this being a great place for hybrids. Everything else is crackling paper in my ears.

Cade and Gypsy move past us as they help the attendants carry the remaining bricks out of sight while Ari is talking with his staff. Julian is going on about something to do with someone, a vampire, I think, taking to the sun. It sounds important, and I want to pay attention, but I can't. One of Ari's attendants points to his office, and I see his face brighten.

Excuse me. I'm not sure if the words even come out of my mouth as I nearly knock Julian down to see what has Ari smiling like a kid on Christmas. Has he ever looked at me like that, I wonder? But I force the jealous thought aside.

Try as I might, jealousy rears its ugly head in high alarm when I see a gorgeous creature standing in the doorway leading to his office. With luscious caramel skin like silk and thick, lofty brown curls, I'm not sure how this voluptuous deity arrived unnoticed. Although, now, they have become quite the spectacle, adorned in a hooded red cloak. With eyes that shine like diamonds, it's no wonder Arius is all smiles as he rushes to the back hall. He gives a brief look over his shoulder, but his eyes go right past me. He's not checking for me. And why would he be?

Be sure to wear the red one. I remember his phone call from before. This must be who he was expecting.

He said he wants out of the friend zone. He said there'll be no more blurred lines after tonight.

Well, he's officially out of my friend zone, because I've never seen clearer than I do right now.

CHAPTER 30

Arius

I spent longer than expected in my office. I hated to rush, but there's no way I'm leaving Des at the mercy of those salivating bastards.

Most spend their time either staring at her cleavage or her ass. Sure, she's a sight, that's for damn certain, but what she is is mine. In all our years together, I've never felt more territorial than I do right now.

I nearly knocked the door off its hinges when I burst into the bar. My eyes are like missiles, aimed at every mangy-pawed prick eyeing Desephone like she's on a silver platter.

"So, what did I miss?" I huff, brushing my hair away from my face and adjusting my collar as I make my way to the huddle.

Des rolls her eyes, smacking her lips instead of responding. Her eyes travel to my unkempt clothes, obviously annoyed with my disheveled appearance. I haven't had a chance to clean myself up since the brawl, but she's looking at me like she doesn't understand I was just fighting only moments ago. While most of these asshats have had a chance to primp themselves, I haven't been as fortunate.

"Oh, we were just waiting for you so we could get started on the next round," Queen Persephone replies kindly as she takes graceful steps to my side.

She's nursing a glass of Cristal and seems giddier than she has been all night. Cade has also taken an apt place beside her, and the two have become quite a pair since the first round began.

"My apologies for the wait, Your Highness," I say as my eyes drift to Des. She resumed her conversations with that guy, Julian, and a few others. I try not to seem as bothered as I should be, so I keep my attention on the queen for now. "We can get started now, if you're ready."

"Perfect!" she exclaims merrily. "Dearest," she says, tapping Des on the shoulder. Des spins on her heel after laughing, very unconvincingly, with that blond asshole, Donovan. She's sure to throw a darted look my way before turning her attention to her mother. "Mr. Knight is ready to commence the next round."

"Oh, is he?" Des quips, her lips curling some as she regards me. Her eyes are threatening, heat-seeking missiles of their own as she stares at me. I'm not sure if she's mad I interrupted her time with Julian earlier, but I thought I made myself perfectly clear. I have no intention of staying in the fucking friend zone. "I thought Mr. Knight would be too busy with his guest," she snips.

So that's what crawled up her ass?

I almost want to laugh aloud, but hearing the drip of jealousy in her tone tells me all I need to know.

Only a small smirk wanders to my face, and I rub the stubble on my jaw as my mind runs amuck with ways to torture her with what she doesn't know. Sure, I could clear this up right now, but since this impacts more than me and Desephone, I hold off. Now isn't the time.

My eyes roam around, and I see Gypsy giving the barroom attendants instructions to set the table upstairs with hors d'oeuvres. Knowing she's busy lets me know I can drag this out and make Des sweat just a little.

"No, Princess, I've done all I need with my guest for now. We can proceed."

Her eyes singe with every dark intention imaginable. I'm sure she expected I'd let on about who is in my office or that I'd deflect. The fact I'm being a whole asshole right now is setting her ablaze, which will only mean I'll be rewarded with her rage when the time comes. I look forward to that with more delight than she can imagine.

"Splendid!" Queen Persephone whirls one last gulp down of her champagne and sets it on the serving tray as one of the attendants passes by.

"No!" Des barks as she stomps toward me. Her eyes are dark misty pools, and the black veins bleeding through her skin reveal the monster beneath I've come to adore. "Enough, Arius!" she shouts.

The queen lets out a small nervous laugh. "You're making a scene, dear," she quietly rebukes Des while squeezing her shoulder.

Desephone breaks from her mother's hold. "Mother, please!" she groans, biting her lower lip, trying to restrain her otherworldly form from taking over. "Look, while I appreciate *Mr. Knight* for commencing the Culling tonight, I think it's time we release him from the court. I mean, there's really no need for him to proceed."

"Well, dear, that's not really how this works. I mean, he still bears the flame," the queen continues, pointing at me. Des darts her eyes to me, her lips tightening when she sees I still have all three flames resting on my chest. "The fact that his flame is still kindled means you must want him here."

Tearing her gaze from me, Des looks around the room. Her lips curl once more, but there's something calculating in her eyes I cannot discern. "Then it would seem I want the rest of them as well, Mother. Their flames still burn for me," she sneers with a devious little smirk. I should be offended, but it's sexy as hell.

The queen looks over her shoulder, her eyes carefully marching past each suitor. Leaning into her daughter's ear, she whispers, "But only the Bulwark's fire shines brightest, dear."

Desephone's armor cracks a little as her mouth parts when the queen speaks. Once more, her eyes narrow, and I know she has thought of yet another way to be rid of me.

"That may be, Mother, but since he fired off Epirus, don't you think—"

"Do you question me, dear?" the queen fires back, annoyed and her buzz wearing off. "Or do you think I could be fooled by the mere charmings of an ancient relic–a Bulwark?"

Ouch.

The venom in the queen's words stings my heart just as much as it does her daughter's, but I remain quiet.

"But Mother, I–"

"If I may, Great Queen," Donovan inserts himself, slyly coming to Desephone's side. He wraps his arm around her shoulder, rubbing her skin with his slithery palm, startling her as he does. By the look on her face, his touch is both unexpected and unwanted, but right now, she hates me more, so she plays along. "The princess may be onto something."

The queen's dark brows cave together against her pale skin, her face hollowing into a ghastly, phantom-like state. I step back as she looks at him. Whatever fury she hurls his way is not meant for me.

"What is it, wolf?" she lashes, her eyes cutting to her daughter, blaming her for this interruption. I wish I could soothe the angst I see on Des' face. I will soon enough.

"It's just that during our time at the brick station, we were commanded to strike down the opposing stations to our right. Mr. Knight was on my right. However, I discovered he used his Bulwark enchantments to fortify his station. Hence, my rage upon learning it and the fight that ensued, so—"

"So you see, Mother, Donovan is right. Ari used his Bulwark powers. That cannot be fair."

The queen looks down her nose at me and the other contestants. I'm sure she's worn with us lesser earthbound supernatural beings. Her face crinkles some as she regards me, but she shifts from her phantom features, back into her mortal form.

"Let me ask you, Mr. Donovan," the queen says wistfully as she saunters slowly through the crowd. "Did I not detect the sun-spun color of your eyes as your wolfen form took over?"

"Well, yes, I did bid my wolf, but—"

"So then you expect Mr. Knight to fight a wolf as a mortal then?"

"Well, no, Your Highness, but his station–"

"Ah yes, his station," she continues, turning quickly on her heel to take a glance at the lighthouse. "So you contend that since he used enchantments, he cheated?"

"Yes, Great Queen," he answers.

Turning back to the crowd, the queen waves her arm around. "And do any of you feel the same?"

Some of the guests nod in agreement, while others remain neutral, too fearful to respond.

"Tell me, vampire," Queen Persephone says, pointing to the curly, ginger-haired vampire in the corner. "Did you use your speed and strength to put together and defend your station?" He tips his head in the affirmative. "And you, hybrid?" She turns to Julian.

"Yes, Your Highness. The strength of my wolf was certainly at play," he answers dutifully.

The queen continues down the line, making every man admit to using his powers. With each response, Desephone's posture stiffens, her shoulders slouching as she grows unsure of herself in her mother's presence. The thought of her feeling less-than sickens me.

I wanted her to squirm, not shrink.

"Great Queen, a word," I say before she has a chance to call out the last two men. I can't just stand by. "If the princess wishes I not continue... then I'll concede—on one condition."

Desephone's eyes grow wide, glassing a little, as though she regretted her words.

"What is your condition, Bulwark?" the queen snaps, equally irritated by my interruption.

"But Mother, I–" Des rushes forward, but her mother raises her palm, halting her motion.

"First, let me call for my associate. Gypsy!" I shout up into the balcony.

Gypsy hangs over the balcony. "What? I'm busy up here."

"Please come down."

Gypsy huffs but hops over the railing, landing in the center of the bar. She makes her way to my side, casting wary glances between me and the others. "What gives?"

I look over to Cade, shooting him a wink, and he quickly springs into action and heads to my office.

"The princess is not the only one seeking a mate. For some, finding a mate is a difficult task. But when your friend finds someone they love and care for, you just want to see them happy. You'll do whatever it takes to make sure your friend finds the love they deserve, even if they won't do it themselves. And that's what tonight is all about."

Desephone looks at me, her eyes big and round and dancing with hopefulness. "Ari, I–I–"

"Stevie!" Gypsy squeals racing to the side of the bar, where Cade stands in the doorway with Gypsy's partner, Stevie. Stevie's arms are outstretched, a wide smile on their face as they welcome Gypsy into their arms. "You're here! But how? And I thought—but how?"

Stevie places a doting finger over Gypsy's lips. "It's okay. Arius called me." They shoot me a wink.

Gypsy turns around and smiles, a lone red tear running down her face. Seeing my friend happy is all I ever wanted.

CHAPTER 31

Desephone

Mother cuts in between the shared gaze between Gypsy and Arius. She has grown tired of the intrusion to our evening. "This all seems well and good, Mr. Knight, but I don't understand how any of this is relevant, least of all your waitress and her gorgeous little plaything in red," she says, waving a dismissive hand.

"Perhaps I can explain, Your Highness," Cade offers with a bright tone. "Gypsy has been too shy to fully let herself be with Stevie for fear she'd interfere with Stevie's choice between becoming a wolf or a vampire. Arius let Stevie know how Gypsy felt because he knew she never would on her own. All night, he has kept her busy only so he could sneak Stevie in as a surprise."

I feel like an idiot. How could I be so wrong?

"You did all that for me, Knight?" Gypsy rasps.

"I'd do anything for my friend. You know that," Arius answers with a warm smile. "Now, you two run off. I don't want to hold the festivities up any further."

Gypsy turns to leave with Stevie but stops short and spins on her heel and throws her arms around Ari's neck. "Thank you, you big lug!" she says, smacking the back of his head.

"So then do you still wish to concede, Mr. Knight?" Mother asks dryly once Gypsy and Stevie head to the back office.

"I–"

"No!" I interrupt Ari before he has a chance to finish. "There is no need to concede. Besides, I was wrong. Mr. Knight has every right to use his power as Bulwark just as any other creature here tonight. I was wrong to despair."

"There was no harm done, Your Highness," Arius protests, quickly making his way in front of me before Mother can answer. "This is your Culling. I, as well as all the others here tonight, are simply afforded the pleasure of your company. If you permit me to stay, I promise I'll be on my best behavior."

"Then can I ask we get on with the festivities, Great Queen?" Donovan snips, sauntering now to the queen's side.

"Well said, wolf!" Mother agrees, albeit a tad off put by Donovan's familiar tone.

"To the axes!" Cade cheers, clapping his hands and shooing everyone forward.

Arius moves on with the others, and I wish I could pull him to the side and clear things up further. Even more, I wonder if he meant what he said about getting out of the friend zone. And there's still the issue of his phone call. *Was he talking with Stevie?* If not, then who?

"Dearest!" Mother shouts, and I flinch as I'm pulled from my thoughts. "It's time!" she orders with a pointed finger at her side.

Once more, I rush next to her, pushing aside my own inclination.

Arius leans against the far wall, allowing the other men to crowd around us. His arms are folded over his chest. There's a faraway look in his eyes that I can't discern. For a moment, I wish he was close enough for me to search his soul. Although I've never done so with him, I'd give anything to know what he's thinking now.

With one thunderous clap, Mother reclaims the center of attention. Even the attendants quiet their chatter and still their movement throughout the bar. Mother smiles, thankful to have all eyes on her.

"Now that you've showcased your masonry and ability to protect what you have built in the first round, now comes the moment of pure skill. In order to win this round, you will be given one chance, for a ruler of the Underworld must be quick and decisive in not only his judgements, but his delivery. He mustn't fumble over trivial matters or pursue idle intentions. He must rule, alongside his bride, hard and fast. You'll be given a single opportunity to make it to your target. Take the next few moments to warm up. When I call your attention again, you will be put to the test."

With that, Mother claps her hands once more, and every man scurries to his station. Arius saunters slowly to his station. He doesn't seem as peppy as before. Instead of picking up his ax and wielding it around a few times, he spends time giving it a spit shine. Using his shirt to buff the blade, he rolls it over in his hands a bit before putting it back on the holster.

I think of our time back at the warehouse. Ax throwing wasn't his best. It took him quite a few tries to finally hit his target. This time, however, he'll only get one chance.

My heart sinks, knowing how hard I've been on him today.

Although I'm not sold that he wants to spend forever with me, I know he cares for me. Perhaps that's what this is about. He said as much to Gypsy earlier. He'll do anything for his friends. Maybe that's what this is about–he just wants to help a friend.

I want out of the friend zone.

Or perhaps he's hoping someone will finally take me off his hands. I'm sure being my friend over the years has been exhausting..

I'm sure that's why he offered to concede earlier.

Well, one thing I'm sure of: once this round is over, he'll be out of the zone.

A small pat on my shoulder pulls my attention. I'm surprised to find my mother next to me. The last time I saw her, she was talking with Cade. I'll have to ask her later how they became such fast friends.

"Are you okay, Dearest?" Mother asks in an unfamiliar syrupy tone. Her soft eyes roam over me, and she fusses with my hair some, tucking a loose strand behind my ear. "You seem distant."

Is this my mother? Asking me if I'm okay? She has been so boorish this evening, I hardly thought she cared how I was doing.

"I'm fine," I answer quickly. I know too well not to let her sweet words disarm me.

"It'll be over soon. Just another round to go," she soothes. "But may I offer a suggestion?"

And there it is. I knew she couldn't resist a moment to tell me what I'm doing wrong, especially after my earlier outburst. "Well, I know you'll tell me anyway, so let's hear it," I quip, brushing her hand off and taking a small step away from her.

Mother's face falls, but she doesn't let it detract from her goal. "I only wanted to propose that you invoke some soul searching this round. You have quite a few contenders left, many of whom will likely pass to the next round should their flames still find favor in your eyes. That way, you only keep who you really want."

My throat clenches. Mother doesn't know I haven't mastered this skill yet. Sure, I searched Perry's girlfriend, but she's mortal.

They're pretty open already. But supernaturals, especially wolves and vampires, are exceptionally masterful at cloaking themselves.

Still, she's right. I need to get this over with.

"Yes, Mother," I say. I don't know how I'll do it, but if it takes everything I've got, I'll see it done.

A proud smile crosses Mother's face as she takes my shoulders in her hands and gives them a squeeze. "Splendid!" She gives my cheek a quick peck before spinning on her heel and heading back to the candidates.

My nerves wrangle into knots in my gut as Mother calls the attention of everyone. "Remember gentlemen, you only have one chance. As the petals fall, please line up in order. Only he who hits the target is certain to move forward to the final round. The only other way to remain is if the Princess fancies you and your flame still burns. Is this understood?"

Without another word Mother waves her arms around in a circular motion as she speaks in the ancient tongue. Lovely pink petals fall, seemingly out of nowhere. Their enchanted fragrance wistfully wands through the air, cutting through the thick scent of bourbon and beer nestled in these walls.

Each petal falls, one by one, into the hand of each suitor. I watch in awe as the petals handpick the order in which the candidates will wield their ax. I feel the pace of my heart quicken in fear as Ari remains the only one without a petal, but when he catches the last one, I release an anxious breath.

Ari doesn't seem as worried as I am that he won't make the final cut. In fact, he hardly seems to pay me any mind. His countenance remains sullen and his eyes distant as he picks up his ax and heads to the end of the line.

Mother and I take our seats across from the target, allowing us a clear view of the target and the candidates. I'm surprised when Mother directs Cade to call up the candidates, but I leave it alone. I suppose since Ari is a prospect it only makes sense for someone neutral to give instruction.

The first suitor comes forward. His efforts are fair, but his ax remains in the white space. Mother looks at me, her eyes questioning. I know she's wondering if I read his soul, but his flames dissipate the moment he's done. Cade quickly dismisses him and an attendant leads him out of the room. Thankfully, I don't have to read him, but I know I won't be as lucky with the next one.

Mother's eyes stay pinned on me as the second suitor approaches. I lock in on him. He's a vampire. A beautiful dark-skin man with a clean shaven head and a thick beard I'd love to tousle my fingers through. As he rears his arm back, his eyes deepen into the target and feel him open himself. This is my chance.

Looking into his soul, I see nothing of concern. He values honesty and is a man of his word. But it's the nothingness that bothers me. His soul is riddled in apathy. He's not connected to anyone or anything. If he had a bumper sticker it might read, *I can take you or leave you. Your choice.* I can't imagine why a man like him would even consider coming tonight, but his soul is right about one thing. I *do* have a choice. And he is not it.

My choice is made just as he releases the ax and the flame burns through his skin. He hollers, expletives flying out his mouth as the fire spreads over his shoulder. The vampire manages to douse the flame, but he sorely misses the target and a roaring curse blares from his mouth. He kicks over a few chairs on his way out of the bar.

"Wonderful, dearest!" Mother chuckles at my side, delighted by my skill. Shock and awe fills me as I watch the wicked machinations brewing in my mother's mind.

I had no idea I was capable of such foresight but I'm certainly not opposed to see where this goes.

One by one, the candidates make their way to the stand. Some wield with perfection, yet still miss the target. While others barely make the target, I concentrate my efforts on reading their soul. Only Mother and I are aware of what I'm doing and how it's affecting the candidates. I do suspect Cade has figured it out, but most seem to attribute their fading or bursting flames to their lack of skill.

And while the outcomes are the same every soul is different. From apathy to abusive tendencies, thievery, and murderous hearts, I've found very little to endear me to the selection here tonight. Now that only three remain, my spine folds like jelly knowing I'll have to read Arius's soul. But I want to do more than read it. I want to know it. Intimately.

CHAPTER 32

Arius

It's taking everything within me to hold my peace. There's a volcanic yearning inside of me, needing to explode and melt everything in its wake. Everything except Des.

If I could protect her from having to go through this dog and pony show I would. But I can't. I have to stay here, lined up like a good little boy and wait my turn in line. Once this Culling commenced all bets were off and I had no other choice but to let things play out.

Even then, I'll still have to convince Des to choose me. That alone will be a hard task considering how much I've pissed her off tonight. All I can do now is hold out hope that she knows how much I love her.

Although, I am happy to see how many have either missed the target or had their flames go up in smoke. That can only mean Desephone's interest is waning. Sure her pretense lasted longer than I thought she could hold out, but I'm glad she's finally seeing through the bull these asshats are serving up on silver platters.

"Next we have Mr. Donovan McKay," Cade announces to Queen Persephone and Des.

Gesturing for him to come forward, the queen offers a regal tip of her head and Des does the same. Donovan flexes his muscles, making a show of his wielding prowess. The queen seems pleased as her eyes flutter a bit like a schoolgirl as she watches him.

He places the ax down on the side table. "If you don't mind, Your Highness," he says slyly as he takes off his blazer, giving her the show she so obviously desires.

I'm only comforted to see Des keeps her sights forward, her eyes narrowed like she's concentrating hard. It's the same look she had in her eyes when she was talking with Perry's girl at the warehouse.

"Take your time, Mr. McKay," the queen replies, biting her fingernails. Her eyes take him in greedily, transfixed on the way his large biceps bounce as he lifts the ax.

With both hands on the thick hickory throat of the handle, Donovan rears back, lifting one leg as he prepares to throw. As he does, I notice he's turned slightly, not directly toward the target. His torso angles just enough that his body is in line with Des.

Releasing the ax, Donovan roars aloud. I watch, as if time stood still as Desephone's eyes grow wide in horror as he hurls the ax in her direction.

"No!" Loud shouts ring aloud. I don't know who's shouting, but I flex fast, shifting into my Bulwark form.

With my wings outstretched, I dive in front of Des and her mother, shielding them from the blow. Both women stare at me horror struck and in shock as they lay nestled safely within the cavity of my wingspan.

Desephone's now darkened eyes lock with mine. Looking at her I can tell she was prepared to shift as was the queen as I take in her ghastly form.

"Are you both okay?" I ask, my eyes scouring both women from head to toe.

"Yes, Ari," Des mumbles, her gaze carrying over my shoulder to the sound of scuffling behind me. I know she can't see through the blackened veil of my wings, but it's evident something is happening.

"You sure?" I have to be certain.

"Get a bloody towel!" I hear Cade yell behind me. "He's gonna bleed out!"

"What the fuck?" I make out Gypsy's voice from across the room.

I still don't know what's going on, but the sound of struggle tells me we're not done.

"Hold him the fuck down!" Cade shouts as snarling and hissing sounds ring throughout the bar.

I give the women one more look, assuring myself they are safe. Slowly, I let down my wings and they retract into my back as I return to my mortal form. Both Des and the queen relax their other-worldly nature as we all jump to our feet.

My servers have Donovan pinned down on the ground. They're holding him by his arms and legs and two attendants keep a tight hold on his torso, ensuring he won't shift.

Cade, however, is kneeling down beside Julian. The ax is bound to his abdomen. There's blood everywhere. Even worse, I'm certain the ax is the only thing keeping him animated.

Des rushes to kneel at Julian's side. Her small fingers trail his jawline as she closes her eyes and whispers a small prayer.

"She calls to Hades," the queen says, so that only I can hear.

"What in the hell happened?" Gypsy says, making her way beside me with Stevie on her heel.

"This son of a bitch tried to kill the princess," Cade reveals, pointing to Donovan. "And this old bloke threw himself in front of the fucking ax. *Dumbass*," Cade snips, shaking his head. Coming from Cade we all know this isn't a snide comment. It's just his way.

"But Des can't die a mortal's death," Gypsy quips, shaking her head.

"Obviously these idiots didn't know that," Cade huffs.

Des is still calling out to her father when Julian reaches up and squeezes her hand.

"Please tell me, will I see her?" His voice is almost muted by the blood running from his mouth. Even a lone tear rolls down the side of his face but he manages a weak smile.

Both Gypsy and Cade stare at one another confused, but I keep my attention on Des. I'll get to that bastard Donovan in a minute.

"Yes, Julian," Des smiles. "She's waiting for you," her voice rings with a woeful lilt. A shimmering dark light exudes from Des as she places her hands over Julian. A look of peace washes over Julian's face as he takes his last breath. "Good journey," Des whispers and Julian fades into the dark light Des emits. "They will be reunited soon," she smiles sweetly as a few loose tears drop to the place where Julian just lay.

"Who?" Gypsy asks.

I could care less. All of my attention is fixed on Donovan.

I help Desephone up from the ground. She uses the back of her wrist and wipes her face. "His wife, Catherine. His one true love. She was a vampire and died by the sun some time ago. Julian spent years grieving her loss. He missed her. So much so, he hoped to bind himself to me in the Underworld just to see her one more time. In fact, that's the only reason he jumped in front of the blade. Mother and I were already saved by Ari. But Julian wanted to see her. And so he shall."

"How beautifully tragic," Stevie croons, leaning into Gypsy.

"More like beautifully asinine. Don't you ever do something so stupid for me!" Gypsy counters, and throws a quick kiss on Stevie's round face. Stevie grimaces some, but they pull Gypsy into their arms instead, choosing not to argue.

"Now what about this asshole!" Cade sneers, pointing to Donovan.

"He's all mine!" I roar aloud, marching toward him.

"No!" Desphone shouts, making her way in front of me.

"Move out of my way Des!" I bark. "He will pay!"

She shoves a heavy hand against my chest. "He's already paying the price, Ari."

"What the fuck?" Cade calls out behind us.

Side stepping Des, I continue forward. "The bastard hasn't begun to pay!" I bark over my shoulder.

"Ari!" Once more Des is in front of me. "Baby, don't! He's not worth it."

Fuck.

Did she just call me baby? She sure picked a hell of a moment to come around.

Desephone's eyes widen, revealing the beautiful misty pools I'd give my soul to dive in. If I let her, that sweet heart-shaped smile of hers will have my stony heart melt into a puddle at her feet. Damn this woman for trying to soften the parts of me meant to be strong for her.

I take her in. Our eyes lock together as the shared revelation of all we are to one another comes into full view. Her warm, soft eyes roam over me, sending chills up my spine while giving rhythm to my heart.

I feel my stance relax some, but not hardly enough. "Move." I ordered Des. I hate speaking so curt to her, but she doesn't push back. Gracefully as ever, she steps aside but her hopeful doe-eyes stay trained on me, pleading with me not to kill this asshole on sight.

My staff keep Donovan in their grasps as I stand over him. Cade flanks my side with Gypsy on the other side. Stevie remains behind us with the queen as they watch from afar. It's moments like this when I'm glad I no longer employ mortals. Having other supernaturals around has always benefitted me when situations get sticky.

"Get him up!" I shout and they quickly bring Donovan to his feet.

He's bruised pretty badly after the beating my team put on him. But he's not letting up. Snarling and gnashing his teeth, I can tell he's begging me to rip him in half. And yet the tears in his eyes are telling me there's a story I don't quite understand.

I swear if I didn't know Des was looking at me right now, I'd rip him in half and never think of him again. But damn if I don't want to be a better fucking man for her.

"You've got a few seconds to explain to me why I shouldn't put this worthless dog down right now!" I shout over my shoulder without taking my eyes off Donovan. I refuse to look at Des yet. She'll just soften me like butter and that's a risk I cannot take.

"He wants revenge for what we did to his brother." Her answer is hasty, as if she feared I'd literally strike him dead this instant.

"What? Who in hell is his brother?" Gypsy asks, stepping to my side, looking up at me.

I hunch my shoulders, and shoot Des a quick look.

"Derek!" Donovan squeaks out only to receive a sharp blow to his gut by Cade. "You killed my brother!" Donovan continues, caving in at the waist in pain.

"Who the fuck is Derek?" Gypsy rattles off.

My mind goes blank. I've taken a few lives in my short life, and I remember every face. Only one face comes to mind, reminding me why Donovan felt so strangely familiar.

Flashes of me standing in front of Petals ripping a wolf in half just before sunrise flickers through my mind. More memories implode my brain and I see a large, dusty blonde wolf, walking arm in arm out of my bar with Des. The cheeky look he gave me over his shoulder as his sun spun, golden eyes blared my way remind me of the same ones looking at me now.

"That was your brother?" I muster, as my mind replays images of me tearing Derek in half, over and over again. My eyes cut to Des, horrified that I invited this trouble into her life.

CHAPTER 33

Desephone

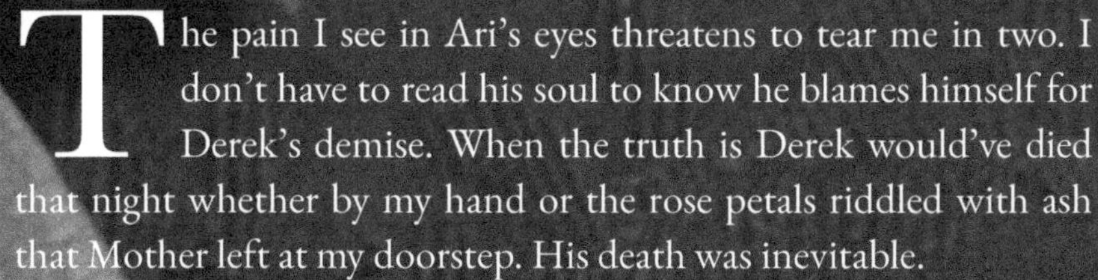

The pain I see in Ari's eyes threatens to tear me in two. I don't have to read his soul to know he blames himself for Derek's demise. When the truth is Derek would've died that night whether by my hand or the rose petals riddled with ash that Mother left at my doorstep. His death was inevitable.

"My baby brother!" Donovan grits through his teeth. "And you killed him in cold blood!"

"Wait a minute!" Gypsy steps in front of Ari, her eyes laced in confusion. "Why would you kill anyone, Knight?"

"Derek attacked Des," Arius states dryly, still keeping an eye on Donovan.

"Lies!" Donovan shouts but receives another blow to the chin by one of Ari's attendants.

I step forward, I need to end this.

"No, Donovan," I start, my eyes peering deep into his soul. "You exiled your brother because he slept with your wife. The wife you in fact stole from him. She doesn't love you. She loved Derek. You knew it, but you staked your claim on her using your role as Alpha. But she and Derek couldn't stay away from one another. In your jealousy, you sent him away. That's how he ended up in the Dram Deaux."

Thick tears rush to Donovan's chin, his bloody lips curling as he gnashes his teeth, still denying the truth.

"But how–how did you know?" Gypsy wonders, her gaze shifting between me and Donovan.

"Because an Alpha can feel every wolf in his pack. So when Derek took his last breath, the telepathic connection between them allowed Donovan's wolf to see his brother's final moments," Stevie answers, now coming closer to our huddle. Their bright amber eyes flash toward us and it doesn't take much to know that Stevie is a hybrid. *Just like Julian.*

"Derek may have been the bane of my being but he was my brother!"

Ari growls at Donovan, his nose flaring and I see his marbled skin shining through. "And she is mine! And your brother tried to take her away from me. You should thank me for ending him so quickly!"

"Ari!" I protest. "Please, we're better than this."

"Are we?" Ari huffs, stepping back some, trying to maintain his composure. "I'm not above killing anyone who tries to hurt you."

"He's already suffering, Ari, look at him!" I plead, taking Ari's wrist in my hand. I can only hope my touch soothes the ache I see in his eyes.

"Not only did his brother try to hurt you, but so did he. Now you want me to just let it go?" Ari groans. His jaws are rigid and I know he's trying to restrain himself.

"There's also the fact that he's an Alpha," Stevie interjects. "If you hurt him now, you'll have his entire pack seeking revenge."

"Do you think I give a fuck about his pack?" Ari shouts over his shoulder at Stevie.

Gypsy jumps in front of Stevie, her red eyes flashing at Arius in warning. She issues a stern look Stevie's way, bidding them to stay out of it.

"Stevie's right, my friend," Cade adds. "If you hurt him–"

Ari yanks his arm away from me, roaring aloud as he does. He grabs his ax from the floor, turns toward Donavan and lunges it through the air. I watch in fear as the blade soars through the sky, past me, Cade, and Gypsy. I can barely make out the muted screams of protest echoing around me as they're drowned out by Donovan's screeching yelp.

I press my eyes tight, knowing all too well what comes next. Death. I smell it in the air. Like fallen autumn leaves, molded beneath the dry earth, its stench permeates the air and sours my stomach.

But just as quickly as the putrid scent hits my nose, it dissipates just as fast. My eyes pop open and I'm surprised to find Arius standing with the tip of the blade pressed in the center of Donovan's skull. Only a small drip of blood falls between his thick brows but his eyes cave with dread.

He knows he should be a dead man. And he also knows it is only by the steady hold of Ari's grip that he is alive.

My eyes widen as I see Ari as I've never seen him before. With the ax in his hand as he holds it against Donovan's head and his darkened gaze narrowed, his stance wide, I see a man in complete control. In the blink of an eye, he somehow managed to not only release the ax but catch it before striking Donovan dead.

"Do you feel it now, wolf?" Ari grits through his teeth. His eyes are as black as night, his face resting between both his mortal and Bulwark features. The sharp, pointed ridges of his wings are teasing at his back, waiting for permission to spread full. Bulking muscles threaten to tear his silk shirt and blazer off his body if he shifts in full, but he still keeps his composure. "I could end you this instant!"

Donovan snarls, grinding his teeth as his canines tear into his bottom lip. "Do it!" he scoffs.

Ari smirks that damn panty-dropping smirk. It's full of hubris and haughty arrogance, and I love him for it. "No," he says, pulling the ax from Donovan's skull. "But you'll always have something to remember me by. And when you think of me, you'll know it wasn't my mercy allowing you to live, but hers," he tips his head over his shoulder toward me, "the love of my life." He turns his head toward me, bearing a cocky smile that twists my stomach in knots.

"But be warned," he turns back to Donovan, "if I ever see you around this bar again–if anyone from your pack wanders through here seeking revenge, if you ever even think of Desephone again–-you won't have to worry about what Hades will do to you in the Underworld. You'll never make it that far. But you'll long for death. You'll beg for it. And you'll never get it. Do you understand me?"

Tears race down Donovan's face as he nods in understanding. "Yes," he manages, his lip quivering in fear.

"Get him out of here!" Ari shouts to his staff. Two of his attendants keep a tight hold of his arms while another stays guarded at Donovan's back as they lead him toward the door.

"Wait!" Mother yells from across the room. She lifts her hand and sends a lightning bolt of fire into Donovan's shoulder. He screams in pain, and we all watch as a black mark sears his flesh. "Now you've been marked. When the day of your passing comes, you'll be afforded no quarter in the High Place or even the purgatory of Purgia–no, foolish wolf, your soul is marked for the Underworld. Whether it be Hades or my daughter, Desephone, this mark ensures you shall receive a torment fitting for someone of your soul. Now, get out of my sight!" Waving her hand once more, a gale sweeps through the bar, opening the door and slamming it shut as they leave.

"Baby, are you okay?" Ari says, his voice much calmer as he saunters toward me.

"So it's *baby* now?" Gypsy teases. Stevie pulls Gypsy to their side and places a hand over her mouth.

"Took long enough," Cade grouses, shaking his head with his hands on his hips as he looks around at the mess in the bar.

"I'm okay," I smile, extending my hands toward Ari. He places his hands in mine, and a warmth I've never felt before covers me from head to toe. "Are you?"

Ari leans into me, the crown of his head touching mine. "All better now."

"Ah-hem," Mother issues a hearty throat clearing.

Ari and I share a knowing smile as we turn to face Mother.

"Does anyone want to explain?" she grumbles, gesturing her hand toward us.

Ari steps forward, "Great Queen, I–"

"No, Ari," I stop him, placing my hand on his chest. *Let me*, I mouth. Ari tips his head to me in understanding, and I turn to face Mother. "Great Queen, we no longer need this Culling. In fact, we never did." I look up at Ari and smile—really smile. I can't believe it took this long to get here, but here we are.

"Is that so?" Mother grouses, her lips drawing into a thin line. "Unfortunately, Dearest, that's not quite your decision to make. It's mine."

Arius

I expected this.

From the moment I met the Queen of the Underworld, I knew I'd have an uphill battle to finally make Des mine. But I came prepared, and I'm here for every rocky hill I must climb.

"But Mother–" Des fires back.

This time, it's me stepping in front of her. "If I may, Queen Persephone," I say, casually sauntering toward her. She affirms with a stiff nod. I haven't completely won her over, but I'm thankful she's willing to hear me out. "I know that once the Culling has commenced, it must be completed, no matter what," I say with a quick glance to Desephone. I see the worry in her eyes, but I press forward.

"You are correct, Bulwark," she says pointedly. "And?"

"So, if that be the case, it would seem we only have one final round to go. Well, that and the more intimate matters, but we needn't speak of that in shared company," I state. I can feel both Cade and Gypsy's eyes boring into me, but I do what I can to keep my sights on the queen.

"How can you say we only have one round to go when this station has yet to be completed?" the queen huffs as she takes her seat, unmoved.

"I beg to differ, Your Highness. As it were, all the other suitors had their go, all except for Julian, who gave his life for the atrocities committed tonight, but after him, I was the only one who remained after Donovan was, shall we say, disqualified," I explain, hoping she understands where I'm going with this. She doesn't seem moved, so I keep going. "And well, in all fairness, the goal of this station was to hit the target. I hope it isn't too bold of me to say, Your Highness, but when I aimed for my target, even you can attest that I did not miss."

"Hmm... I see," she quietly groans. Her eyes stayed trained on me, as though she's reading my soul. I hope she is.

I hope she sees how much I love her daughter. I hope she knows how long I've cared for her, protected her, befriended her. I hope she sees how I've built everything in my life with her in mind. I even hope she knows that if I thought there was a better man for her daughter, even though I love her so much, I'd step aside. That's what I hope she sees.

"And are you now professing your love for my daughter, Mr. Knight?" she asks, plucking her fingers as she bounces her crossed leg.

I look at Des as she looks up at me, her caring gaze assuring me the time is finally right. "Yes, Your Highness." My answer is sure and my conviction steadfast.

"Then do tell me, Mr. Knight, if you loved my daughter so much, why did you wait so long to finally profess your affection?" the queen bites back, her eyes darkening.

"Mother, please!" Des protests, but I take her wrist in my hand.

"No, Des," I gently admonish as my thumb runs along her knuckles, hoping to soothe her angst. "The queen deserves an answer. *So do you.* I did wait too long. At first, it was because I never thought a woman like Des could ever see me as anything more than the Resident Bulwark, protector of Biloxi. But as our friendship grew, I thought I was doing the right thing as Bulwark in ensuring she was not only safe but could find a mate. Years went by, and I realized the mate I hoped she'd soon discover was me. For a time, I thought it was all in my head, until even my friends noticed I was in love with my best friend, and I couldn't deny it any longer." I pause, looking back over my shoulder at Des before returning my attention to her mother. "I only ask that you do not count my hesitation against me, Your Highness."

"Oh, quite the contrary, Bulwark!" she spits back. "For you are not simply asking for my daughter's hand, but to also rule at her side. A ruler of the Underworld must be quick and decisive, and you've waited the better part of fifty earthbound years."

"Yes, Your Highness, earthbound years," I quickly counter. "And if my Netherworld math is correct, that would only mean about five months. So, in theory, my hesitation was not hesitation. In fact, it was quite expeditious." My tone is a bit brusque, but the sharp curve of her mouth as she looks at me now tells me I'm beginning to dent her armor.

Still bouncing her leg, she leans forward, pointing a condemning finger my way. "And now, with countless lives lost all because you've waited until what you perceive is the opportune moment, you expect me to just hand my daughter over to you?"

"Well, it is as we both agreed earlier, Your Highness, the Princess is worth dying for. Whether it be my death or any other, I value no other life above hers. I never have before, and I never will."

Queen Persephone casts a cagey grin as she sits back in her chair, calculating her next move. "Sage words, Mr. Knight. Then, what about your residency? I thought Bulwarks were forbidden to mate."

"Oh, Ari! I forgot about that–" Des rasps, her face falling some as she bites her fist.

I pull her hand from her mouth, bringing it to my hand and adding a small kiss. "I didn't." I thread my hands through hers and rest them at our sides. "Since I knew the topic would inevitably arise, I did a little homework. While Bulwarks are forbidden from marriage, I discovered this restriction does not extend beyond the earthbound realm. Should the Princess accept me as her mate and we venture to the Netherworld, the restriction will no longer apply."

The queen stares at me a bit, her mouth curving into something that almost resembles a smile, but she purses her lips, still resigned. "And what of you, Desephone?" She turns her head away from me to Des. "Do you share Mr. Knight's affection?"

"Yes, Mother, *I do!*" Desephone's voice rolls like thunder through the room. I even detect a whiff of smoke as her shadowy form flashes forward the moment she answers. Still, she maintains her mortal appearance as she stands proudly at my side.

"Well damn!" Gypsy shouts, clapping her hands and rolling her fist like she's watching a basketball game. "It's about time!"

"I second that!" Cade chortles in agreement.

Even my attendants cheer along with Gypsy and Cade, whistling and clapping in agreement.

The queen raises her hand and stands up from her seat. She

takes graceful strides toward us, her doting gaze pinned on her daughter. Once she reaches us, she smiles, giving me a once-over from head to toe before returning her gaze to Des.

Persephone glides her pale palm up to Desephone's chin, lifting it until her own eyes glass with water. "I'm happy for you, Dearest."

"Thank you, Mother," Desephone cries into her mother's palm. She still keeps her hand glued to mine and I can feel the heat rising from her skin. This feels so damn good.

Slowly, the queen pulls her hand from Desephone, and she darts her gaze between us. "Of course," she begins, casually sauntering around the bar. "I already knew," she says as she turns back to us. "I mean, it was quite obvious to anyone with eyes how you felt about one another the minute you walked into the flower shop. But some-times, Fate dictates things play out as they do. Yet, as you've said before, Mr. Knight, now that we've commenced the Culling, we must complete it."

"Wait!" Des pushes back, releasing my hand as she marches toward her mother. "There's no one left but Ari. There is no longer any competition!"

The queen shakes her head with her chin lifted high. "Alas, the rules are the rules. Mr. Knight must continue to the prisms. If he passes the final station, then you two have my blessing."

"But–"

"I'll do it!" I exclaim. Des turns to me, disappointment filling her face. Yet, all I can do is smile when I see her. "Whatever I have to do to make you mine, baby, is what I'll do."

"Splendid!" Queen Persephone squeals with a hearty clap as she brings her clasped hands beneath her chin. "Well, now that we have an accord, we should–"

"I invoke *vita ad vitam*! A life for a life." Des breaks into the queen's rant. "If Ari has to go through the prisms, so do I." Vita ad vitam is the highest sentence of death in the Underworld. I'm not sure if the queen is more shocked that Des even knows the term or that she is willing to risk her life for mine.

"But Dearest, if either of you fail–" Nothing but horror fills Persephone's face, but Des isn't done.

"Then we die. But if we are to tempt such a fate, we'll do so together. That's all I ever wanted."

CHAPTER 35
Desephone

The feel of Ari's hand around my wrist as he tugs to turn me toward him sends shivers up my spine. All I've ever wanted was Ari, and now that I have him, I can't imagine life any other way.

"Baby, what are you doing? I can do this," Ari grouses, his eyes slanting in that let-me-take-control way that always turns me on. But I won't let him pull me off course.

"Correction: *we* can do this. It's together or nothing, Mr. Knight," I snip, shooting him a fiery gaze of my own.

Mother blows through the bar like a gentle breeze as she makes her way back to my side. "Dearest, do you know what you're saying?"

"I do," I say as my eyes lock with hers.

"Very well then." Mother's tone is a bit jilted, not accustomed to this side of me.

Ari gives me a look, his jaw tense. I take his left hand in mine, cupping it in my grasp. "It's okay, Ari. I know we can do this. You already prepared me, remember?" I let out a small giggle, hoping to ease the worry I see in his eyes. His expression softens some, but I know he's not fully convinced.

"If anything happens to you because of me—"

"The best thing to ever happen to me is you. That's all I know. You give me strength I never knew I had. You gave me just what I needed to see this day through. What better way to end it than with us doing this together?"

Ari runs his hand softly down the side of my face. "Together. I like the sound of that."

As much as I wish we could stay here for a little while, the sound of Mother's hearty clap pulls our attention back to her.

My eyes go straight to the prisms. The three oddly shaped contraptions sit in the midst of the bar near the dance floor and jukebox. I think of the times I've taught Ari new line dances. He's never one to dance in front of others, but the night he saw a bear shifter dancing the Cupid shuffle with me, he forced his way to my side.

Arius Knight has always made his way to my side. Even though all these years I've been too blind to see it. Now, however, I couldn't picture it any other way.

Mother and Cade are standing near the prisms in the back of the bar. Both Gypsy and Stevie are seated across from the prisms with some of the remaining attendants. It feels different now that the other suitors are gone. I'm more relaxed. Knowing I'm no longer on display helps keep the butterflies swarming in my gut at bay.

But Ari and I walking hand-in-hand, with everything laid bare, is all I ever wanted. Sure, there's still so much we need to say to one another, but knowing he wants this as much as I do brings the consolation to my heart I've always needed.

"Are you two ready?" Mother asks sweetly, her eyes dancing with a hopefulness I've never seen.

"Yes!" Ari and I declare in unison.

A few giggles roll around the room. I indistinctly hear Gypsy making some offhand remark about Ari, but he just shoots a playful grimace her way as we move forward.

"Now, Mr. Knight," Mother begins, "you'll still need to use Epirus to light the prisms. However, once you do, you'll have to quickly make your way through them with the Princess. I can't imagine that being too difficult a task, seeing as you caught that ax before it had a chance to split that wolf open like a melon." Her eyes are kind as she stares at Ari. Knowing she always sensed there was something between us, it warms my heart to see her take so well to him now. "Do you understand?"

"Yes, Your Highness." Arius nods in understanding. Turning to me, Ari kisses my knuckles once more before heading to the front to fire off the bow.

Taking a deep breath, Ari flexes, shifting into his full Bulwark form. Extending his wings at his sides, he roars as his muscles break through his shirt. Rotating, he arches his arms in position, and Epirus appears in his grip. This time, however, there are three small arrows notched in the bow. He releases the arrows all at once, and they burst like fireworks into small flames.

Once we enter the prisms, our lot is our own. An iridescent fog will shield us from the view of everyone else. Only Arius and I will know what trials the prisms reveal.

The first arrow booms past me, landing on the first prism. Lifting above the floor, I allow my Nether-form to take over as my shadows carry me to the first prism.

A cool spray of water springs up from the prism, trapping me inside its misty flume. I turn about, looking for an exit, but I don't see a way out as the water builds, dampening the soot and ash exuding from me. Panic swells within me as I try to summon my own dark force to break through the prism, but I cannot. I'm trapped.

Just before my fear grows into something worse, a bright warm light pummels through the prism, forcing the water to either side of the walls, creating a hole big enough for me to escape.

I'm not surprised when I see Ari's hand extend through the prism. The luminous glow of his palm rivals that of the sun. There's a steady wind coming from just outside the prism. As Ari's wings flap hard against his back, he creates a tidal force so strong, it sweeps the spray against the prism walls, holding it back just enough for me to get out.

As he pulls me out, I cave into his chest. The security I feel in his arms as his wings and large, muscular arms envelop me assures me I am not alone.

I never was.

Still, I don't have time to marvel at the strength of his embrace when another arrow bursts into flames, igniting the second prism. Ari's eyes lock with mine, and he gives me a reassuring nod as we press forward into the next prism.

For a moment, there's nothing. We're standing eerily still within the prism walls. Ari is fully alert as he looks around, but I can't get my eyes off him, how regal he looks in his full Bulwark form. He is a gorgeous creature to behold, but I don't have time to idly stare at the man I love when the foundation of the prism shakes and a loud sound rumbles around us.

Ari wraps his arm around my waist, pulling me so I'm in front of him. His wings curve inward, no room for his full wingspan, but he keeps me covered.

"I've got you, baby." Ari lowers himself to my ear, and the cool tingle of his breath prickles my pores. I push back against him, allowing my head to rest against his shoulder. As much as I'd like to do nothing but rest in his arms, the feel of his hardened member pressed against my backside has my lady bits doing somersaults. A small moan escapes me, and Ari presses forward, ensuring I feel the steel strength of him. "Not yet, Princess. That comes later."

I barely have a moment to process what he means when I feel the prism shake once more.

Shaking side to side, Ari and I slide from one end of the prism to the other across the smooth floor. It's hard to keep our footing within the triangular shape, but Ari keeps a sturdy grasp on me.

"Hold onto me, Des!" he shouts when I almost slip out of his hold.

Grabbing his forearm, Ari pulls me back into his embrace as the seismic tremors continue to rattle the prism walls. I toss my hands around his neck, and he lifts me so my legs are wrapped around his waist.

Our eyes lock with one another when the feel of his rock-hard length pushes against my sex. I let out another small yelp. Even with his trousers on, what I feel bucking beneath the fabric makes me desirous for him in ways my mind is too muddled to comprehend.

The room shakes again, and this time, Ari uses it to his advantage as he presses me against the wall. I can feel his hardness even more in this position as he's now aligned with my clit. Wetness gathers at my center, and my needy sex spasms, eager to feel Ari once more.

My eyes must tell him all he needs to know as he bucks against me, ensuring his length hits my spot every time the prism shakes.

"Is this what you want, princess? To be trapped in this prism with my cock pressed against your sweet little–"

"Ari!" I moan, wishing I could just kiss him right now, but it's too soon to tell, and I won't hurt him.

Once more, the prism shakes, the walls narrowing around us, pressing Ari harder against me.

"Yes," I groan against his ear, desperate. I grind against his steel shaft, and he bucks into me, making the prism shake more.

"You want me to make you come? In here? Like this?" he growls, looking at me with those piercing dark eyes that seem to see into my soul.

I don't respond. I just keep grinding.

This is what I need. This is what I dreamed of, and I'm not leaving here until I get it.

CHAPTER 36

Arius

Fuck.

If I had known running prisms with Des would be like this, I would have done this a long time ago.

But here we are. I have her pinned to the prism wall with her legs wrapped around my waist. She's grinding her greedy little pussy against me like she's trying to start a fire.

The feel of her heat moving on me now gives me all the assurance I need to know what will come later could set the world on fire, but I don't care. I say, let it all burn.

If we were alone right now, I'd plunge my finger inside of her and work her until she came violently against my palm. For now, though, this will have to do.

I'm much bigger in this form, but she doesn't seem to mind. In fact, the calculating look in her gaze tells me she's quite pleased with my size.

"Ari!" Des whines as she jerks against me, bouncing up and down, ensuring the hard curve of my cock hits her spot.

"Take what you need, baby," I coax her along, slamming myself into her with every tremor of the prism. "Your first one was supposed to be on me, but I'll let you have this one."

"Thank you... *Fuck*!" she cries out, and I know she's nearing her peak as her large breasts bounce against my chest. Damn, if I don't want to pull one of her breasts into my mouth right now, but I know this Culling has to be complete first.

One more thrust, and Des combusts with a shout, curses and promises flowing out of her mouth like dirty poetry, and I love her for it.

I could've exploded in my pants too, but I held my composure. This was for her, but I need something too.

The tremors lessen, and I let Des slide down my body as she comes down from her high. Her eyes are a misty haze of lust as she stares at me, and I've never seen her look sexier.

"Thank you," she moans again with a silly little smirk. "I think I need a cigarette," she chuckles.

"Maybe later," I smile, taking her hand in mine and giving her wrist a kiss. "Right now, I need something else."

"What?"

"Just a little something to keep me going for the next round," I answer darkly.

"Anything, baby," she croons, running her free hand through my hair.

Taking her hand, I hike up her dress until I find her lace panties. Her breath hitches, and her eyes pop open.

"Ari, baby, wait!"

"Just trust me," I breathe back.

Guiding her hand, I take her pointer finger and trail it over her sex. I nearly get goosebumps knowing I'm so close to where I truly want to be, but I know I have to wait. I push her finger inside, just enough that I hear the wetness that awaits me at her entrance.

"Fuck!" Des moans, biting her lip at the pleasure. As she does, a loud rumble pummels through the prism as the floor shakes once more.

Picking up my pace, I swirl her finger around a bit, and she folds into me as I make her fuck herself against the wall. "These are the sounds I heard you make for me outside your window at night."

Her eyes pop open at my reveal.

"Ari, baby..." she coos, and I keep swirling her finger around.

"Now, give me what I want," I demand, pulling her finger from her sex as I bring her hand to my mouth.

"No, Ari! What if–"

"Are you still afraid I'll die if I fuck that bratty little hellcat of yours? What about if I taste it? Surely a little taste can't hurt." Before she has a chance to protest, I suck her finger, letting her sweet flavor explode across my tongue. She has no idea the plans I have to feast on her tonight.

Her face blushes red, and she makes a purring sound as the foundation rumbles once more. "I like the sound of that. You should know that making my little hellcat purr is my sacred duty."

Des keeps her eyes glued to mine. There's fear in her eyes, but there's also something else. Hope. She wants me to live.

I continue sucking her finger, swirling my tongue around the tip until I take in all I can muster. Desephone tastes like the sweetest candy, and I know I'll never get enough, but I slowly pull her finger from my mouth.

"Delicious," I growl, leaning my head against hers.

Des presses her eyes tight, biting her lip with that cute little smirk I've come to love over the years. "What am I going to do with you?"

"Whatever the hell you want."

The shaking foundation of the prism settles, and we're left standing with our heads still resting together. Neither of us wants to leave this prism, but when we hear the final arrow burst near the last one, we ease our way out.

As we do, I take the opportunity to stretch my wings. It was a tighter fit inside the prism than I anticipated. I suppose the prisms are usually meant for singular use, but from this day forward, Des and I will do everything together.

The last prism blazes with fire like a volcanic eruption. Scorching flames of orange and blood-red shoot up from the center of the prism.

A lava-like stream runs from the prism's walls, closing in near our feet. I lift Des, flapping my wings just enough to keep us from the fiery stream, but when sparks of fire hit my wings, I bring us back to the ground.

"Ari, are you okay?" Des asks worriedly as her hands trail over my injured wing.

Grimacing a bit, I manage a strained grin. "I'll be fine, but we need to get out of here." Prisms may be a mystical illusion of sorts, but the effects are very real.

Just then, the floor rumbles from the last prism, causing the lava to flow toward us faster.

Des looks behind us at the last prism and again at the flaming prism ahead of us. "If this keeps up, we'll have a heap of fire on us in no time."

I look over my shoulder and spot the first prism. I notice there's still water sprouting up, and inspiration strikes.

"Baby, I need you to be you right now. Bring that rage only my little hellcat can."

Des shrugs her shoulders as her brows raise in confusion. "Rage? Right now? That's your idea?"

"Just trust me, baby."

Sucking her teeth, she gives me a hearty eye roll before summoning her dark force. As she does, a dark gale whips around her, creating a plume of ash and smoke. Her shadowy chasm whirls around me like a phantom, and I watch as the lava seems to parry her movements.

"That's it, Des. You lead the fire, baby!" I shout toward her. She looks down at me with a slight nod. Her darkened features would frighten someone else, but the sight of her like this only makes me love her more.

I run toward the last prism and ram my shoulder into the wall. The foundation shakes, and the lava stream trickles toward the prism. Des twirls around the flames, enveloping the fire until nothing is left but smoke. The remaining lava travels to the second prism as I shake the foundation once more. I channel an orb of light to my hand, shooting the first prism until the walls break like a dam. Both the water and fire meet in the center of the second prism, balancing each other. As I lean against the wall, it finally hits me: Des is my balance, and I am hers.

CHAPTER 37

Desephone

As we walk out of the other side of the final prism, my heart bubbles within me, knowing Ari and I conquered the prisms together.

The old ones always said prisms are more about learning about one's true self than training one to use their powers.

If anyone asked me what I learned about myself during our prism exercise, I'd tell them the truth: Arius Knight and I are meant for one another. Not only are we the best of friends, we complement each other.

Ari isn't afraid to let me be my true self. I know that not only will he always protect me, but even in chaos, he'll meet my needs even in the most intimate of ways.

How I've gone so long without truly acknowledging all that we are and have been to one another is beyond me. Yet, no matter how long it took for us to get here, I wouldn't trade it for anything.

Once more, Ari brings my hand to his mouth, planting a doting kiss on my knuckles before letting our clasped hands fall back between us.

We're greeted by a series of cheers, claps, and shouts. Gypsy and Stevie are the loudest, along with some of the servers. Cade wears a proud smile, clapping like he just witnessed his youngest brother walk across the stage.

Mother is the most surprising. She's whistling, actually whistling, as we emerge from the smoky prism chamber. Her smile is wide, and her bright eyes shine like sapphires as we come into full view.

A whizzing sound, like that of crackling fireworks, booms around us, and Ari and I turn to see the elemental prisms shimmer behind us. They pop and fizzle until there's nothing left but brass triangular posts. It still amazes me how something that looks so ordinary can bring about such extraordinary strength, but I'll never question its power again.

Leaning my head into Ari's embrace, I smile when I feel him kiss the top of my head. I've never been happier.

"Desephone!" Mother cheers aloud, surprising me. She rarely says my name in front of others. With her arms outstretched, she immediately pulls me in for a hug, nearly ripping me from Ari. He doesn't seem to mind, but he keeps close with his hand on the small of my back. But the Queen of the Underworld won't see her future son-in-law left out. Opening her arms a bit more, she gives room for Ari to find his place at my side. "I am so happy for you, dearest. Both of you," she corrects herself.

"Yeah, Knight, you finally manned up," Gypsy teases, hitting Ari's back. "But since some strange sounds were coming out of that second prism, you two might need to go back in there and try again—"

"Gypsy, stop it!" Cade shoves her shoulder. "I, of all people, want no repeats of whatever happened in that prism."

My eyes are stunned as I look up at my mother. She gracefully looks away from me, only to give a quick eye roll to Gypsy. Stevie bumps Gypsy's hips, hoping she'll catch the drift. Ari shakes his head, pursing his lips, but he keeps his attention on me.

"So, did we pass?" I ask, needing to get the attention off Gypsy's comments.

"Yes, darling, yes!" Once more, my mother throws her arms around me. This time, Ari backs up, letting us have this moment.

"Well done, my friend," I hear Cade say as the two slap hands.

"For real, big guy, I'm happy for ya!" Gypsy exclaims, and I hear another loud pat on his back.

Mother squeezes me tighter. "This is what I've always wanted for you, my darling." I feel a splash of water hit my shoulder, and I pull my face up just enough to see a single line of tears from her eye. "You deserve all the happiness in the world."

"Thank you," I cry into her embrace. She has never held me like this before, but I'm not going to ask her to let up.

"Oh dears," she squeals with a flustered shake of her head. Straightening her posture, she pulls away, patting her face to gently wipe her tears away. "I'm making such a fuss."

"It's quite alright, Your Highness," Ari says with a dutiful tip of his head. "I'm sure you'll get no objections from this one." He smiles down at me.

"Not a chance!" I yelp, throwing my arms around my mother's waist one more time for good measure. I don't linger, but I'm simply happy enough that she doesn't pull away.

"Well, Mr. Knight," Mother begins, lifting her chin with her hands clasped at her waist. "You've made quite an impression today. Not only have you proven to be an exemplary member of your class, ensuring the peaceful residency of supernaturals in Biloxi, but you've also befriended and shown love and genuine affection for my daughter."

"You can say that again!" Gypsy snips.

Cade quickly wraps his hand over her mouth to muffle her interruption. Ari lets out a small grunt of disapproval in her direction, but Cade firms his hold on his friend, reassuring us he'll keep her quiet. Even Stevie wraps an arm around Gypsy's waist to keep her from any other outbursts.

"Thank you, Great Queen. I love Desephone. I always have, and I always will."

Ari's words strike me straight in the heart. I always knew he cared for me, but now more than ever, I see him as I've never seen him before.

"I love you too," I say, rising to the balls of my feet just enough for him to kiss the top of my head.

"And now that love will be put to a greater test," Mother continues, her voice a bit more restrained. "With the full moon tomorrow, you must fully commence with the final exercise: the mating ritual."

"Didn't they do that already?" Gypsy's muffled words manage to break through Cade's grip.

"Gypsy!" both Ari and I snap over our shoulders.

Although we laugh it off, I cringe inside thinking about what everyone might have heard while we were in the second prism. Thankfully, we were shielded within the orb, the sound muted by the rumblings of the prism, but it's not hard to guess something went on between us.

Still, I have no regrets. We were long overdue. Besides, we're all adults. Monsters, even.

"This is a good time for us to adjourn upstairs." Mother seems to ignore Gypsy's outburst. Waving her hand toward the attendants, she points to the upper room. "If Mr. Knight's staff wouldn't mind leading everyone to the reception, I would greatly appreciate it."

The staff quickly disperses. Some head upstairs while a few others begin leading Cade, Stevie, and Gypsy upstairs. Although she never made it clear, both Ari and I know instinctively to stay behind.

"Now that we're alone, there are a few things we should discuss." Mother pauses, her gaze drifting between me and Ari, ensuring we follow. "While I am happy you two have made it this far in the Culling, the time has come for you to complete the most important part: the mating."

I gulp as Mother speaks. It's not that I'm uncomfortable discussing this in front of her, it's that I understand the weightiness of it all. More importantly, I realize the position I'm putting Ari in.

"Not only must you be in perfect harmony, but all must be laid bare. So, if there are any doubts, now is the time to reconcile your concerns. Do you understand?"

"We understand," Ari boasts proudly, his eyes beaming with assurance. I nod, thankful when Ari firms his grasp on me. It gives me more confidence than the butterflies in my stomach suggest.

"Yes, Mother," I add, forcing a bright smile. Mother's nose twitches some as she looks at me, but she gives a smile that softens her usual hardened expression.

One more shared hug from Mother, and she shoos us out of the door while she continues upstairs to the reception. The door slams behind us as we exit the Dram Deaux. Our shared gaze immediately marches to Petals across the street, but I don't have time to linger when Ari pulls me into his arms. I could stay like this forever.

CHAPTER 38

Arius

Desephone curves into my embrace like she committed to memory every nook and crevice. With her head planted at the center of my chest and her small arms wrapped around my torso, she presses herself tight, and I can hardly tell where she begins and I end.

"Are you ready?" I whisper against the crown of her head.

She doesn't reply; instead, she squeezes me tighter. If I was mortal, her hold on me would hurt.

"Baby?" I groan, pulling back some. I need to see her face.

Still, she squeezes me hard, preventing me from breaking away.

"No! Not yet!" she grumbles into my chest as she uses all her might to keep me in place.

"Des, baby, are you okay?" I ask when I hear a muffled cry. She loosens her grip, and I pull back so I can see her face in full. Two dark tears race down both sides of her face, and I lift her chin until her eyes pop open. "Baby, please, tell me what's wrong."

"Are you sure about this, Ari? Like really? I mean, I am death incarnate. What kind of future can you have with death?"

I wipe her stray tears, marveling at the trust beaming from her wide, doe eyes as she looks up at me. "Baby, I die a little bit every time I'm not with you. But right here, right now—all I see is my future, here with you."

Shaking her head, not fully accepting my sentiment, Des uses the back of her wrist to wipe her face. "I'm sorry, Ari."

"You have nothing to apologize for."

She folds her arms over her waist, pouting as her brows arch inward. "But I do. If it's not bad enough that people still died for me tonight—despite everything I wanted—now I'm asking you to possibly do the same. I love you too much, Ari. How can I risk losing you after finally making you mine?"

A small smile crosses my face. I know it's bad timing, but damn it, I don't care. I've waited forever to hear her say that. "Well, if I'm yours, you can never really lose me, can you?"

"Ari," she grouses, rolling her eyes. "I'm being serious here."

"So am I, Des." I give her a pointed stare, and her posture relaxes some. "Listen, folk dying here tonight, that's not all on you. I had something to do with some of that, remember?"

"Well, it's on both of us. If we'd gotten our act together sooner... "

"Don't do that, Des. There's enough should've, would've, could've to go around, but none of it is going to make you feel better. The fact is, despite how long it took us to get here, we are here. You know how I feel about you—how I've always felt about you. I love you, and you love—"

"Then what about the other woman?" Des fires back, her wide, round eyes almost accusing, but there's something else. Insecurity. I've never known Desephone to be insecure.

"What other woman?" I answer, confused. "Who, Stevie? They're with Gypsy, not me. I explained–"

"I'm not talking about Stevie, Ari. Your phone call earlier. I heard you tell someone you loved them. I know it wasn't Stevie. So, who was it?"

A small laugh escapes me. I'm relieved. "Damn, I forgot you came in when I was on the line."

Des raises a brow, and her neck does a cute little roll as she leans her head to one side, awaiting my reply. I've never seen her do this with me before but fuck, if it doesn't turn me on even more. Sassy Des is sexy as hell.

"Yeah, I heard you on the line, Ari, so spit it out."

Then, it hits me. "Wait a minute—you can't tell me you're actually mad at me right now."

Her gaze narrows, and blackened veins crouch around her eyes. "Does it look like I'm mad?"

"I'm not talking about how you look, beautiful. But I'm just saying, my phone call didn't seem to bother you when we were in that prism." Her eyes widen and her stance softens. I take a step forward, closing the distance between us. Running my hand up her arm, to her neck, I finally rest my palm against her cheek. She folds into me, and I firm my grasp. "When you pressed your pus–"

"Stop, Ari," she breathes back, slowly pulling from my hand. "Don't do that. That's not fair."

"Not fair?" I groan, inching closer. "So tell me, what's fair?"

"I'll tell you what's fair when you tell me who you were confessing your love to. Because there's no point in us going further if you have feelings for someone else. If you're in love with someone else. And you're right, I should've thought about that sooner, but I'm thinking about it now. Too many have died already. I won't have your death on my conscience, especially if you're in love with someone else."

"Well, let me put your mind at ease, Your Highness. You did hear me confess my love to someone else." I pause as I watch her eyes go wide in horror. "But it's not what you think. She–"

Des turns away from me. "I don't need to know any more!"

I grab her wrist, turning her back to me. As I do, I quickly shift into my Bulwark form. I hardly care to check whether anyone is looking. I'm putting this and Des to bed, once and for all.

"Oh, you need to know, Princess. And after I'm done explaining it all to you, I'm taking you back to Petals so I can fuck you senseless!"

Color drains from her face, her eyes brightening in shock. "Ari, I–"

I don't give her a moment to protest when I scoop her up in my arms, lifting her into the night sky.

Once more, she wraps her arm around my waist, but she doesn't fold into me as she did before. She's rigid and stiff, only holding on enough that she doesn't fall. I don't like this strain between us, but I'm hardly letting her go without laying all the cards on the table.

Persephone said for this to work, we have to be honest with one another. I've kept too much of myself hidden from Des for too long. All for good reason, but tonight, when we make love for the first time, there'll be no ambiguity, no pretense, no blurred lines. Straight, no chaser. That's how my baby likes it.

I'm not a fan of flying, never have been. For Des, I'll make an exception. I'm grateful for the cloud cover to keep us from prying eyes, although I wish I could spend the time pointing out the lovely sights of the city as we breeze through the sky, but Des is hardly in the mood for smalltalk. I feel her loosen up a bit as we pass the lighthouse, and I make a note to stop by on our way back. I want this night to be special.

Thankfully, Gulfport is just outside Biloxi, so we're not in the air long before reaching our destination. This is not how I planned for this portion of the evening to go, but here we are.

"Where are we?" Des grumbles, backing away from me the moment I place her on the ground. I barely have a chance to shift back into mortal form before she reclaims her grumpy stance.

"It'll all make sense soon," I shoot over my shoulder, adjusting my clothes. Shifting is such a chore. "Follow me." I reach out my hand.

But she just stands there with folded arms, narrowed eyes, and pouty lips. "Not until you tell me where we are."

"Can you just please trust me for once?"

Her eyes blaze with fire. "For once? What's that supposed to mean?"

"It means I know you like to have everything labeled from A to Z and scrutinize everything in between before you take a plunge into the dark, but I'm asking you to trust me. Trust that I won't lead you astray. Trust that I'll never do anything to put you in harm's way. And most of all, trust that no matter what you heard earlier, it's you and only you I want to spend eternity with."

Desephone's fiery gaze fades like a stormy sea, her eyes welling with tears as she looks at me. "Ari, I–I–"

I pull her close to me. "Yeah, you love me, I know." There's an apt smirk on my face meant just for her. It might annoy her a little, but deep down, I know she loves it.

"You're an ass, you know that, right?" Des shoves my shoulder and giggles.

I wrap my arms around her shoulders, smiling down at her. "I'm yours." I nuzzle my nose against hers. "Now quit all of this stalling, Princess, and come meet my mom."

"Your mom?" I shriek, using the force within me to break from Ari's hold.

"Calm down, Des," Ari says, chuckling as he grabs my wrist and pulls me back to him.

"Don't tell me to calm down, Ari. You just told me I'm meeting your mother–your mother!"

He laughs, still keeping a good grip on me. "Well, who else would I be professing my love to?"

My mind is doing somersaults, but I do what I can to settle the racing of my heart. While I'm glad there's no other romantic interest I need to worry about, meeting his mother wasn't on my list. Not that I think she'll outright reject me, but after dealing with

Persephone today, I'm not sure I can take another round of mother knows best.

Looking around, I finally take a moment to get my bearings. I need to calm down. Thankfully, Ari gives me the space I need to take it all in.

We're under a massive oak tree. The leaves hang around us, some falling into a lovely Autumn array of gold, orange, and red onto the lush green carpet beneath us. There's a large metal sign that reads *Solatium: A Pinnacle Place*.

While I know the first word is simply *comfort* in Latin, there's something familiar about the second part I can't place. Even more, I can't fathom why his mother is here or that she's still alive altogether.

"Ari, I don't understand," I plainly say, slightly panting at the thought of meeting his mother.

He smiles—a genuine one, not that sly, sexy grin he normally shoots my way. "It'll all make sense soon. Now, come on. I have less than twenty-four hours to make love to the love of my life and cement my place at her side. I don't want you meeting my mom to throw off the mood too much."

"Well, somebody's got a one-track mind tonight," I laugh, shaking my head. He's not the only one, but I won't let him in on that secret.

"You better know it," Ari grunts, pinching my chin.

Ari doesn't give me another opportunity to protest when he loops our arms together and leads us to a round brick building with a glass and steel roof. Once we reach the door, he quickly punches a few digits on a keypad, and the door opens.

As we enter, the scent of lavender and jasmine hits me, along with the cooling fragrance of eucalyptus. There are two large waterfalls on either side of the wall, with a large fountain in the center of the lobby. The colors are bright but neutral, creating an inviting and comfortable environment. It reminds me of some of the luxury hotels I've been to, but even better.

"What is this place?" I ask, tugging on Ari's arm.

Ari opens his mouth to speak when another set of doors opens, and a tall woman with long red hair greets us.

"Mr. Knight!" she exclaims, happy to see him. "I'm so glad you came, but I told Vicki not to bother you. I promise, we've got Ms. Tala under control."

I feel Ari stiffen at my side. His arm drops to his side as he steps in front of me. "Ms. Reed? What do you mean you have my mother under control? And why would Vicki need to bother me?"

Ms. Reed's eyes brighten in alarm as her brick-red lips part in a gasp. "Oh–oh! I'm sorry, Mr. Knight," she rasps, placing a hand over her heart. "I–I thought Vicki told you, but–"

Ari doesn't wait for her to say another word before he marches past her, slamming his way through the set of double doors. I rush around her to keep up with Ari. I want to ask him how I can help, but I don't. I do just what he has done for me all day: be here. Be whatever he needs, however he needs me.

"Please, Mr. Knight, I promise she's okay!" Ms. Reed calls behind us.

As we make our way down the hall, the setting changes some. I notice people dressed in scrubs, but the stylish, expensive kind. We pass rooms where I notice elderly people and some who seem to require medical attention. There are some hooked up to oxygen tanks, while others have intravenous blood bags.

It doesn't take a genius to note that almost everyone here is of some supernatural descent. From the golden and crimson eyes staring at me to those of amber and even the color of lightning, I can sense their power as I move along the corridor.

Several staff persons pause reverently as they see Ari coming down the aisle. From startled gasps to a few rounds of *Good evening, Mr. Knight* and *How can we help you, sir,* and even, *Oh, doesn't he look handsome tonight,* it's clear Arius carries quite a bit of weight around the facility.

I try not to let the varied expressions throw me off as I focus on keeping up with his quick pace. As we near the end of the hall, the sound of a growing disturbance pulls my attention away from the onlookers.

We reach another set of doors, but this one leads to a patient room. When Arius bursts through the door, I don't immediately enter, but I stand on the threshold, holding the door ajar with my hip.

I see a gold nameplate that reads Tala Knight on the door, which I suspect is his mother's name. There's a teal chiffon curtain hanging on either side of the door for privacy. I want to cross the curtain, but I also don't want to intrude.

There's commotion on the other side of the curtain, sounds of about three voices and another voice, crying out in distress. Then, there's Ari's voice. He keeps asking what happened, but no one seems to immediately answer.

I feel so powerless. I don't know what to do or if he'd even want me on the other side of the curtain. I haven't formally met his mother, nor do I know if she is prepared for company.

Still, I don't have a moment to think about it when Ms. Reed yanks the door open behind me, presses by, and swings the curtain open.

And then, I see her.

Tala Knight. Ari's mom.

She's seated in a rocker, hugging herself, rocking back and forth. Her face is small, framed by beautiful, thick salt and pepper hair that's more salt than pepper. She's adorned in a silky red robe. It reminds me of a kimono, but I know it's a bit different. There are black and silver etchings of stars and dragons laced throughout her robe. Then, it hits me: *she is the one in red.* It wasn't Stevie or anyone else. It was her. It has always been her.

The thought puts a smile on my face.

But that smile quickly fades when Tala makes a low, wailing sound that pinches my heart.

"Mom, it's okay," Ari says, kneeling beside her. "I'm here," he coos, patting her hand, hopeful she opens her eyes.

Slowly, her eyes open, and a look of relief washes over her face. Tala's dark, crescent eyes stare up at Ari with a child-like glow.

"Evander," she whispers as her small hand grazes Ari's face. "Oh, Evander, I've missed you," she cries softly.

"It's okay, Mom, it's me. It's Arius," Ari says, his eyes tender and kind as he regards his mother.

"Arius?" she frowns, pressing back in her seat. "Arius," she screams.

"Mom? Mom?" he tries to regain her attention.

Tala rocks side to side. "Call Arius! Please! Tell him! Tell him! They took Evander! He's gone!"

"Mom, I'm right here!" Ari says, lifting until he catches her eye. "Ari is here."

Tala's eyes pop open, and she reaches for his collar, pulling her close to him. "Arius, you can do it. You must do it now. They've done it. They took him from me! They killed your father, and they must pay!" she shouts, pointing an accusing finger at Ms. Reed and the nurses. Her eyes drift to mine, and she manages a small smile. "And she can help you. She can send them to hell."

Arius

This is not how I expected tonight to go. I've wanted for so long to introduce my two favorite ladies to one another. I've waited because deep down I've always known it would go like this.

Mom has been pretty poorly for a while, but lately, it has gotten worse.

Her dementia is beyond medical intervention or even supernatural explanation. Still, she's my mother, and I'll do anything to keep her safe and comfortable. I just wish Des could have met her on better terms.

"Has she had her medicine?" I say over my shoulder to Ms. Reed. I need to know more about her condition for the evening before I invite Desephone closer. She's keeping close to the curtain, and if I know her, she'll wait until I extend an invitation before coming to my side.

"Yes, but–" Ms. Reed begins.

"But what?" I snap. Mom hasn't taken her eyes off Desephone, and it's starting to freak me out. Des doesn't seem to mind, and I'm thankful it's keeping mom settled.

"Well—"

"One of the new landscapers knocked over your father's chimera in the garden," Vicki rattles off, jumping in front of Ms. Reed. "I tried calling you at the Dram, but the folks said you were out and not reachable for the evening."

I blow out a sigh. I can't fucking win for losing tonight.

Rising from the floor, I keep a hold of Mom's hand. She's still gawking at Des like an infant looking up at a twinkling mobile. She looks like she's lost in a trance. Then again, she's staring at Des the same way I do, so I get it.

"How in the hell did that happen?" I snap.

"Well, sir, it's a new company, and they–"

"Mortals, Grace. Don't forget to mention they're mortal!" Vicki reveals, her golden eyes shining bright. Wolves are always a bit testy on the eve of a full moon.

My head whips in Ms. Reed's direction. "You hired mortals?"

She shrugs her shoulders. "I'm sorry, Mr. Knight, but as you know, we didn't receive funding from the Civility Center last quarter, and we—"

"Then you let me know. That's what the fu—" I restrain myself for my mother's sake. Dementia or not, she'd whack my ass one good time if I cursed in her presence. Tala may be a tiny woman from a small village near the mountains of Manila, but she has always been a force. "So, what are we doing about it?" I ask, doing what I can to curb my frustration.

"I put in a call to Trieu," Ms. Reed answers quickly. "She said she can look into something, but she doubts anything can be done."

"Of course not!" I shout back. "My father was literally in repose in his chimera. And now you've let some fu—some mortal split him in half. He has been suffering for over seventy-five years, Grace. You know he's all she has left! No wonder she's a wreck!"

"I'm sorry, Mr. Knight, truly, I am. If there was anything I could do–"

"Where is he?" Des' small voice cracks from the back of the room.

"Who is she?" Vicki snips, waving a dismissive hand toward Des with a disapproving frown.

Des doesn't look at Vicki; she keeps her sights set on Mom. For Vicki's sake, I'm thankful.

"Who she is is someone who can vacate your soul before you could blink. She's also my fiancée," I bark back.

Ms. Reed smiles wide, clapping her hands wistfully. "Oh, how wonderful, Mr. Knight!"

I'm not sure if Ms. Reed is truly happy for me or just thankful to stick it to Vicki. Vicki has always made overtures my way, but I've never paid her any mind. Not only do I not mix business and pleasure, but she's not Desephone.

Vicki's mouth gapes wide, and she fades back near the window.

"Evander's chimera is just outside in the garden," Ms. Reed says, pointing through the glass balcony doors. "We keep him in earshot of Tala. She likes him to be the first thing she sees in the morning and the last thing she sees at night."

"Take me to him," Desephone says sweetly, smiling as she keeps her eyes fixed on Mom.

"Oh, but it's so dark out," Ms. Reed continues.

Des breaks her intense gaze with Mom for a few seconds. "I'm hardly fearful of the dark, dear." As she speaks, her eyes fade to black as dark veins form around her face.

Both Vicki and Ms. Reed step back, fear glazing their faces as they stare at Des.

"What are you thinking, baby?" I ask.

My mom squeezes my hand until she gets my attention. She smiles up at me, and for a moment, I see a light in her eyes I haven't seen in over seventy-five years. "She's bringing Evander back to me," Mom announces cheerfully as she brings my hand to rest on her chin.

A stinging ache threatens the corner of my eyes, but I fight back the urge. Instead, I keep my sights on Des. She's the only thing that has kept the tears at bay all these years. Apparently, she has the same effect on my mother.

"Des?" I take a step forward, narrowly blocking Mom's view of her. I'm not sure if it's Mom's dementia at work here, or if Mom is on to something.

Des pops her eyes to mine, peeping over my shoulder just enough to wave at Mom. Mom waves back and lets out a girlish giggle. "Take me to your father, Ari," she answers sweetly.

Ms. Reed doesn't wait for me to ask, but she takes her key from around her wrist and heads to the balcony door. She unlocks it and opens the latch on the opposite side so the French doors open wide.

Mom claps her hands, patting her small feet on the floor like a kid waiting ready to blow out the candles on their birthday cake.

"We'll stay with Tala," Ms. Reed says, gesturing her hand for Des and me to go outside.

I bend over and give my mom a kiss on the cheek. "Give us a few minutes. We'll be right back."

"Okay, I'll be right here," she says as she kisses me back.

I extend my hand toward Des as she takes a few graceful steps my way. Both Vicki and Ms. Reed stare in awe as Des saunters forward. Des doesn't look in their direction, instead keeping her sights on me, flashing intermittent smiles at my mom. Mom smiles wide, like she just met her new best friend.

Desephone stops to look at the Juliet Rose flowers on Mom's nightstand. Her eyes bounce up to mine, and she covers her mouth in a gasp.

I throw her a quick wink. "I order them from a lovely little flower shop every week. They're pretty expensive, but I'm in love with the shop owner, so..."

She only shakes her head. I caught her off guard, but I'm sure she'll give me an earful later.

Des places her hand in mine, and I lead us across the threshold leading into the back garden. As we march down the cobblestone pathway, my heart drops to the pit of my stomach when I see my father's broken chimera lying in the grass.

I kneel at my father's side, running my hand along his stone-carved form. For his love of my mother, he was cursed to live in repose as a gargoyle for the rest of his days. Shortly after, Mom slipped into a state of dementia, and she never recovered.

For years, I avoided love because I never wanted to end up like my father. But when I met Des, something changed. I finally understood why my father risked all he was for not only the woman he loved, but the life he wanted. That's what I finally tapped into. Like my father, I've found the love of my life. Now, I intend to live each and every moment I have with her.

CHAPTER 41

Desephone

Looking down at Ari, my heart wrenches into knots seeing the tearful pain now marring his face. Ari is always so strong and sure of himself; it hurts seeing him so broken. Over the years, Arius has done everything possible to be a rock for me. He has protected me, challenged me, been my best friend. Even today, he put aside his own feelings just to prove how much he cares for me.

I've never known anyone to love me like Arius Knight, so I'll be damned if I don't do what I can to offer some love to him in return.

"Ari," I say, kneeling at his side. I rub my hand along his back, hopeful to soothe some of his pain away. I notice the tip of his wing forging its way outside of the blazer, and I can still see the bruise from earlier. The thoughts burn through me when I think of everything he has done for me today. "Baby," I call to him once more.

He finally turns toward me, his face a stunning red and his eyes riddled with tears. Quickly running his hands over his face, he forces an unconvincing smile. "Some first introductions, huh?"

I run my hand through his hair while using my free hand to dry his tears. "Maybe I can help," I say, adding a squeeze to his shoulder.

"How?"

"Just trust me." I give a quick wink.

I can see he's confused, but he doesn't argue. Instead, he sits up on his knees and looks at the scattered pieces of his father's chimera laid across the lawn.

I go to stand, and Ari hurriedly rises from the ground to help me up.

"You should probably stand back," I say as I begin circling his father.

I notice a heap of ash in the center of stone, and I bend over and scoop up as much as I can. Ari lifts a finger to say something, but he covers his mouth and steps back.

A dark shroud forms around me, shimmering iridescent embers, reminiscent of the stars twinkle, forming a misty haze. Whispering a prayer, I lift the ash into the iridescence and free it from my hand.

The tiny particles find their way to each twinkling light, creating brilliant beams like connecting the dots. Another wave of my hand, and the stone pieces lift from the ground. Although I'm not touching them, I can feel the weight of them in the depths of me. Evander wasn't a small being by any stretch. Ari is well past six feet, but his father was obviously taller and bigger. Tala's petite frame must be the differentiator in Ari's size.

Slowly, Evander's fragments come together, bit by bit. As he does, Ari's eyes loom in wonder, but I'm not done yet. As the stone pieces fit together, I whirl my hands around once more, summoning his ashen hull back into his frame.

It's not an easy task to weave each piece into place, but I do so carefully, ensuring not one grain is missed.

As all the pieces form Evander's chimera, a bright white light exudes from his casing, and a low rumble shakes the entire garden. Evander's eyes flash bright, and Ari steps in front of him.

"Dad!" he gasps in awe. Evander's eyes shine only briefly before they are once more covered in stone.

"Not yet!" I warn, ensuring Ari stays clear of his father as the makings of his deathly curse cleave to his being. Ari keeps his place, but I can tell he's chomping at the bit.

Once more, I whirl my hand around, reciting ancient words too hauntingly beautiful to tell. The shimmering mist hovers over Evander for a few seconds, only to cover him completely just as I bring my hands to my sides. For a moment, I see him. Through the misty haze I see Evander as he was before he was relegated to stone. Smooth dark skin, and piercing gray eyes, steely, but kind just like Arius.

I barely have time to admire Evander before I fall to my knees. It's not often I endure my own enchantments, and now I remember why. It takes too much out of me.

"Baby!" Ari breezes to my side, catching me before I fall onto the grass. "Des, are you okay?"

Cradling me in his arms, Ari's tender gaze sweeps over my face, and I still can't believe I've taken so long to see him as I do now. This isn't the first time he has looked at me like this, like I was precious, important, *his*. I never want him to look at me any other way.

"I'm fine," I say, trying to push myself up in his arms.

"You are amazing, that's what you are." He brings me to his chest and holds me tight.

"She is definitely a good one, son," I hear a small, smooth voice say behind us. "Don't mess it up."

I manage to look over Ari's shoulder to see Tala and Ms. Reed standing behind us.

"Mom?" Ari seems surprised to see her outside.

She's still wearing her robe, but she has it pulled to her chin to keep her warm. I notice the cute gray bunny slippers she's wearing, and I can't help thinking she's probably someone who enjoys cartoons and silly shows.

"Yes, Arius," she answers with a warm smile. "Doesn't he look beautiful? Like an angel," she breathes, clasping her hands beneath her chin.

We all stare up at Evander. He does look angelic. With broad wings twice the span of Ari's and a foreboding frame, Evander reminds me of everything I learned of Bulwarks of the old world. His chest is brawny with muscles and his legs are massive, rivaling the trunk of the oak in front of the facility. Evander has one, well, two things Ari doesn't have: horns. Two small horns peek from his clean-shaven head, and his tail is thicker than Ari's.

Since Ari is only half-Bulwark, I'm sure he has taken much of his mortal form from his mother.

"Yes, Ms. Tala, he is beautiful," I reply, keeping my eyes fixed on Ari. Thankfully, everyone is too busy looking at Evander to notice how I'm gawking at Arius.

Ari offers his hand to help me up. "Mom, I'd like you to meet someone."

"Ah yes, the lovely lady I met over there. I hope this is the Des you've gone on and on about," she chuckles.

"You heard that?" Ari frowns with a curious smile.

Tala pats his shoulder. "A mother always knows," she says while shooting him a quick wink. "It's very nice to meet you, Des."

"Very nice to meet you too, Ms. Tala."

Tala swipes a quick hand through the air. "Please, just Tala. I'm not hardly one for formalities," she says sweetly. "But I am happy to finally meet you."

"Well, Mom, I wanted to introduce you to Des because we're soon to be married," Arius says proudly as he wraps his arm around my waist.

Tala claps her hands wildly beneath her chin. "Oh, Arius! I am so happy for you! Both of you!" She turns back to Ms. Reed and smiles. "Isn't this joyous news, Grace?"

"Very joyous, my friend," Ms. Reed answers.

Reaching out for our hands, Tala squeezes our hands, and I'm surprised by her sturdy grip. "Now listen, Arius. I know you've been biding your time, looking after me, but I'm glad you finally realized you needed to move on with your life. I'm not sure what jump-started your engine, but it must've given you a swift kick in the ass!"

"Mother!" Ari leans back, surprised.

She lifts a brow and gives his hand an extra tug. "You heard me." Ari doesn't respond; he just stands in awe of her. "But truly, I'm happy for you. Any minute now, I will be back to riding shotgun in my own soul, but one thing I want is for you to live your life. I lived mine and so did your father. We found each other. We created a family. We created memories. That's the only thing I miss. The memories. Seeing Evander broken like that–well, it threatened to take the memory of him from me, but your pretty little bride here gave all those beautiful memories back to me. Now, it's time for you to go and make some beautiful memories of your own. So, if you've come for my blessing, please know you already have it. I love you, son."

"I love you too, Mom."

CHAPTER 42

Arius

Things went far better than expected.

When Desephone put my father's chimera back together, it awakened something in my mother. Damn, if I didn't know how much I missed talking with my mother with her memory intact, but it was the gift I didn't know I needed.

Although it only lasted a short while before Mom reverted back into her shell, I relished in the new memories we created in that moment. Ms. Reed insisted on taking a picture of us, all four of us. My parents, Des, and me. It's not a picture I ever thought I'd get, but it's the keepsake I'll keep with me forever.

Not only did I have a moment with my mother, but I got a flash of my father. It has been seventy-five years since I've seen his eyes— his real eyes, not those carved in stone. It may have only been a few seconds, but it felt like he shared a lifetime of memories with me.

Memories of the first time he saw Mom in Manila to when he held me in his arms and so many moments in between flashed before my eyes. Even more, there was an apt sense of pride exuding from him I always hoped to find. He never got to see the man I've become, but tonight, I am confident he is pleased with how I turned out.

My heart leaped a little when I saw Mom and Des huddle in the corner while I went over a few things with Ms. Reed. For years, I've wanted the two to meet, but to see them hitting it off right away made me the happiest man in the two realms.

Still, I made sure to clear up a few things with Ms. Reed to ensure my father's chimera remains a permanent fixture for as long as Mom is on this earth. There will be a new iron railing added to his place in the garden to prevent the landscapers from accidentally knocking him over. Desephone assures me the charms she added to his stone are far sturdier than what he had before, making him almost impossible to break.

I also let Ms. Reed know that guardianship of the facility will fall to Perry Bossier. He's already accustomed to many of my business dealings, and he's the only other person I trust wholeheartedly with my mother. I love both Cade and Gypsy dearly, but their blood-thirsty nature presents a challenge with caring for my very human mother. Plus, being an orphan himself, Perry has always looked at my mother like family.

~

Now that we've arrived back at Petals, there's an anxiousness brewing inside me I didn't anticipate.

"Thank you, Ari," Des says quietly as she places her hand on the doorknob.

"For what?"

Hunching her shoulders, she smiles. "For trusting me enough to meet your mom. She is a lovely woman."

"I wish the two of you could've met sooner, but it should be me thanking you," I say, taking her free hand in mine. "What you did back there with my dad, and the way you were with Mom—you're one amazing woman. Thank you."

Des doesn't respond; she just blares her usual sweet smile and turns to open the door.

"Looks like your mother added more petals." I point to the ground.

She turns and looks at me for a moment, like her mind is elsewhere. "And you're still not burning. That should've been my first clue."

"What do you mean?"

"Well, the Great Mother, Demeter, used petals to not only denote the ground a bride walks on, but also her mate. From the beginning, she charmed the petals so anyone found unworthy would burn, marking them unsuitable for mating."

"So that's why Derek was burning earlier?"

"Yeah, and it's also why you're not burning now." She shoots me a wink. "So, are you ready to come in?"

"Absolutely," I answer, placing my palm in hers as I cross the threshold. As I do, I feel a whistling sound behind me, and I'm surprised to see the petals blowing up in the wind.

The door closes behind us, and more petals fall from the ceiling.

Des shakes her head, rolling her eyes and laughing. "Mother has such a panache for the dramatic."

"Well, it's not every day you can finally be with the person you've been secretly in love with for fifty years."

Des chuckles, squeezing my hand. "You haven't been in love with me all fifty years, have you?"

"Okay, maybe I didn't know I was in love right away, but that's probably because I didn't know what love felt like until you came along. I never wanted what I wanted with you with anyone else."

She runs her free hand up my chest. "And what do you want with me, Ari?"

"Forever."

Her eyes glass with tears. "That's what I want, Ari. But are we sure? If anything goes wrong—"

I place a finger over her lips. "The only thing that can go wrong is waiting another minute."

Not waiting for another protest to pour from her pretty pouty lips, I scoop Des up in my arms. She laughs in surprise as she wraps her arms around my neck.

"Ari!" she squeals.

"I've got you, baby," I groan into her ear.

As I take us upstairs, my senses are overloaded by the sweet smells of orchids, vanilla, and lavender. The scent permeates the air, prickling my pores, invoking just the aphrodisiac needed for our time together, although I hardly need anything to get me in the mood.

Just looking at Desephone is enough to rev up my engine.

Aromatic candles light up the walkway to Desephone's room, and another spray of petals greets us as I kick open the double doors to her room.

In all our years as friends, I've only been to her bedroom once. She purchased a heavy, floor-length mirror from an estate sale, and she asked me to bring it up for her. Although I've spent quite a deal of time hovering outside her window at night, I've never come as close as I am now at seeing her room in detail.

Slowly, I let Des down once we're inside, and we stand there, staring into one another's eyes.

Everything in me is demanding I claim her now, but she isn't some mere prize for the claiming. She isn't a possession. No, it's her possessing me, and she deserves everything I have to give.

"I'm not going to kiss you yet." I make my intentions clear. She gasps, her eyes wide, but she doesn't say anything. "First, I'm going to take care of you. Get the day off you. And then—"

She presses her eyes tight, pursing her lips into a cute little button as I trail my hand along her shoulders. "And then what?" she breathes back.

"Give me a second," I whisper against her ear.

I lean over her, inhaling the sweet smell of coconut and almond in her hair before stepping around her. I make my way to her bathroom, roll up my sleeves, and start her bath. I'm not surprised Persephone has adorned her ensuite with more flowers and candles.

There's a basket of crushed flowers beside the tub, and I sprinkle them and the honeymilk into the water, allowing it to fill the dark chrome clawfoot tub. While the water continues, I make my way back to Des. Before I do, I make note of the toothbrushes left beside a small tray of mint leaves and paste. I chuckle, knowing Des has always been a stickler for dental hygiene. I'll find a way to add it to our evening.

Des is still waiting for me in the center of her bedroom. With her hands clasped at her waist, I can sense the nervous energy exuding from her pores. I have every intention to soothe every doubt and fear away.

"It's time!" I announce merrily as I reenter the room. "Time for me to open my gift."

CHAPTER 43

Desephone

Arius takes slow, calculating steps toward me, the hungry gaze in his darkened eyes reminding me of a panther waiting to pounce.

He throws off his suit jacket, and it lands perfectly in the chair near the window. There's a burning gaze in Ari's eyes as he stares at me as he steps out of his shoes. I'm almost glad he doesn't look outside. If he did, he might notice I have a straight view into his bedroom.

Oh, the nights I've seen him leaving his bathroom dripping wet, and the things I've done to myself in response. They're not my finest moments, but they sure are some of my happiest. To have him here now rivals every dream I've had of Ari over the years.

"Your gift?" I wish I could remove the nervous lilt in my tone.

"That's what you are, Des: my gift. I've waited patiently. Now, I finally get to unwrap my present."

I bite my lip when I feel his heavy hand once more on my shoulder. Slowly, Ari pulls my sleeves down the side of my arms, rolling them past my chest until my breasts spill out.

"Perfect," he croons, gently rubbing his thumbs over my hardened nipples.

Ari continues rolling the dress down my body, stopping short when he reaches my hips. Kneeling, he places himself front and center as he pushes the fabric past my hips, down to the floor, until I'm left in nothing but my thong.

A low rumble bounces through his chest as his eyes lock on my sex. "May I?" he asks, looking up at me with those steely, sexy eyes that steal my breath away. I want to say something, but my throat can't even manage a hum. An eager nod is all I have to offer as Ari quickly hooks his fingers around the lace and slowly eases the thin fabric off my body.

His eyes are locked on my sex, and he lets out a growl as he grabs my butt, forcing his face to my sex.

"I'm going to feast on this pussy... *soon*," he moans against the small patch of curls sweeping his mustache. He's on his feet before I have a chance to think, but he still has a hand on my backside. "First, we're going to get cleaned up. Then, I'm going to finally taste that sweet little pussy I've been dreaming about." He clenches his eyes shut. "Then, I'll touch every part of you. And then, I'm going to–"

"*Fuck me senseless*," I urge him on.

His eyes flash like lightning. "I was going to say kiss you as I made love to you, but if you'd rather I fuck you first..."

"Earlier," I moan, pressing my body against his as my fingers unbutton his shirt. "You promised to fuck me senseless, so—"

"Is that what my baby wants?"

"Yes, but you can kiss me too."

"Soon," he breathes against my mouth as he works himself out of his shirt.

I've seen Ari shirtless before, and each time, I've had to catch my breath. Now, knowing what we are to one another, seeing him like this takes on a whole new meaning.

From his sculpted abs to his chiseled chest to the dark wavy trail that leads below his waistline, Arius Knight is the personification of perfection.

And while I'm thankful for the perfect gentleman he's being right now, he could also slam me on the bed, call me his filthy little whore, and fuck me until I forget my name, and I'd still wake up and serve him breakfast in the morning.

But I'll keep that secret close to the vest for now. I have a feeling once he knows, he won't show me an ounce of mercy.

Ari leads us to the bathroom, where I see Mother has been hard at work. He stops the water just before it fills too high, and he adds two towels to the warming rack.

Offering me his hand, Ari helps me into the tub. The water is hot just like I love. Steam rises from the water as I sink beneath the soft, silky petals.

Ari walks over to the sink and grabs a glass of water and a few mint leaves. He tosses a few in his mouth and hands me some. I chew the leaves as I hang over the tub.

"Spit," Ari says, offering me his hand. I look up at him and frown in protest. He pushes his hand forward, insisting. I do as he says, and another low rumble churns through him. "That won't be the last time." He gives me a swig of water, and I swish and spit once more into his hand.

He washes his hand at the sink and rinses his mouth. As he makes his way back to me, he unbuckles his pants and pulls them off. He kicks them out of the bathroom and closes the door.

My eyes stay glued to his waist, in awe of the well-hung cock swinging between his legs. He's not even fully hard, and his size alone rivals anything in my imagination.

"Like what you see?" he asks, donning that smug-ass smile of his that has my head spinning. At least I know he has something to back up his cocky attitude.

"You'll find out soon enough," I say, trying not to sound too eager.

Arius taps my back, letting me know he's joining me. He settles in behind me, and I nearly lose my mind when he sits me between his legs. His thick, hard dick is pressed against my butt, and I'd give anything for him to ram himself into me right here, right now.

He grabs the sponge and adds some soap before pulling my hair to one side. Gently, Ari scrubs my back and arms, massaging me with one hand and cleansing me with the other.

"Just relax baby," Ari whispers against my ear. "I feel you bouncing around. You want me to fuck you now, don't you?"

Once more, I'm nodding eagerly as his soapy hands run over my breasts and stomach.

I grab the other sponge and start cleaning him as well. I'm noticeably not as methodic in my movements, but Ari lets me roam his body.

I pop to my knees as I watch his cock spring up from under the water. His eyes are glued to my breasts as he takes them in his hands. "So big and pretty," he groans, allowing his thumb to circle my nipples.

"So big," I moan, dropping the sponge in the water and taking his hard length in my hands. The motion takes him by surprise, but I'm not done surprising him when I lean over and take him into my mouth.

"Baby," he moans, ripples of shock cracking his voice as he palms the back of my head, keeping me in place. "Fuck!" he growls as I lick around his tip, eagerly wrapping my mouth around his crown.

I run my hand down the base. I almost wonder if I've taken on more than I can handle when I have difficulty wrapping my fingers around his girth. He's big, bigger than I thought he'd be in his mortal form, but he'll hear no complaints from me.

I suck hard and fast, faster when the taste of his sweet and salty flavors grazes my tongue. I know Ari has a plan, but I have a plan of my own, and that's to get his dick in me as fast as possible.

"You deserve this," I moan around him. I think of how he protected me, cared for me, believed in me, not just today, but over the years. He even let me have my first orgasm with him in the prism today. Ari has never been selfish, and he deserves to be rewarded and lavished with all the love I can give him.

"Damn right!" he growls, smacking my wet ass as it bounces up and down. Now I know I have him just where I want him. I move up and down, letting my butt dance along the water as I swirl his cock in my mouth. "Fuck, Des, I'm about to come," he roars, and I take him as far as I can handle until I feel his spend tickle the back of my throat. "Ah, baby," he moans as I lick up every drop, thankful for the honor.

I pull up from his lap, hovering over him as his hooded glare locks on me like a heat-seeking missile. Ari straddles me over his waist, just above his erection, as he pulls my left breast into his mouth while massaging the other. He lifts us from the tub, holding me in his arms, my head hanging over his shoulder as he carries me to bed.

CHAPTER 44

Arius

Laying Des in the center of her bed, I take a moment to appreciate just how beautiful she is. With her wet, messy mane spread across the white duvet, she looks like an angel as she waits for me.

There's just one problem.

"That's cute," I chuckle.

She frowns, looking over her legs at me. "What?"

I lean over her. "How you sit there hugging your knees together when they should be apart." Taking her knees in my hands, I slowly spread her legs, hungrily eyeing the way her perfect little pussy opens for me. "Now that's fucking beautiful." I shake my head in appreciation.

With sweet dark curls on top, her fat little pussy lips spread just enough for me to see a glistening sheen of wetness waiting for me. I lick my lips as I crawl over her, placing her legs on my shoulder.

"I'm going to feast on this pussy like it's my last fucking meal," I growl against her sex. She smells so good, like a sweet rose.

"Ari..." She says my name, and there's a hint of warning in her tone. Des grazes her hands through my hair, holding me just enough to stop me from what I truly want.

I look up, and the worry I see in her eyes almost freezes me, but I'm too far gone. I sit up a little so I have a better view of her face. The longer I stare at her pussy, the less I give a damn about anything else.

"Baby, don't be afraid," I say, hopeful the softness of my voice calms her fears. "I've already tasted you, remember? And I'm still here. Besides, I'm not him." I didn't want to go there, but damn it, this is where we are.

"What?" She frowns, pushing up on her elbow.

"You heard me, Des. I'm not him. I know the pain of the past clouds your thoughts, but you don't have to live in that hurtful place. Not anymore. Not with me."

"But I– What if–"

"What if we make glorious, passionate love? What if I let you rain everything you have on me? What if you rode me like there was no tomorrow? What if I *fucked you senseless*?"

Her breath hitches, and I reach between us to stroke her pussy. It's soft and plush as I guide a finger to her entrance, enjoying the wetness there.

"Is this how you touched yourself at night as you thought of me?" I ask as I thrust a finger inside. "Or is this how you touched yourself?" I add a second finger.

"How... How–" she breathes wildly beneath me as I run my finger against her clit. "How did you know?"

"I watched," I finally admit. "I sat outside your window, listening to you pleasuring yourself as you called out my name."

"Baby," she moans, her eyes rolling back as her back arches, making her breasts jiggle.

With my opposite hand I move a digit around her ass. Her eyes pop wide when she feels me circling both holes.

"Ari!" Des grunts, tightening up a bit.

"Just relax, my little hellcat. I'm exploring all of you tonight. Nothing goes untouched. Not even here." I pop a digit inside and she blows out a breath. "That's right baby, I'm just priming you up a bit. But don't worry, my tail is far gentler than my hand. You need to know I can be at two places at once."

Des moans beneath me as I explore her depths. She feels so damn good. If we keep this up, I'm going to rut through her like a wild boar, and something tells me she'd be fine with just that.

I pull my hand from her backside and focus on her pussy. It's so damn pretty. And pink. *And mine.* All mine.

I twist my finger around, working her into a fit. Damn it, I'm going to get what I want, once and fucking for all. Throwing her legs over my shoulder, I bring my face back to her pussy.

Her eyes pop open. "Fuck me, Ari! Damn it. Fuck me right now!"

"A man's gotta eat first," I growl back.

"Please don't die, Ari," she pleads beneath me..

Her words send a sting down my spine, but it's not fear—it's fucking conviction. I know who I am and who we are to each other. I'm not one of those limp-dicked bastards who just wanted to check her off their fuck card, and I'm certainly not some pureblood vampire who thought his aristocracy alone was worthy enough to be loved by this amazing woman.

No, I'm more, and so is she.

"Shh," I hush against her sex. I lick between her sweet folds and am immediately rewarded with her honey. I kiss her lower lips like I'll do when I kiss her mouth, tonguing her pussy walls with deliberate strokes.

Desephone whines beneath me, moaning and grazing her hands wildly through my hair. I continue my assault, sucking down her juices while nipping at her sensitive skin. She must like the way it feels, because she picks up the pace, grinding against my face just like she did in the prism.

I don't let up, thinking of how long I've wanted this—*us*— makes me ravenous for her in unexplainable ways. Desephone and the sweet sway of her hips own every part of me, and I plan to feast on her every chance I get.

I feel her pulsating heat against my lips, and I invest all my energy into driving my tongue against her clit until I'm finally rewarded with a generous spring of her sweet honey dripping down my throat.

She screams my name with a mix of expletives in a language too ancient to discern. I drink down everything she offers, but I refuse to let her off easy.

This is exactly how I wanted her.

Spent. Incensed. Horny.

I position myself over Des, keeping her limp legs over my shoulders. I line my cock up with her drenched pussy, and my crown easily makes a home at the nook of her entrance. I could shove myself in one hard and fast stroke, but I wait for her eyes to bounce to mine. I need her to know what's coming her way.

Des looks up at me with clouded eyes and those perfect pouty lips that were just wrapped around my cock.

"I've tasted this sweet pussy, and I'm still alive. But know this, if making love right now meant I had to die, then so be it. I swear to you, your pussy is worth my whole life, Desephone. I'd give my whole life just to have a taste of your sweetness. I won't just die for you, Des—I'd live for you. I'd live to have your heart. Do you understand me?"

She nods eagerly as I slap my dick against her slick entrance. "Yes, Ari, baby." She lifts her hips, trying to pull me in.

"I love you, Des," I confess as I finally slide into her depths. "Fuck!" I shout as her walls masterfully massage every ridge, up and down. "Shit!" I cry out. I've never felt anything so damn good.

Crushing my mouth to hers, Des wraps her arms around my back, driving me deeper. I can taste myself on her tongue, as I'm sure she can taste herself, but she doesn't seem to mind. I may be fucking her, but she's owning this kiss as her tongue tames me into submission.

Her hands press against my ass, forcing me deeper, and I take the plunge. She's tight as fuck and the resistance I feel as I go deeper surprises me.

"Please fuck me, Ari," she begs against my mouth.

As I press forward, she squeezes her eyes tight, biting my lower lip as she makes sexy mewling noises beneath me. Purr, my little hellcat, purr. Her sweet sounds give me what I need to thrust forward until she cries out when I reach the hilt.

But I don't stop. Neither does Des as she ginds against me, her newfound wetness leaking to my balls. I find new walls to hit as I pound into her mercilessly, over and over again. Every wanton stroke makes her breasts bounce wildly in my face, and I alternate from her mouth to her tits.

We go on like this until I feel my body warm from the inside. If I didn't know better, I'd say my blood was literally boiling. It feels like the hot lava in the prisms, but this time, the lava is inside me.

It burns and it's hot as hell, but I keep thrusting, working Des into a fit beneath me.

"Ari?" Des groans, her face twisting with worry as she runs her fingers over my chin. "You're burning up!" she shrieks, but I don't give in. She feels too good, and I love her too damn much.

A throbbing headache shoots through me, and I close my eyes, still grinding deep. A dark, shrouded figure burns in my mind, and it doesn't take a genius to know who I now see staring back at me.

It's Hades. His dark, fire-ridden eyes stare back at me as he lets out a cunning cackle. But if he thinks I've come this far only to let the love of my life go, he doesn't know who I am.

"Ari, please!" Des cries beneath me.

I pop my eyes open, and the worry I see in her gaze should force me to quit before I'm laid bare before Hades' feet, but knowing Des loves me the way she does and all we mean to one another, I'd be a fool to let go of what we have. So, I hold on tighter. I'm not giving up.

Now I know how Hades scared all those punks away, searing their minds with thoughts of unending punishment and doom, taking their lives. But I am not like those men.

Roaring, I only know one way to conquer anything set before me. I think of how much I love this woman. I think of how she loves me for all that I am. Thrusting hard against Des, I shift into my Bulwark form, forcing my wings to expand. My marble skin shimmers, cooling the burning red inferno building in me. My tail whips at my back, but it finds a resting place as it plunges into Desephone's ass.

She cries out from both pleasure and pain as my wings wrap around her, lifting her from the bed.

This is a first for me. I've never fucked anyone with my tail. I've never fucked anyone as a Bulwark. Only Desephone. Something like cum leaks from my tail as it flicks around her tight little hole, lubricating her opening as I make my way inside.

"That's it, baby," I coax Des along. "Look at you, taking me so well. *This ass.* This pussy. Both mine. See how I fuck them both?"

"Yes, baby!" Des cries out, her head resting on my shoulder. I know it must hurt, but I always keep my promises and I promised to fuck her senseless.

Once more, the stinging ache in my head tries to lull me back to Hades, but I ward him off, using the same boundary enchantment on my mind that I used at the door of the Dram, but this one is a thousand times stronger.

Fuck you, Hades, I groan within myself, and the pain pops like a bubble, melting away.

I'm lifting Des from the bed with my wings as she folds around me. I'm fucking her like a ragdoll. My engorged, stone-hard, gargoyle-sized dick is plunging into her pussy, my tail in her ass, my wings feathering her breasts.

She's mine for the taking, and I'll have all of her.

I thrust hard and fast as we hover over the bed, our bodies wedged within the tray ceiling. I pound her so hard, she reaches for the crystal chandelier to hold onto as I unload everything I have into my beloved.

It's the rage room all over again, just a bit more intimate, I think to myself.

"Ooh, Ari," she moans, rubbing her hands against my head as we hover over the bed.

"What?" I slowly shift us back down to the bed.

She moves her hands around, grazing something I've never felt before. "You have horns!" she shrieks with a bright smile. Her fingers dance over my scalp, touching the pointed tips. The feel of her holding my horns while riding my dick, is sexy as hell.

As I lower us back onto the bed, I turn us so we're positioned in front of her large, floor-length mirror and I can see my new horns. They remind me of my father, and the thought makes me proud. But what makes me happier is seeing Des straddled over my waist. I'm still lodged as hard as a brick inside her sweet little pussy, my tail still holstered between her ass cheeks. She looks completely radiant staring back at the monster who'd defy the gates of hell just to be with her.

Even more, she knows this monster would do more than die for her. He'd live for her.

CHAPTER 45

Desephone

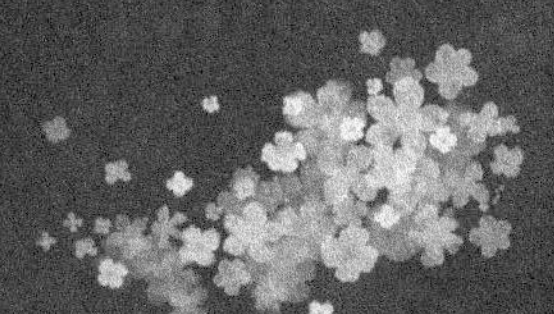

We made love for hours.

This was a first for me. Usually, if a guy even gets to third base, he bursts into flames before he even has a chance to enjoy it.

Tonight was the first time I've actually gone all the way. I feel like a damn teenage girl who just got her cherry popped by the cutest guy on the football team.

"You're still smiling," Ari croons in my ear as I rest on his chest.

"How can you tell?" I lift my face, plastering a ridiculous grin.

He smiles and plants a small kiss on my cheek. "Oh, just a guess, I suppose," he teases, looking up at the ceiling.

"Okay, can I admit something?"

Ari shrugs his shoulders. "You can tell me anything, baby."

"Tonight was my first time…you know, going all the way." I pull the covers over my face. I almost feel silly saying it.

Ari lifts the covers, pulling them off my face. His eyes are wide, almost surprised. "It's okay, baby. I must say I was a little surprised myself. But I have to admit, I'll forever be grateful for the honor."

"Oh, Ari," I breathe against his chest. "It's no big deal." I try to laugh it off.

Ari isn't convinced. He lifts my face to meet his. "It is to me."

My brow lifts. "Why?"

"Well, it certainly isn't because I'm some neanderthal cherry-popper, if that's what you're thinking. But because I know why I'm the only one to do it."

I sit up on my elbows, curious. "Why?"

"Because I'm your friend. Your best friend. And you value friendship as a level of intimacy. The Culling taught me that. We learned things about one another that took that level of intimacy even higher. Look, I know you cared for Cecil, and maybe a few others, but can you honestly say they cared for you. To know you–understand you–intimately. I take that responsibility seriously. I always will."

"Damn, Ari, I love you so much right now." I want to say more, but I just use this moment to kiss him. "But you're right, baby, no one has ever made it that far. You can't imagine how much it crushes the ego to know you're a fucking black widow."

"You're no black widow, baby." Ari's tone is serious. He has never been fond of me putting myself down, and I know he won't put up with it anymore.

I poke out my bottom lip. "I'm sorry. This has just been so annoying over the years! I mean, couldn't you sense my, um, frustration?"

He lets out a small laugh. "I suppose you were a little eager. I would be too after three thousand years."

I throw my head back on the pillow. "Gah! Don't remind me!"

"Oh, I'm not complaining. I can see why they didn't make it that far. Hades is scary as hell. Besides, no guy I know, supernatural or otherwise, wants to see his lady's father when he's um–" He purses his lips.

"Fucking her senseless," I tease, poking his shoulder.

"Yeah, that part," Ari grins, pulling me back onto his chest. "Now, let's just hope he doesn't kick my ass when we get to the Underworld."

I feel Ari tense a little. He's not completely worried, but he's no fool. "I wouldn't worry about that, baby. Besides, you have Persephone in your corner. If she likes you, he'll love you, that's for sure."

"So stay on your mother's good side. Good tip."

I kiss his cheek. "Yeah, but you have nothing to worry about, Ari. I promise. And now that I've learned more about you and there are no skeletons in the closet or secrets between us–"

"Secrets?"

"Okay, well in your case, it's like your closet of good deeds. You know, how you own a medical facility to house your mother and other supernaturals with health conditions. Or how you're actually my number one customer, ordering flowers to send to your mom. Or how you own properties in the Warehouse District to help disadvantaged supernaturals train. And how you love me."

"Well, that's no secret. I've always loved you. In fact, I'm sure my friends are happy I finally had the balls to make my move."

"If there's anyone proud of your balls, that would be me," I say, reaching down to his crotch. Ari lets out a cute grunt, running his hands through my hair. "Any other secrets you care to share with me?" I rub my hand along his smooth, sculpted chest; it feels like an odd question, considering how much of himself he showed me last night.

"Now that you've met my mother, you know I'm half Filipino. My father is Afro-Panamanian."

"Nice!" I respond. "I kinda figured that out a while ago when I heard you speak Tagalog." Ari laughs and rambles off a few words. It's never been a secret that we are both biracial. We never talk about it because supernaturals come in all ethnicities. We're more focused on our otherworldly origins. "Anything else?"

"Well, I am named after a heretic, so that's something you didn't know," he smiles, adding a soft kiss to the top of my head. I pull him in until our lips lock again and I can taste myself on his tongue. I love how far we've come—friends to lovers, now fated to forever. "Now, your turn."

"Okay, I'll stick with the same theme. I'm named after both of my parents." That was too easy, I know.

Arius shakes his head in laughter. "Makes sense. A heretic and a hellcat. What a pair we make."

"What a pair indeed," I murmur before crushing my lips to his once more.

My hands find their way back to his shaft and I find his erection ready and waiting. I straddle his waist and slide down on his rock-hard cock. It still hurts to take his size, but the reward is certainly worth the pain.

"That's it, baby," Ari coaxes me, guiding me down with his hands on my hips. "Take me all the way."

"Ah!" I scream when I finally reach the base. He grabs my butt, thrusting himself further, forcing me to lean over him with my breasts dangling in his face.

Taking both my breasts in his hands, he circles his thumbs over my nipples, enhancing the stimulation. He pulls both of my breasts to his mouth and alternates between both, licking and sucking in such a fluid motion, I can barely think straight.

Ari pushes himself back against the headboard so I'm still sitting on his dick, giving him more leverage to intensify how he pounds into me.

With my back arched and my head tilted, Ari uses the opportunity to continue lapping at my breasts like a starved man. But I don't have a moment to enjoy it when he flips me over and thrusts himself into me from behind.

Ari smacks my butt hard and pulls out. I almost wonder if he's going to shift again, but when I don't feel any movement, I look over my shoulder, wondering if something *is* wrong.

"Don't mind me, baby. I'm just admiring this pretty little pussy." He smacks my butt again on the opposite side. "Fuck! That's too pretty. I love watching it bounce just for me," he growls before he pounds into me once more. "And it's all mine. Say it's mine!"

He smacks my butt again, and I cry out. "It's yours!"

"Damn right!" he says as he slams into me, over and over again.

"Are you okay?" Ari asks as he places gentle kisses along my backside.

"Yes, baby. That's the third time you've asked me. I promise you, I'm okay."

He rubs my butt a few more times and then flips me over. "I'm sorry I got carried away. I don't ever want to hurt you."

"Oh, baby, I don't mind if you hurt me a little," I tease, biting my fingernail. "I know you're not trying to harm me. There's a difference."

Ari opens my legs and looks appreciatively at my sex. His fingers roam over me as he slides a finger inside. He twists until I let out a little yelp when he hits my G-spot. Pulling out of me, Ari brings his finger to his mouth and sucks off my slick.

Leaning down, he takes a long, slow lick before kissing the top of my pussy. "Damn, Des. You taste so good. You better cover up before I fuck you again."

"What if that's what I want?"

"You really want me to fuck you senseless, huh?"

I smile, knowing it's time I finally reveal my true intentions. "Ari, you can tie me up, hang me out to dry, bite me till I bleed, and fuck me until I can't remember my own name, and I'd still wake up and serve you breakfast, begging for you to do it all over again. You asked me if I trusted you earlier. Well, I want you to know that I trust you with every inch of me."

Ari lines himself up at my entrance. "Then I'll give you every inch of me."

CHAPTER 46

Arius

One year later.

It seems like just the other day that Persephone said, "I'm giving you one year to wrap up your earthly dealings. You'll wed upon my arrival. Make all your preparations."

Des and I have spent the year planning the wedding, closing out our respective businesses, and getting to know each other on a more intimate level.

If left up to us, we would've married right away, but the only way I don't succumb to the same fate as my father is to go to the Netherworld once Des and I officially marry.

I'm glad we took the extra year. I had a chance to formally bury Mom in the gardens next to my father. His chimera seemed to harden once she passed, and Des said she believes the two are finally together.

She once asked Ms. Reed how it was that my mom, a mortal, lived to be one hundred and sixty-three. Ms. Reed thinks she was afforded some charmed elements by carrying me. If it wasn't for the dementia, she might have lived longer, but I wouldn't wish that for her. She loved my dad too much to be in a world where he no longer existed.

Des later told me she could pick up the stench of death lingering on my mom when she first met her, but she didn't want to say anything just in case she was wrong.

"Are you ready, asshat?" Perry grumbles as he comes into my office. "Or are you still looking at yourself in the mirror, pretty boy?"

"Oh, don't tease him," Cade laughs as he straightens my bowtie. He pats my shoulder, giving me a final once over before stepping to the side so I can see myself in the mirror.

"At least my reflection doesn't crack mirrors." I chuckle, looking over my shoulder at Perry.

He laughs and gives me a little shove at my back. Both Perry and Cade stand behind me, smiling proudly. They're the brothers I never had and damn if I won't miss them when Des and I head to the Netherworld. But I have a sneaky suspicion I'll see them again.

"Well, we had better get you to your bride before she sends us all to the Underworld." Cade pats my shoulder once more and turns to open the door.

"Hey, do you have the–"

"Ring?" Perry cuts me off with a smile. He pulls the small velvet box from his tuxedo jacket and shakes it. "Of course! You know I've got your back."

"Thank you." I take one last look around my office and smile, knowing Des is waiting for me.

Desephone

"**A**re you ready, dearest?" Mother asks, still fussing with my hair.

I step back a little and glance at myself in the mirror. "So ready." I grin eagerly.

"You look beautiful. Truly lovely," Mother gushes over me with her hands beneath her chin. "I'm so happy for you, dear."

"Thank you," I say, giving her a small kiss on her cheek.

"Knock, knock," I hear Gypsy call from my doorway. She covers her eyes, waving her hand away.

Mother and I laugh as she grabs my bouquet from my chaise.

"Gypsy, I think it's only bad luck if the groom sees the bride, not the groom's friends," Mother chuckles.

"And since you're also the bride's friend, I think you're fine," I add.

Gypsy pulls her hand from her face, her eyes brightening as she looks at me. "You look fucking gorgeous!" she shrieks. "Damn, Knight is gonna lose his shit when he sees you!"

"Gypsy!" Mother admonishes her, shaking her head as she walks to the door.

"I should hope so," I giggle as I take one last look at myself.

Mother had this gown hand stitched in the Soleil, just as she did Ari's tux. Since we can't enter the Netherworld in anything earthbound, she gifted us with our wedding attire.

My gown is white and black, with shimmering black tulle on the bottom and a long, white and black ruffled train. There are hand-stitched dragon scales along the seam and diamonds that run over my shoulder and breast. Mother even took the liberty to dust me in gold from head to toe. It's a normal practice among women of status in the Netherworld, so I'm honored Mother is treating me to the best.

We don't wear veils in the Netherworld, since that earthbound practice has more to do with a "purity reveal" that is quite frowned upon among our kind. Since mating happens prior to the wedding ceremony, wearing a veil seems quite silly.

"All set?" Gypsy asks with a sweet smile on her face.

"Yep," I say and make my way toward the door. I stop in the doorway in front of Gypsy as Mother continues downstairs. "Gypsy, thanks for being such a great friend to me and Ari all these years. I know we haven't been the easiest to endure, but we wouldn't be here without you in our corner. Thank you." I give a quick kiss to her cheek and we head down the stairs.

CHAPTER 48

The Wedding

All Hallows Eve.

A perfect setting for a perfect pairing—a pairing so perfect, one might say Persephone planned it herself, though she might have had a little help from a hybrid vampire with his own reasons for having a friend in the highest of low places in the Underworld.

There are pretty, pretty petals everywhere. Pretty autumn leaves adorn the steps leading into Desephone's garden behind her flower shop. There's a lovely fountain at the end of the garden outlined by hydrangeas, lilies, and an array of orchids, stems of lavender throughout.

Candles and fiery torches outline the treeline leading to the dark altar where the two will share their vows to eternity.

Arius looks out from beneath the wilted rose arch made of thorns, his eyes beaming with pride as his bride descends from the darkness. Under the cover of moonlight, she strides into view with graceful steps along the dried path of petals leading to her beloved.

With a long stride wrought with anticipation, she makes her way forward as her shadowy familiars hover about in a misty plume, carrying her to the edge of the garden.

Queen Persephone is at the helm, her smile from ear-to-ear as she awaits to proclaim the two man and wife. Words she's been eager to announce since the day Hades crafted the princess in his image.

The Grandmère Bulwark, Melvina, is also present, along with a handful more, like Stevie, Gypsy, Ms. Reed, Cade, and Perry. There are two unfamiliar faces among those gathered: Kharon, the Ferryman, Prince of the Netherworld, and his wife, Lady Rae Vereen. Queen Persephone procured her daughter's transport beyond the earthbound plane sometime before these two became lovers, but these are secrets she'll keep close to her heart.

Still, despite the guests gathered, all eyes remain on the bride and groom.

"Dearly beloved, we are gathered here to witness the union of Desephone, the Daughter of Hades and yours truly, and Mr. Arius Knight, son of Evander and Tala Knight. The two have prepared their own vows, which we will hear at this time."

Arius takes a deep breath, blowing out a small air of nerves as he takes Desephone's hand in his. "Des, you are the light of my life, the joy of my world, and the holder of my heart. I promise to love and cherish you for the rare, exquisite treasure you are. I will keep you close and always protect you." He turns and takes the ring from Perry. "And now, with this ring, I bind myself to you in life, death, and everything in between. I love you."

Desephone lets out a nervous giggle as Arius places the ring on her finger, and her eyes glow like lightning. "Ari," she breathes, catching her breath. "I love you. Not just because I know you'll always protect and care for me, but because I see you—the man who serves others, putting everyone ahead of his own needs. I've never needed to read your soul because I see it. You are the most caring, loving, and selfless soul I've ever known. I trust you with my whole heart, my body, and my soul. I promise to remain faithful at your side. Forever and always, I am eternally yours." In the same manner, she receives a ring from Gypsy, and she guides it on his finger.

A loud crack of lightning pierces the night sky, and roaring thunder rolls through the air. Everyone looks around in wonder, but the bride and groom keep their eyes fixed on one another.

"And now, with the power vested in me as Queen of the Underworld, I now pronounce you husband and wife," Persephone announces merrily to a cheerful round of claps and whistles. "You may now kiss your bride."

Bringing her face to his, Arius and Desephone share their first kiss, united as one.

Turning to their crowd of friends who've now become family, they smile, kissing one another once more.

Soon, they'll take their descent into the Underworld and begin their happily ever after. However darkly, their happiness shall be, though, is still a story that remains to be told.

Thank You

Thank you for reading 'Till Death Do Us. Use the QR code below to leave a review on my direct buy site, Amazon, Goodreads, BookBub & more!

You can also support the book by purchasing merchandise such as hoodies, tees, and sweatshirts at: https://www.bonfire.com/store/lc-son-books/

Acknowledgments

First, and always, I want to thank my Creator for sharing the gift of creativity with me. I do not take this gift lightly. To my husband and children, thank you for being such supportive and loving humans. You remain my greatest gifts.

Writing *'Till Death Do Us* was exceptionally challenging for me. During the writing process I experienced death and loss in unimaginable ways. I lost my aunt, uncle, and brother over the course of six months. My tears were endless pools and my grief—well, I'm still grieving. So writing about grief, and death, and loss was both cathartic and painful. But because I knew there was a happy ending waiting for Desephone and Arius, I pressed forward. I needed to see, feel, and experience their happiness as if it were my own.

It wasn't easy.

As if death itself wasn't hard enough, here comes dementia. Having a parent with dementia is soul crushing. For a person who literally gave you their face to look at you like a stranger is the most heart crushing thing I've ever experienced. Yet, here I am. I decided to include Tala's dementia into the story because, like Arius, I know what it feels like to want to make a safe place for mom while still trying to pursue your own dreams. It doesn't come without difficulty. But I needed to see it work for Arius, even if only to live vicariously through him.

If you or someone you know needs help or is struggling with dementia, please check out the following resources or reach out to a trusted medical and mental health provider.

*Alzheimer's Association 24/7 Helpline- (800) 272-3900 www.alz.org

*Alzheimer's Foundation of America (AFA) Helpline (866) 232-8484. https://alzfdn.org

Still, none of this would have been possible without my wonderful Beta readers, TDDU Hype Team, ARC readers, my fabulous editor, Alexa, and my wonderful formatter, Megan. To all of my author pals, especially Mary, Molly, Jess, and K.C., thank you! I appreciate your friendship. You encourage me more than you know.

To all of my readers, both new and those who've been riding with me for a while- I love ya!

Dream Well,
LC

* Websites and contact information provided is not solicited by aforementioned. All information discoverable via the internet as of September 2024. Author not liable for services rendered*

More from L.C. Son

EXPLORE THE BOOKS AND SHORT STORIES OF
THE BEAUTIFUL NIGHTMARE UNIVERSE:

Books

Beautiful Nightmare (Book One)

Hearts Eclipsed, A Beautiful Nightmare Novella

Awaken: Beautiful Nightmare (Book Two)

Untamed: A Beautiful Nightmare Story

Beta Rising

One Winter's Kiss: A Beautiful Nightmare Story

Fire Kissed & Fire Born Duet (Netherworld Series Debut)

Vengeance Born: A Grim & Reaper Netherworld Tale

Coming Soon

Beautifully Dark Things- TBA

Dawn of Descent: Beautiful Nightmare (Book Three) TBA

Short Stories

I AM NO WITCH: A Beautiful Nightmare Short Story

With Clipped Wings of Butterflies: A Beautiful Nightmare Short Story

With Hearts Like Fire: A Beautiful Nightmare Short Story

Untamed Afterlife

For more info on my books, visit: My Books & Short Stories - L. C. Son
Books (lcsonbooks.com)

Remember leaving reviews makes you an MVP!!

Thank you!

About L.C. Son

Known for her Amazon Best Seller *One Winter's Kiss*, and the series starter, and epic fantasy novel, *Beautiful Nightmare (Book One)*, L.C. Son is the happy wife of more than twenty years to her high school sweetheart and a loving mom of three.

Growing up, she spent hours reading comic books she "borrowed" from her older brother, which inspired her love of heroes and all things fantasy and paranormal. Much like the characters she adored, she lives a duplicitous life. By day, she works tirelessly to champion the employment of persons with severe disabilities. By night, she puts on her wife-mom cape, sharing with her husband at their church and juggling their kids' highly active schedules.

Presently, she's working on the next installment of monsters, myths, and misfits.

For the latest info and to join the member-only newsletter, visit: www.lcsonbooks.com.